JANA DELEON

Chapter One

At 7:00 a.m., on a perfectly good Thursday, I stared at the mass of people on Main Street in dismay. The Fourth of July is cause for a big holiday celebration in many places, but when you combine the Fourth with a contested mayoral election, in Sinful, Louisiana, it's apparently cause for mass chaos. I dodged people shouting, snow cone stands, children screaming, and people hanging streamers until I reached Francine's Café. I hurried inside, expecting to see a similar scene, but was pleasantly surprised to find the regular early-morning breakfast crowd in their usual seats.

I smiled and headed for my corner table, waving at Ally as I crossed the café. She popped over with coffee a minute later. "Given what I saw outside, I figured this place would be a madhouse."

"So did Francine," Ally said, "which is why she doubled the prices on everything and has forbidden anyone from only ordering coffee."

"And she gets away with that?" I definitely appreciated the strategy, but couldn't fathom her stance not causing a riot.

"Most everyone is scared of Francine," Ally said. "If she closed up shop, half the people in Sinful wouldn't have a good meal again. And she gets offers all the time from restaurants in New Orleans. Bakeries would kill for her banana pudding recipe."

"I bet Celia's not afraid of her."

Ally frowned. "You're right there, and with her being elected mayor, there's going to be nothing but trouble. Any news on the election recount?"

"Marie has hired an auditing firm out of New Orleans to do the job. It will take several days, though."

"In several days, Aunt Celia could bring this entire town to the brink of insanity."

"Given that it's mostly already there, that's not exactly a big leap."

"True, but Celia's brand of insanity is more…mean than most."

I nodded. Ally's aunt was the equivalent to a bipolar cat lady. Lived alone, didn't like anyone and they didn't like her, and her mood and allegiance shifted by the minute. Just a couple of weeks ago, I'd saved her life and she actually seemed grateful. One incident with wieners and hound dogs, and she promised to run me out of town. Today she might be knitting blankets for seniors and tomorrow she'd be calling a group of Girl Scouts ugly and fat. I'd given up trying to figure out what made her tick. If Gertie and Ida Belle hadn't figured it out in fifty-plus years, I certainly wasn't going to manage it in a month.

"We'll just hope she's too busy celebrating to get right down to nasty business," I said, but I knew it was a wasted sentiment. Celia had probably been up all night plotting ways to make her sworn enemies miserable. The worst part was, in settling her personal scores, she would ruin Sinful.

Ally nodded. "Do you want your usual?"

"No. Just egg whites this morning. I saw a funnel cake vendor out there. I may have to go grazing in the sweets after breakfast."

"Funnel cake?" Ally sighed. "That's so unfair. Like testing

my own baking isn't problem enough, now I'll be out there after my shift's over, playing cattle like you."

I grinned as Ally headed back to the kitchen. Staying in shape had been a constant problem since my arrival in Sinful. If it hadn't been for the shenanigans I got into with Gertie and Ida Belle, I probably would have gained far more than the five pounds I'd already put on. Between Gertie's dessert gifts, Francine's fantastic and fattening meals, and Ally currently living with me and creating new bakery items every day, I was probably consuming enough carbs and sugar to induce a diabetic coma in an inert person.

I took a sip of my coffee and looked outside the picture window at the fray. There was no way this day would end without a problem that required law enforcement intervention. The sheer number of Sinful residents celebrating combined with homemade hooch and questionable IQs spelled certain disaster. I hoped Carter didn't allow himself to be pulled back to the job. Dr. Stewart refused to release him to work for another week, and that was only if he had a clean scan showing no remaining swelling in his brain.

Not that Carter paid a lick of attention to what his doctor said. He'd left the hospital two days before and gone straight into the bayou looking for a gunrunner and murderer. The fact that he saved Ida Belle, Gertie, and an ATF agent was the only thing that kept his mother from yelling at him, but it hadn't stopped her from calling Dr. Stewart and passing the phone to Carter so that he could yell at him.

Carter had taken the doctor's orders seriously yesterday and spent most of the day sleeping with me in my hammock, then we had a nice dinner that Ally prepared, and afterward, he actually agreed to go to bed early. He would never admit he wasn't a hundred percent, but I could tell his strength was waning by evening. I'd had a head injury before, courtesy of a slight miscalculation when I tried to jump from a bridge onto the yacht of an escaping gunrunner. The week I'd been forced to sit around in my condo hadn't been the most thrilling, but when taking a shower required sitting for twenty minutes to recover, it was hard to argue about the forced time off. Especially when your job included carrying a gun.

I took my time over breakfast, chatting with Ally when she could stop by and getting a couple more chapters done on the thriller I'd started reading the day before. Finally, I paid my bill and walked outside to see what was going on.

Main Street was just as crowded as before, but was starting to take on the shape of minimal organization. Streamers and balloons were attached to all the light poles, and stands lined both sides of the street, residents busily putting up their wares. I spotted Ida Belle and Gertie across the street at a booth in front of the General Store and crossed over to where they were unpacking boxes of Sinful Ladies cough syrup.

"You're selling your moonshine right here on Main Street?" I asked.

Legally speaking, Sinful was dry, meaning no bars and no sale of alcohol, which meant the men in town either risked their wives' wrath by going to drink at the Swamp Bar or they brewed their own. The female residents of Sinful elected the less strenuous option of purchasing Sinful Ladies cough syrup, which would indeed cure the worst of coughs, but mostly by scaring bacteria right out of your body.

"Walter sells it at the store," Ida Belle said. "What's the difference?"

"Celia is mayor," I said.

Gertie frowned. "Don't remind me. I sat up all night with some of the ladies, alternating burning candles and praying with burning pictures of Celia and drinking. I have the worst hangover ever."

"You're lucky you didn't burn your house down," Ida Belle said. "The lot of you have no business combining alcohol and fire. It's like daring the universe to do something."

"You mean like selling hooch on Main Street when Celia is mayor?"

Ida Belle gave me a dirty look. "It is not the same thing. I like Gertie and wouldn't want to see her go up in flames. Celia, on the other hand..."

I grinned. "Apparently, making Celia mad is what I live for, so pass me a crate."

Ida Belle slid a crate to me and I hefted it onto the table and started unpacking the wares. "Hey, this is a new one." I held up a bottle labeled "Sinful Ladies Atomic Blast Cough Syrup." The tagline read, "When regular cough syrup just won't do."

"That one's one-ninety proof," Ida Belle said.

"Jeez Louise, are people supposed to drink it or use it to strip paint?"

"I've used it for both," Gertie said, "and to remove some rust off my barbecue grill."

"That one is best added to a cup of coffee," Ida Belle said. "A very large cup of coffee if you plan on walking the rest of the day."

No doubt. I put the bottle on the table, reminding myself to stick to regular only. I was sorta attached to my liver. I finished unpacking that crate and was about to ask for another when I heard a commotion behind me.

I turned around in time to see Sheriff Lee ride into the center of Main Street on his burro. But instead of his normal slacks and button-up shirt with the sheriff's department logo, he was decked out in a sequined Uncle Sam costume, complete with top hat. Holy crap, maybe a swig of the hard stuff wasn't such a bad idea.

"Oh, look," Gertie said. "There's Sheriff Lee in his Fourth of July outfit."

"He has a special outfit for the Fourth of July?" I asked.

"He has a special outfit for all holidays," Gertie said. "You should see his costume for the May Day festival."

"I'm afraid to ask," I said.

Ida Belle nodded. "Smart woman. May Day has its roots in fertility rites."

Residents crowded around sheriff and burro, some posing their kids in front of him to get pictures. "Looks like the crowd likes it," I said, reminding myself that there was no accounting for taste in Sinful, Louisiana.

Ida Belle waved a hand in dismissal. "Those idiots eat it up. They'll take any opportunity to take another picture of 'Little Tommy and Mary' and post them on Instagram. The whole thing is a snooze fest."

"What do you know about Instagram?" I asked. I'd only learned about it the week before when Ally was taking pictures of her latest baking to post to her account. She'd insisted on setting me up an account because she'd be moving back to her own house soon and she didn't want me to miss out on any of her new stuff. My thighs were certain I needed to miss out on her new stuff, but my taste buds overruled them and told her to go ahead, with the caveat that if she posted anything I couldn't live without, she had to bring one over. She'd agreed, set up the account TroubleMagnet, and gotten me some friends or whatever. I had yet to post a picture.

What the hell. Maybe I should start.

I pulled out my cell phone, zoomed in on Sheriff Uncle Sam Lee, and snapped a pic, then posted it to my account. There you go—one thing accomplished today. I could officially spend the rest of the day goofing off.

I slipped the phone back into my pocket and turned around, only to collide with Deputy Breaux. The young deputy was nice, but also inexperienced and mostly afraid of his own shadow. With Carter officially on medical leave, he was probably about due for a nervous breakdown. Sheriff Lee didn't exactly set the world on fire with his law enforcement prowess—or at least, hadn't in the last hundred years or so—and without Carter on duty, that left Deputy Breaux to handle Sinful. It was a losing proposition right out of the gate.

"I'm sorry, Fortune," Deputy Breaux said. "I've got to get to the sheriff before she does."

"Before who does?" I asked, but Deputy Breaux had already taken off across the street.

My question was answered when Celia Arceneaux stepped into the street and marched straight up to Sheriff Lee. Deputy Breaux froze, his panic so apparent that I elbowed Gertie and asked, "Do you have defibrillators handy?"

"Why?" Gertie straightened up and looked across Main Street. "Oh. That doesn't look good."

"We better go see what it's about," Ida Belle said.

We hurried across the street right as Celia stepped up to the burro and handed Sheriff Lee a piece of paper.

"What the heck, woman," Sheriff Lee said. "You know I can't read this without my glasses on."

Celia pulled herself up straight and glared. "Don't call me 'woman.'"

"Why not? That's what you are. It would be downright silly to call you 'man.' Not to mention incorrect."

Celia snatched the paper from him. "It says… Oh, never mind." She shoved the paper back at him. "It says you've been relieved as sheriff due to mental incompetency."

Sheriff Lee's face turned as red as the stripes in his outfit. "The hell you say."

"You rode a burro on top of a federal agent's car. The city just received a bill for it. Until which time your mental health can be assessed and proven to be sound, you are no longer in charge of law enforcement in Sinful."

"And just who is in charge?" Sheriff Lee asked. "Carter's out on medical leave and Deputy Breaux isn't qualified by a long shot." He shot a look at the still-frozen Deputy Breaux. "Sorry, son."

Celia gave him a smug smile. "In the interim, my cousin Nelson will be filling in."

Gertie gasped and clutched my arm. I didn't know who Nelson was, but I had a feeling I wasn't going to like him.

Sheriff Lee's jaw began to twitch, and the longer Celia stood there wearing that smug smile, the worse the twitching became. Then, in a move far faster than anything I'd ever seen him do, Sheriff Lee pulled out his pistol and aimed it directly at Celia's forehead.

Most of the crowd took a step back and several women started to cry.

"Don't do it, Sheriff," one man said. "She ain't worth it."

"She wouldn't die anyway," a woman said. "You can't kill Satan."

I leaned down to Ida Belle. "Should we do something?" I whispered.

Ida Belle shook her head. "You heard the man. He's not wearing his glasses."

Even though it was Celia, and she was our sworn enemy, I couldn't just stand there and watch the sheriff shoot her. The problem was if I tried to tackle him or threw something at his arm, I ran the risk of his accidentally squeezing the trigger and shooting someone in the crowd. That would be worse than shooting Celia. At least she sorta had it coming.

"I've wanted to do this for a long time," Sheriff Lee said, his finger tightening on the trigger.

I gathered myself to spring but it was too late. He pulled the trigger.

A loud *pop* sounded and Celia collapsed into the crowd behind her, taking down five other people and sending her skirt over her head, exposing her big white granny panties.

Sheriff Lee began to laugh like a lunatic, and I whipped my head around and saw the "Bang" flag hanging out of his fake pistol. The crowd, finally catching on that Celia hadn't really been shot, started to chuckle. Deputy Breaux came out of his stupor and fled the scene. Clearly he was smarter than people gave him credit for being.

Gertie shook her head. "She just can't seem to keep from showing her wares, can she? You'd think after last time, she'd start wearing pants."

Ida Belle whipped out her cell phone and took a picture of Celia in all her white cotton glory. A couple of Celia's crew rushed over to help upright the new mayor, who was starting to regain consciousness. A couple seconds later, my phone buzzed and I saw an Instagram notice from HotRodMama.

Sinful's new mayor shows her ass in public.

It was like a sea of white on my screen. I grimaced and turned my phone off. It was bad enough the first time. Now it was immortalized on the Internet. Gertie, who'd been digging in her enormous handbag, finally pulled out her phone and saw the same picture on her screen. She howled with laughter and some other people giggled. I scanned the crowd and realized all of the gigglers were holding their cell phones. Good God.

"Hey," Gertie said, "the *Times-Picayune* just picked it up. The first official press photo of our new mayor."

I couldn't hold in the grin any longer. "I bet you're proud."

"I'm something," Gertie said.

Celia grabbed two of her friends' arms and practically dragged herself up from the pavement, glaring at a grinning Sheriff Lee. "You'll pay for that," she said.

Sheriff Lee responded by turning his burro around until the animal's butt was smack in front of Celia's face.

"That's enough, Lee." The male voice sounded from behind me and I turned to see a man making his way through the crowd.

"Thank God you're here, Nelson," Celia said, taking a step back from the burro's butt. "I want him arrested."

So this was the new sheriff in town.

Midfifties. Five foot ten. Two hundred fifty pounds. Hadn't lifted anything heavier than a beer can since he was a teen. Only a threat to an all-you-can-eat buffet.

"Arrest him for what?" Gertie asked.

Celia pointed. "For having that unruly animal in the middle of Main Street."

"The law says burros are allowed as transportation on the Fourth of July," Gertie said. "Unless he exchanges that animal for oxen, he's perfectly within his rights. One would think the mayor would bother to learn the laws."

"Oxen?" I looked over at Ida Belle.

"Only on Christmas Eve," Ida Belle said.

"Of course."

"He created a public disturbance," Celia said.

Gertie snorted. "So did you. Unless you passed a law that it's okay to expose yourself on Main Street."

Celia's brow creased. A little girl, maybe twelve years old, tugged on her sleeve and lifted her phone to Celia's face. Celia turned red, then purple, and for a moment, I thought she was going to either cycle through all the colors of the rainbow or her head was going to explode. Finally, she sputtered "Handle this" to Nelson and took off toward the Catholic church.

"How many Hail Marys does mooning call for?" Gertie called after her.

Nelson took a step closer to Sheriff Lee. "Get down from that infernal beast and come with me."

Sheriff Lee backed the burro up into Nelson's face. "One more word and I give him the signal to relieve himself. He's been gassy."

Nelson hopped back, suspiciously eyeing the burro's hind end. "This isn't over, Lee."

"Oh yeah it is. It was over before it ever started." Sheriff Lee gave the burro a nudge and it stepped backward again, pinning Nelson's foot underneath its hoof.

Nelson howled in pain and shoved the burro's rear, trying to force it off his foot. Not a good move when faced with a gassy burro, who took the hands on his butt as a signal to eliminate part of his load right on Nelson's shoes. Apparently, relieving himself made the burro frisky and he kicked up his legs, lifting a good bit of his "relief," and smacked Nelson right in the center of the chest with both hoofs. Nelson clutched his chest and fell onto the concrete, gasping for air. The former Sheriff Lee and the burro strolled away without so much as a backward glance.

"Now do we need the defibrillators?" I asked.

Ida Belle walked over and bent down, placing her fingers on Nelson's neck. "Get up, you big baby. Your heart's fine." She looked over at us. "Funnel cake?"

"I thought you'd never ask."

Since everyone had gravitated to the sheriff-and-burro show, the funnel cake trailer was free of patrons. A young woman smiled as we approached. "Ida Belle and Gertie…I haven't seen you guys for years."

Thirtyish. Five feet four. Hundred twenty pounds. No apparent disabilities, except for the smile.

"Kayla?" Ida Belle said. "I almost didn't recognize you."

Kayla blushed. "I've lost a couple of pounds since high school."

"You've lost more than a couple," Gertie said. "All you young people are on those fad diets."

"I went on the college boy diet," Kayla said. "They didn't go for chubby girls, so I lost the weight, and had a makeover—new hair, fixed my teeth—you know the drill."

"Your teeth look great," Gertie said. "Are those veneers?"

"Some veneers and some crowns. I was wishing I'd taken better care of them when I got the bill."

"I'm thinking of getting some work done," Gertie said.

Ida Belle rolled her eyes. "You've worn dentures for ten years."

Kayla laughed. "Anyway, I heavily invested in the whole makeover thing."

"And did it work?" Ida Belle asked.

"Worked like a charm." A man's voice sounded behind them. They turned to look as he stepped by them and jumped over the table and into the booth with Kayla. He stuck out his hand. "I'm Colby, Kayla's husband."

Ida Belle and Gertie introduced themselves to Colby and then pointed to me. "Sorry we completely forgot to introduce our friend, Fortune. Her great-aunt was one of our best friends. She's here this summer settling the estate."

"Oh, I'm sorry," Kayla said.

"It's okay," I replied. "We hadn't seen each other in quite some time."

Like never.

"You didn't come back to Sinful just for the celebration, did you?" Gertie asked.

"Sort of," Kayla said and waved a hand at the trailer. "This is our business. We travel around to different events, selling funnel cakes and snow cones."

"Sounds like a lot of work," I said. The whole idea of moving to a different place every week and dealing with random people all day was enough to make me itch.

"It is," Kayla agreed, "but it's fun, too. Colby and I both love to travel, and the business does quite well. We have a motor home that we can pull the trailer with, so we're always at home, so to speak. Lots of times there's days in between events, so one of us drives our truck and we check out the local sights."

"Speaking of running the business," Colby said. "I forgot the extra paper plates in the truck. I'm going to run get them."

"Okay," Kayla said and flashed her million-dollar smile at him.

"He's a real cutie," Gertie said. "Weren't you dating one of those twins in high school?"

Kayla rolled her eyes. "Doug. I actually married him my freshman year of college. Lasted a whole month before I caught him sleeping with my chemistry lab partner."

Gertie shook her head. "Well, looks like you got a good one now."

"The best," Kayla agreed.

"How's your mother?" Ida Belle asked. "I haven't seen her around in a while."

"She's good," Kayla said. "Goes to visit her sister in Denver a lot. She likes the cooler temperature. I get back here for short visits as often as I can, but it's hard when we're booked solid. But enough of my rattling. What can I get you?"

"Three funnel cakes," Gertie said.

Kayla sprinkled powdered sugar on the fresh cakes that Colby had just removed from the fryer and placed them on the table in front of us. "That will be fifteen dollars."

"No wonder they can take time off," Ida Belle grumbled.

"I got it," I said and passed her a twenty. She gave me my change and we gathered our dessert and headed back to the Sinful Ladies booth. "Do you have to man the booth all day?"

"Heavens no," Gertie said. "We just set it up and then the other ladies take it from there. They have a schedule so that everyone has plenty of time to enjoy the festivities."

Sure enough, two of the Sinful Ladies were already at the booth finishing up the unpacking. They looked up as we approached.

"We heard Celia made a fool of herself," the first lady said.

"Heard it and saw it," the second one said and made a face as though she'd stepped in dog poo.

"It was hilarious," Gertie said. "And then the burro crapped on Nelson's shoes and kicked him."

Both ladies giggled, then they sobered. "We also heard Sheriff Lee has been benched," the first one said. "Nelson can't take care of a cactus, much less this town."

"Technically, Sheriff Lee can't either," Ida Belle said. "But we all keep voting for him because we know that means Carter will be taking care of things."

"I wish Carter would run for sheriff," Gertie said.

"He's always said he wouldn't until Sheriff Lee retires or dies," Ida Belle said.

"If Sheriff Lee hasn't died by now, I don't think he's going to," I said.

Ida Belle nodded. "It might all be a moot point now. If Celia makes this mental issue stick, then Carter is going to have to step up in the next election. Bad enough we'd be stuck with Nelson for the time being."

"Did someone say my name?" Carter's voice sounded behind us.

Chapter Two

I turned around and he winked. I couldn't help but smile. "You look better today."

"I feel better. It was probably all that rest I got yesterday." He nodded at the ladies, then sobered. "I heard about Sheriff Lee."

"That's just what we were talking about," I said. "What does that mean for you?"

"Nothing yet, but there's no love lost between Nelson and me. If Celia manages to make this mental competency thing stick, I might be looking for another job."

"You really think he'd fire you?" I asked. "You're the only one who knows anything."

"I think he'd fire me in a heartbeat, but before he got the opportunity, I'd walk. No way in hell would I work for a sleazeball like Nelson."

"In case you missed the implication," Gertie said to me, "Nelson isn't exactly popular."

"So what's the deal with him?" I asked. "I've never heard you mention him before."

"We believe that saying his name is like summoning a demon," Gertie said.

"Well, apparently, he's been summoned by his boss, Celia," I said. "You can't make it worse."

"True," Ida Belle said. "Before Gertie launches back to

Genesis, I'll give you the CliffsNotes version. Nelson left town after high school and went to New Orleans."

I stared. The CliffsNotes version started at high school? That was over thirty years of notes.

"He got a job at a garage working on cars," Ida Belle continued. "After a couple of years, he decided he knew everything and moved back to Sinful to open his own garage."

"He thought competing with Walter was a good idea?" I asked.

Gertie shook her head. "Walter didn't have a garage at the time. Only the store."

"In fact," Ida Belle said, "no other garages existed in Sinful at the time, so everyone was happy to have one so close."

"Everyone who didn't know Nelson very well," Gertie said.

"Yes, well," Ida Belle said, "it didn't take long for everyone to figure out Nelson didn't know his butt from a hole in the ground when it came to cars. Sure, he could do an oil change or fix a flat, but God forbid you needed anything more complex."

"I take it he screwed up some cars and people weren't happy about it?" I asked.

"He screwed up all right," Ida Belle said. "The worst one was Sheriff Lee's pickup truck. It was a classic."

Gertie rolled her eyes. "Meaning it was so old, he bought it directly from Henry Ford."

Ida Belle shot Gertie a dirty look. "In any event, that truck was Sheriff Lee's pride and joy. He took it to Nelson for an oil change, but when Sheriff Lee pulled it into his driveway after the work was done, the accelerator stuck and he drove it right through his living room and into the bayou behind his house. Took out his bass boat, too."

I'd been struggling to envision Sheriff Lee in motion on anything that didn't run on hay, but the picture Ida Belle painted made it easier. "And he blamed Nelson?"

"Not at first," Gertie said, growing animated, "but after Sheriff Lee drove through his house, other customers started complaining that their cars broke down after Nelson had worked on them, even though they'd had no issues before."

"Uh-oh." I could already see the writing on the wall.

"Sheriff Lee figured Nelson was jimmying the cars so that he could get more business," Ida Belle said, "but Lee was never able to prove it. Still, the rumors were enough that people started taking their business out of town, and Nelson had to close the shop."

Gertie snorted. "Close, my butt. He took everything that he could hock out of that building and hightailed it out of town in the middle of the night, leaving a bunch of residents who'd invested in his garage without a dime to show for it *and* holding the bag for all the rent and utilities he'd skipped out on for the building."

"Including my grandmother," Carter said.

"The man's a criminal!" I said, now outraged. "And Celia thinks he's the best candidate for sheriff?"

"Given that Celia's only interest is having a puppet who'll do her bidding, yes," Ida Belle said.

"Good God," I ranted. "That woman will single-handedly be responsible for the fall of the entire town."

"Exactly what I've been saying," Gertie said.

"Yes, well, we knew there would be trouble," Ida Belle said, "but I don't think any of us saw this twist with Nelson coming. After he was essentially run out of town, he hasn't been back except for short visits."

"I'm almost glad I'm on medical leave," Carter said. "Maybe by the time Dr. Stewart clears me, Marie will have her recount done and Celia will be out the door."

"That's what I'm praying for," Gertie said.

I was getting ready to suggest something stronger than prayer when a huge *boom* roared through the skies. Everyone whipped around in time to see fire blast upward, sending a cloud of black into the air.

"What the heck was that?" I asked. "That's the middle of the swamp."

Ida Belle and Gertie exchanged a glance.

"What?" I asked.

"Well, um," Gertie stammered, "sometimes swamp gas can—"

"Don't even go there," Carter said. "It was probably a still."

"A still?"

"Moonshine," Carter said.

"Oh!" Everyone knew that the Sinful Ladies cough syrup was moonshine, but I'd never asked where or when they manufactured it. I assumed Carter hadn't either, because then he'd be forced to do something about it. I looked over at Ida Belle and Gertie. Ida Belle gave me a barely imperceptible shake of her head.

So it wasn't their still. But it was somebody's. "Is this common?" I figured the items used to make moonshine had to be highly flammable, but in the time I'd been in Sinful, I hadn't heard much talk about explosions, at least not of the liquor-induced sort.

"It happens more often than one might think," Gertie said.

"Except one who's familiar with Sinful and its residents," Ida Belle pointed out.

I looked over at Carter, who was staring at the smoke cloud and frowning. "So what do you do in these situations?"

"Nothing," he said.

"Really?"

"Yep. I'm on leave, remember?"

"Oh, right. Lucky you."

"Unlucky Deputy Breaux," Gertie said. "With the Fourth of July celebration and the election nonsense, he was already halfway to a heart attack. Then that mess with the sheriff and Celia this morning sent him scurrying for a place to hide. This may be what sends him over the edge."

Before I could respond, the man in question burst into the middle of Main Street, frantically looking around. When he spotted us, he broke out into a run and slid to a stop in front of Carter. He opened his mouth to speak, but all that came out was a choked cry, then he bent over gasping for air.

What the hell? The sheriff's department was across the street, not a mile out of town, but Deputy Breaux was acting like he'd run a marathon.

Gertie patted his back. "It's your asthma, isn't it? All this excitement was bound to trigger an attack. Just concentrate on breathing."

Deputy Breaux rose up and took in a couple huge breaths and blew them out. His face was beet red and he looked as worried as he had been when Carter was shot. Something was seriously wrong. Something more than a still explosion.

"The explosion," he wheezed.

"Yeah," Carter said. "We saw it."

"Scooter called in…him and Walter was fishing near it and Walter got hit with some debris. He's unconscious. Scooter's hauling butt back to the dock, and I already called for the helicopter."

My pulse spiked and I glanced over at Ida Belle, taking in her pinched expression. Walter owned the General Store and was Carter's uncle, a lifelong pursuer of Ida Belle's affections, and my friend. "What hit him? Is he bleeding?"

"I don't know," Deputy Breaux said. "Scooter was in a bad way. I couldn't make sense of everything, and I didn't want him driving the boat and talking to me…"

"Of course not," I said. Scooter was the mechanic for Walter's garage and barely made sense sober and not stressed. He was probably practically incoherent now.

"Then we best get to the dock," Carter said.

The five of us headed to the dock behind the sheriff's department and all stood there in awkward silence. Gertie sat on a pylon, casting anxious glances at Ida Belle, who was trying to play off her worry by wearing her usual stoic expression, but I could tell she was having trouble keeping the mask in place.

"Let's not get ahead of ourselves thinking the worst," Carter said, breaking the silence. "Scooter isn't known for his accuracy or communication skills. I'm sure Walter is fine."

I nodded. "Carter's probably right."

Ida Belle stiffened and pointed down the bayou. "We're about to find out."

I turned to look at the bass boat ripping up the bayou so fast that it created huge wakes that crashed against the bank. Several people fishing on the bank gave Scooter a drenched middle finger, but he didn't even bother to give the obligatory "sorry about that" wave. I hoped he cut his speed soon or he was going to run up the bank and right onto Main Street.

Just when I was about to suggest we clear out of the way, Scooter cut the engine, and the front of the boat dropped onto the top of the water and coasted straight for the dock. I could see Walter lying in the bottom of the boat, a life preserver under his head. He had a big red knot on his forehead near his receding hairline, but I was relieved to see no blood.

Scooter tossed the line to Carter, but Ida Belle jumped inside before it had been secured. She leaned over and spoke

Walter's name. Walter's eyes fluttered and he attempted to move, then groaned and reached up to clutch his head.

"Don't move," Ida Belle said. "The medics are on their way."

"What happened?" he asked.

"There was an explosion," Carter said. "Probably a still. You got hit by debris."

Walter blinked and squinted up at us. "I was fishing with Scooter. Just landed a good speckled trout. That's the last thing I remember."

I heard the approaching helicopter and looked up. "Your ride's here."

"What?" Walter turned his head to watch as the helicopter landed on the bank behind the dock. "I don't need no doctor."

"Don't be an old fool," Ida Belle said. "You need to have your head checked."

"Probably true," Walter said. "Given that I've been chasing a bossy woman for most of my life."

The paramedics came down the dock with a bed and climbed into the boat. Ida Belle jumped back on the dock to get out of the way. The paramedics rolled Walter on his side and slid the backboard under him, then rolled him back onto it and lifted him onto the dock. A couple minutes later, he was in the helicopter, Ida Belle sitting beside him, and they were off.

"We'll meet you at the hospital," I shouted as the helicopter took off.

"Um, I hate to ask"—Carter gave me a sheepish look—"but do you mind driving? I'm still not cleared, and Dr. Stewart already told me if he sees me behind the wheel, he'll readmit me to the hospital."

"No problem," I said.

Gertie perked up. "We should ask Scooter if he knows what

hit Walter…in case there's a cut anywhere."

Carter frowned. "I didn't see any, but you're right. Even a small infected cut on the head is a bad thing."

We headed back down the dock where Scooter was unloading the fishing gear from the boat. He looked up as we approached and there was no mistaking his worried expression. "He's going to be all right, isn't he?" Scooter asked.

"I think he'll be fine," Gertie said. "Probably just needs to take it easy for a couple of days."

"I hope you're right. It was just so strange…that explosion coming out of nowhere."

"We were wondering if you saw what hit Walter? The doctors will want to know."

Scooter's eyes widened. "Crap! I completely forgot. I brought it with me, in case you needed it for that police stuff and all."

He turned around and opened his ice chest and pulled something out, then tossed it on the dock. Gertie shrieked and skipped backward right off the dock and into the bayou. Deputy Breaux whipped around and reached down to help Gertie back onto the pier.

Carter and I leaned over Scooter's offering, then looked at each other.

"Walter was knocked unconscious by a flying leg?" I asked.

Carter stared. "That's what it looks like."

"Is anything ever normal in this town?"

Deputy Breaux stepped up beside me and the blood drained from his face. "Jesus, Joseph, and Mary."

Carter reached over and grabbed the leg, lifting it up to his face. He took a sniff, then blanched. The smell wafted my direction and I covered my nose and mouth with my hand. Deputy Breaux covered his nose with his arm and took several steps back.

"It smells like it's made of stale cat urine," I said.

Carter tossed the leg back onto the dock and turned his head to take in a breath. "Yeah. Which is even worse news than before."

"Why?" I asked.

"Do you know what smells like cat urine?" Carter asked.

"Old Miss Johnson's house," Deputy Breaux said, "but she's got about a hundred cats and both of her legs. I saw her earlier downtown."

Gertie rolled over on the dock and struggled to her feet, sending a spray of water onto us. "Meth labs," she said.

Deputy Breaux uttered a strangled cry. "No way!"

Carter stared at her. "How do you know that?"

"Wikipedia," she said. "There's so much information on the Internet. It's downright amazing, and somewhat disturbing in a lot of cases."

"Yes, the Internet is full of things that help criminals," Carter agreed, "but why were you looking up meth labs? You know what, never mind. I don't think I want to know."

I looked down at the leg. "A meth lab? In Sinful?"

Gertie nodded. "And with Nelson as sheriff, they could be selling the stuff on Main Street and he wouldn't catch them." She shot me a look and I struggled to keep my expression the same. I knew exactly what she was suggesting—that with Carter out of commission, there was no one left to keep Sinful safe.

I didn't want to agree with her, but one person very important to me had already been injured. And if he'd been hit by a piece of flying metal instead of a leg, he might be dead. Not to mention that meth was an insidious evil that could ruin a small community like Sinful in a matter of months. When Carter looked away, I gave her a slight nod.

This was a mission for Swamp Team 3.

We could hear Walter complaining as soon as we entered the emergency room hallway.

"He sounds fine to me," Gertie said.

I gave her a nod. From what I could hear, he sounded the way Carter had just days before. It was either a relation thing or a man thing. When we entered the room, Ida Belle was sitting in the corner, shaking her head. Dr. Stewart was standing next to Walter's bed, looking frustrated. He glanced over when we entered and his frown deepened as he locked his gaze on Carter.

Carter held up both his hands. "Fortune drove. I swear."

"Uh-huh, and at a highly illegal rate of speed based on how quickly you got here. Which means you were either fully dressed in your bed, or you were out roaming Main Street when you should be resting."

"Mom drove me to town and I was sitting."

Dr. Stewart raised one eyebrow. "Really? That's what you're going with? Anyway, I assume you're not here to be readmitted even though it's probably not a bad idea."

"Damn doctors," Walter groused. "Being cooped up in hospitals is what makes people sick."

Carter nodded.

"Is he all right?" Gertie asked.

"He's going to be fine," Dr. Stewart said. "There's no sign of damage other than the knot on his head. The stubbornness was in place before he arrived. Do you know what hit him?"

I glanced at Carter, who hesitated a moment before answering. "Yeah, Scooter thought it would be a good idea to bring it with him."

"Really?" Dr. Stewart looked a bit surprised. "That's a lot of thinking for Scooter."

"Yeah, well, I'm especially glad he had a moment of clarity in this case."

"Oh? Something wrong?"

Carter nodded. "Very wrong. Walter was hit by a flying leg."

"What?" Walter sat upright. "Get me out of this hospital right now. I need to go home and shower for the next day or two."

Dr. Stewart frowned. "I guess from one of the moonshiners."

"I don't think it was a still that exploded," Carter said. "The leg smells like cat urine."

Dr. Stewart's eyes widened. "A meth lab?"

"That was my guess. I brought the leg with me hoping you could do a test…"

"Yes, of course. It's not my area of expertise, but I'll talk to the guys in the lab. I'm sure there's something they can manage."

Carter shifted a bit, looking uncomfortable. "Doctor, if you could keep this between us for the time being, I'd appreciate it."

"I heard about Celia and Nelson," Dr. Stewart said. "Normally, I wouldn't be part of hiding evidence, but in this case, it seems the prudent thing to do. Besides, I had this beautiful Cadillac…" He sighed.

Strike five thousand for Nelson and his auto business. I wondered if there was anyone in Sinful over the age of forty that he hadn't screwed.

"Thanks," Carter said.

"Don't mention it," Dr. Stewart said. "Literally. Don't mention it."

Carter nodded. "The leg is in a cooler right outside the door."

"I'll take care of it and call you when I have something, but you will turn the evidence over to someone responsible enough to investigate it, even if that means calling in the state police. And you'll do all of it from the recliner in your living room."

"Yes, sir," Carter said, and sighed.

"Well, if you don't have any other doom and gloom to lay on me," Dr. Stewart said, "I'm going to grab the leg and head up front to sign release papers for Walter."

Walter hooted and Dr. Stewart shook his head.

"With the condition," Dr. Stewart continued, "that you rest for at least forty-eight hours and call me if you have any changes in your condition. In fact, maybe you should stay with Carter for a couple of days. You two can bitch about me and hospitals from your recliners. Don't make me call Emmaline."

Carter and Walter shot each other a nervous glance and I held in a laugh. Carter's mom was beautiful, smart, and kind, but more importantly, a force to be reckoned with when it came to her family. Dr. Stewart pointed a finger at both of them and left the room.

"Busted," Gertie said, and laughed.

Walter swung his legs over the side of the bed. "Anyone who doesn't want to see my bare butt will exit now."

Carter practically ran me over getting out of the room, and I was close behind. I liked Walter, but I didn't want to see any of his parts naked except for the socially acceptable ones.

"So are you going to call the state police?" I asked Carter as we all huddled in the hallway. He'd already asked Deputy Breaux to keep the flying meth leg to himself for the time being. Something the good deputy had been visibly relieved to agree to.

"I guess I should," he said, but I could tell the idea left a bad taste in his mouth.

Ida Belle shook her head. "The state police will never get anywhere with the locals. It takes somebody who knows those people to get to the bottom of this sort of thing."

"If only Walter had been hit by a flying hand," I said. "At least then you could have gotten fingerprints."

Carter stared at me. "You have the oddest trains of thought for a librarian. What the heck do you read while you're sitting there waiting to check out books for people?"

Crap. "I might read detective books."

He shook his head. "That explains a lot." He looked over at Ida Belle and Gertie. "What's your excuse?"

"I blame television," Gertie said.

"I'm just nosy," Ida Belle said. "And I don't like living with criminals. The regular drunk-and-disorderlies and poachers are one thing, but I don't want Sinful to become the meth lab capital of the swamp."

Carter narrowed his eyes and looked at the three of us. "You three are to stay out of this, understand? I may not be able to arrest you, but if I catch you looking into this, I swear to God, I'll call Celia and tell her to have Nelson put you all in jail."

I glanced at Ida Belle and Gertie. I had no doubt Carter would make good on his threat if he thought it would keep us out of trouble. I had even less doubt that Celia would jump at the chance to put us all behind bars.

"I mean it," he said. "Just days ago, you were seconds away from being shot. If I hadn't shown up when I did..."

"Hey, leave me out of it," I said. "I was at home taking a nap, remember?"

Ida Belle and Gertie shot me dirty looks, and it was all I could do to hold in a smile. The truth was, I'd been right in the thick with them up until the firing squad part. I'd managed to slink away before being discovered and avoid any uncomfortable scrutiny from Carter about why librarians would go after arms dealers. The whole thing was ironic, really, considering an arms dealer was the entire reason I was hiding out in Sinful pretending to be someone else.

"Yes," Carter said. "That's what you keep saying, but what I've never gotten a good answer for is why you weren't there when you've been in the fat middle of everything the other two have been into since you arrived."

"We didn't tell her," Gertie said.

"Why not?" Carter asked.

"On account of you two dating and we were afraid it might lower her chances of getting lucky if you were mad," Gertie said. "I vaguely remember getting lucky. Now I'm too old for anything but a vicarious thrill, so I was protecting my interests."

I coughed to keep from laughing. The look on Carter's face was priceless, and I'd be willing to bet that he'd never venture down that line of questioning again.

"Yes, well," Ida Belle said, "all talk of luck aside, we've got a real dilemma on our hands. Carter is benched and Deputy Breaux is a nice boy but not capable of handling anything of this magnitude. The state police wouldn't be any better. Not with only a flying leg to go on."

"I can do some checking," Carter said.

"From your recliner?" Gertie asked.

"If that's the way it has to be, then yeah."

He said it casually, but I could see the wheels turning. Carter had a plan, but he wasn't about to share it with us. If ever there was a time I wished I had those feminine wiles that Gertie was always talking about, it was now. Unfortunately, so far, my way to Carter's heart had been trying not to give him reasons to arrest me. Even if I knew how to turn on the charm, if I did it now, he'd have Dr. Stewart checking me out for brain damage.

"Then I guess that's that," I said.

Feminine wiles might be off the table, but spying wasn't.

And at that, I was a master.

Chapter Three

After we got Walter ensconced in his recliner for the afternoon, the rest of us headed back to the festival. Gertie and Ida Belle needed to check on the Sinful Ladies booth to make sure they weren't running low on product, and I had promised Carter I'd let him show me the joys that were Sinful's Fourth of July celebration.

I had to work a bit to appear relaxed at the festival, but I didn't want Carter to get the idea that my mind was firmly locked on the explosion. It was somewhat interesting since I could tell he was making a show for me, but clearly, his mind was also on Sinful's current criminal trend. We both pretended to care about really bad singing at the talent show and blue ribbons on candied yams, and a pig beauty pageant—which was actually quite entertaining since the pigs got loose—but neither of us was really engaged. I just hoped my acting was better than his, or that he was too distracted to notice how bad it was.

By late afternoon, I could tell his energy was beginning to wane and commented that I needed to head home and feed the cat, and could use a shower. It was, after all, Louisiana in July. We could easily see the fireworks from my backyard, so he could get some rest, then head over to my house at dark. He looked a bit relieved, and I held in a smile as he headed off with Emmaline, who'd shown up an hour or so earlier. Men.

"I'm glad you finally told him you were going home,"

Gertie said. "He'd have stayed here until his heart gave out before he admitted he was tired."

I nodded. "I know. And it wasn't exactly a lie. I could definitely use that shower."

Gertie pulled at her top, which was sticking to her chest. "Got that right."

"What time does Ally get off work?" Ida Belle asked.

"She's already off," I said, "but she's selling pies at the café booth until eight."

"Good," Ida Belle said. "Let's all head home for a refresher, then meet at Fortune's house…say in an hour. That will give us some time to talk things over before Carter gets there."

"Sounds good," I said and headed through the crowd. I'd been concentrating so much on appearing normal that I'd forced myself to avoid thinking of the current problem at hand. Once I got into assignment mode, I tended to blank out on everything that wasn't about the job. But as I was Carter-free on the walk home, I had the opportunity to let all the facts roll around.

It wasn't a very long roll.

What we knew wouldn't fill a Post-it note. Something exploded. We suspected it was a meth lab, and there was no history of meth problems in Sinful. Heck, that didn't even get me half a block. Given my short-lived history with the town, I wasn't going to be able to offer much in the way of ideas, so I had to hope that Ida Belle and Gertie had some. More importantly, that they were viable.

A long, cool shower was great for my sweaty body, but didn't provide any mental illumination, so I figured a beer and some of Ally's chocolate chip cookies were in order. I set the plate of cookies on the kitchen table and plopped down in front of my laptop. I hadn't heard from Harrison since last weekend, when he'd let me know that Director Morrow had been struck by a hit-and-run driver. Harrison's message implied that Morrow was okay, but also that the attack had been deliberate. Since they'd lost eyes on Ahmad a week or so before, I didn't blame Harrison for not putting Morrow's incident down to coincidence.

I went through the process of rerouting my log-in so that no one could trace anything I did back to Louisiana, and opened up the fake email account Harrison had set up for me before I left DC. My pulse ticked up a notch when I saw a message.

To: farmgirl433@gmail.com

From: hotdudeinNE@gmail.com

I knew you'd be worrying, so I wanted to give you an update on Dad. The doctor says his foot will heal up nicely and no additional surgery is required. The swelling in his head is going down, and he's not having headaches as often. Apparently, he saw the car just before it jumped the curb and managed to leap out of the way, leaving only his foot and head to take the brunt of it. He's lucky as the car was traveling well above the speed limit. The police got security footage from the bank across the street, and I've got to tell you, it made my heart jump when I saw just what a close call it was. Unfortunately, the car was reported stolen the day before, so we'll probably never know who the driver was. Obviously a criminal, so for all we know, he could have been fleeing the scene of another crime. That seems to be the police take on the matter.

In other news, the cool weather still eludes us. The weather people keep teasing us with promises of a drop soon, but so far, nothing has panned out. How are things down on the farm?

I slumped back in my chair and blew out a breath. Harrison's message would seem normal enough to anyone else, but I knew exactly what he was trying to convey. The attack on Morrow was intentional, and he was lucky to have escaped with his life. He might not be so lucky the next time. And with the car being stolen, there was nothing to go on. Which meant Morrow and Harrison would need eyes in the back of their heads until this whole ordeal with Ahmad was over.

Even worse, they still hadn't found any sign of Ahmad. In the five years the CIA had been tracking him, they'd never lost sight of him for more than a couple of days. Either he'd gone deep underground or someone in his organization had taken him out. But if the second had happened, the CIA would have seen movement from the new ruling party. I shook my head. The far more likely scenario was that Ahmad had intentionally disappeared. But for what purpose? Was killing me really that important to him, or was he off pursuing a new business interest?

I drummed my fingers on the table and sat upright when a thought occurred to me. What if he'd gone underground for plastic surgery? That had happened once with a drug dealer in Colombia. He'd dropped off the map for weeks, then a new face appeared at the compound, giving orders like a general. Whoever had done the work had made such a difference in his appearance that none of us noticed the similarities until an operative who did clay sculpture of human heads as a hobby pointed out the bone structure. The facial recognition software verified her observation, and we were still able to get our man.

If Ahmad had done the same thing, he could be anywhere, looking like a totally different person. New facial features, colored contacts, bleached hair, and no one would be the wiser. I doubted he could approach me without all the hair on my body rising, but he could easily blend in a crowd and probably go unnoticed. I leaned forward and pulled the laptop closer to reply to the email.

To: hotdudeinNE@gmail.com

From: farmgirl433@gmail.com

I was worried about your dad. Thanks for the update. I'm glad he is feeling better but frustrated that the police don't think they'll catch the responsible party. I guess your dad was too busy trying to get out of the way, so he didn't see anything. Maybe he needs to take the bus for a while instead of walking. People have gotten so careless with cars. We'd probably all be safer if we got off of sidewalks.

Things at the farm are going good. Nothing is ever simple but things have a way of working out eventually. I'm sorry you still haven't seen your cool breeze yet. Remember when we took that trip back in 2009 expecting cooler weather and it was nowhere in sight? Everyone says it's global warming, but I figure things have always changed one way or another. Hopefully, things will improve soon.

I reread the message to make sure Harrison would understand. The first paragraph was a warning to both of them to watch their backs. I didn't think he needed it, but it never hurt to reinforce an idea, especially with assassins, as we tended to fancy ourselves invincible. I hoped the second paragraph reminded him of the previous target and his plastic surgery. If it registered with him, then he could begin to think about how to track Ahmad's movements differently. And he'd have everyone on alert for any newcomer on the scene.

Satisfied that I'd been as directly vague as I could be, I pressed Send, then reached for my beer. I was on my second handful of cookies when Ida Belle and Gertie arrived. I served them up requested sweet tea, put the plate of cookies on the table, and waited for the ideas to start rolling off their tongues. Instead, they both ate their cookies in absolute silence.

"Really?" I said, finally breaking the stagnant air. "If you guys don't have any ideas, I'm not sure who does."

Ida Belle put down a partially eaten cookie and sighed. "I've been thinking about it all day, and Gertie and I talked on the way over to your house, but the bottom line is that we have never heard of a meth problem here."

"Carter already said that," I said.

"Yes," Gertie said, "but Carter wouldn't be privy to things people intended on keeping secret. Nosy old ladies, however, have ways of hearing about things that law enforcement doesn't."

"I see." I considered this for a moment and frowned. Gertie was right. Unless they got careless, it was unlikely for the sheriff's department to be aware of the dangerous and illegal habits of residents, but it was a whole other thing completely for people like Ida Belle and Gertie to have no one on radar that might be involved.

"Maybe we're losing our touch," Ida Belle said. "Look at all the things that have happened the last month, and all of them going on right below our noses."

"I don't think so," Gertie said. "I think criminals are getting smarter and worse is all."

"They're not that smart," Ida Belle said. "After all, we've caught all of them eventually."

"Yeah, but they're getting smarter than the average Sinful mental acumen," Gertie said, "or they wouldn't have gotten away with things as long as they did. I think it's more of an issue of lack of exposure on our account."

"Gertie makes sense," I said. "I mean, I'm new here, but based on what you've told me, the town never had big issues before now, at least, not that you were aware of. If it was a normal rash of poaching or theft or drunken idiocy, you guys would be all over it because that's what you're trained to clue in on, but this stuff…"

Ida Belle nodded. "You're probably right. Gunrunning, murder, and now meth. I know plenty of people who smoke weed, but aside from the random few who've gone to New Orleans and gotten screwed up on the harder stuff, I don't know of anyone from Sinful who has a problem, and certainly no one who lives here now."

"Who do you know that smokes weed?" Gertie asked.

"I'm not telling you," Ida Belle said. "You'd be silly enough to try it."

Gertie shrugged. "I heard it was good for the eyes."

"For glaucoma," Ida Belle said. "It doesn't cure nearsightedness."

Gertie crossed her arms across her chest. "How many times do I have to tell you, I'm not nearsighted. I just need reading glasses."

Ida Belle rolled her eyes. It was an argument that the two of them would probably take to the grave, even though Gertie didn't have a leg to stand on.

"If I had to guess," I said, "drug problems would start here with the younger generation—probably in high school. You two aren't exactly dialed into the youth of Sinful."

"That's true enough," Gertie said. "Once I stopped teaching, I pretty much wanted the rest of my life to be child free."

"Maybe we should ask Ally," I said. "She's young and may have picked up on something at the café."

"True," Ida Belle said, "but that means telling her about Carter's suspicions, which means getting her involved in something that can't possibly end well."

I sighed. "There is that. Maybe I can figure out a way to broach the subject without asking her outright."

Gertie laughed. "You want to try to coax the information out of her through general conversation…without letting on that you're fishing? You have a lot of skills, Fortune, but lack of directness isn't really one of them."

"I can be vague and indirect," I said. "Sort of. Maybe. Fine, I won't ask."

"Probably best," Ida Belle said, "but your point about taking a harder look at the young people in Sinful is a good one. I just don't know how we go about it."

"There's always the dance," Gertie said.

I frowned. Dancing sounded awful enough. Dancing with a lot of teenagers sounded like some form of hell that was just asking for a Wikipedia page. "What dance?"

"The Fourth of July dance," Ida Belle said. "It's always held on the fifth because of the fireworks show on the night of the fourth. Teens started getting together the night after probably fifty years ago, and the tradition stuck."

"And they dance?" I asked.

"Oh," Gertie said, "there's probably some of that twerking going on, but I doubt many go to dance."

I glanced over at Ida Belle, who gave me a slight shake of her head. Clearly "twerking" was lost on her as well, but since the word originated with Gertie, I felt it best to leave off asking for an explanation.

"Mostly," Gertie continued, "I think they sneak their dads' beer in and stand around a bonfire."

"And what good does that do us?" I asked.

"It's against the law for more than two teens to congregate in public unless they're with an adult or it's a sponsored event,"

Ida Belle said.

"Or unless they're fishing or hunting," Gertie added. "People think teens just hanging out are looking for trouble."

"But teens carrying fillet knives and guns are not an issue," I said.

"Of course not." Gertie looked confused.

"The point is," Ida Belle said, "the town requires adult chaperones for the event, so if we wanted a good reason to mingle among teens without looking suspicious, the dance is it."

"Aren't the chaperones already in place?" I asked.

"Probably not," Ida Belle said. "No one wants to spend their night sweating around a bonfire in July. The mosquitoes are so thick they can carry you off."

Gertie nodded. "That's what they say happened to Lucy Franks back in '84."

Ida Belle sighed. "Sixteen-year-old Lucy Franks ran off with the forty-year-old school janitor who used to be her father's fishing buddy. Her father's a deacon, so he opted to go with the mosquito story."

It seemed reasonable. "So we volunteer for this torture and what? I can barely communicate with adults. How am I supposed to get information out of teens?"

"I don't know that we can," Ida Belle said, "but it's worth a shot."

I blew out a breath. "This is the thinnest line of investigation we've ever had. What about the location of the lab? Surely that would give us something to go on."

"Maybe," Ida Belle said, "but we need a way to get there. Right now, we're completely out of boats and the only one we could easily steal, we already sank."

"What about Walter's boat?" I asked.

"Walter locked the boat keys in his safe after we borrowed

it last time," Gertie said.

"And you don't know the combination?" I asked Ida Belle. "That seems like something that would already be in your bag of tricks."

Gertie laughed. "Despite the fact that Walter's been in love with her since grade school, that doesn't mean he trusts her any further than he can throw her."

That's because Walter was a smart man, but I wasn't about to say so. "Ally's boat is small but doesn't go very fast. I'm sure she'd let us borrow it, but I'm not sure it's a great idea. I mean, if anything happened while we were out there…"

"We'd be sitting ducks," Gertie said. "No speed and no place to hide in a boat that shallow."

"There's got to be something," I said, feeling frustrated.

"Let me work on it," Ida Belle said. "I might be able to come up with something."

A knock on my front door had us all straightening in our chairs. I glanced at my watch. It was only 7:00 p.m.—too early for Ally, and besides, she had a key. And Carter wasn't supposed to be there until dark.

I headed to the front of the house and swung the door open, surprised to see Carter standing there smiling and holding a bottle of wine. "If I had to spend another minute with my mother watching me rest, I was going to shoot her," Carter said.

I grinned. Emmaline had almost lost her son just days before, so she was doing the required hovering, but I knew that to Carter, it probably felt like someone slowly squeezing the air out of him. I'd feel the same way. "Come on in," I said. "I was just having some of Ally's incredible chocolate chip cookies with Ida Belle and Gertie."

Carter frowned as he stepped inside. "You three aren't up to anything you're not supposed to be, are you?"

"Of course not," I said as I headed for the kitchen, glad that he couldn't see my face when I answered. I was an expert liar, but lately, I'd found that my feelings for Carter made it harder and harder to keep a straight face when I was telling him something untrue.

Carter stepped into the kitchen and gave Ida Belle and Gertie the once-over. "Ladies. Fortune assures me you're not up to no good. Since you're awake, I'm not convinced."

"Jeez," I said, "sit down and have a cookie. It will probably improve your mood. And if you must know, the only thing they're 'up to' is wrangling me into helping them supervise some kids' dance tomorrow night."

Carter raised one eyebrow. "You two are supervising the dance?"

"It's our civic duty," Ida Belle said. "Everyone's got to take rotation sooner or later."

"What's the matter?" Gertie asked. "You think we can't handle a bunch of kids?"

Carter shook his head. "I'm more worried for the kids."

"Damn straight," Gertie said and rose from the table. "Let's make ourselves scarce. If three's a crowd, then four is an invasion."

Ida Belle hopped up and gave me a nod, then headed for the front door.

"We can let ourselves out," Gertie called. "But let's do breakfast. That whole vicarious thing…"

I stared after her and Carter laughed at my dismay.

"Do you think video would work for her?" he asked.

"Don't give her any ideas," I said. I turned around and reached for the wine, figuring a big, tall glass would calm me down, but Carter pulled the bottle away and grabbed me around the waist with his other arm. He sat the wine on the counter and pulled me close to him, then lowered his head.

"I've wanted to do this all day," he said as he lowered his lips to mine.

Against all common sense and training, I didn't even try to resist. Kissing Carter was as thrilling as an assignment and, in my case, held the same level of danger. No matter how many times I'd gone over the reasons for why getting involved was a horrible idea, I found myself drawn back in, as if my heart and body had my mind held hostage.

I wrapped my arms around him as I pressed my body against his, my hands running over his muscled back and shoulders. He deepened the kiss, and I felt my knees weaken. Another couple of minutes of this, and I was going to rip his clothes off right there in the middle of the kitchen.

Then my cell phone signaled I'd received a text message.

Under normal circumstances, I would have ignored it and carried on, but nothing about my existence in Sinful was normal, so I was afraid to let it slide. Not to mention that I'd never be able to enjoy the kitchen undressing because I knew my mind would keep slipping off to wonder what the message was.

"I need to get that," I said as I broke away and reached for my phone. I held in a sigh of relief when I saw it was from Ally and completely innocuous.

Staying in town for fireworks. Will be home after.

"Anything wrong?" Carter asked.

"It's just Ally. She's staying in town for the fireworks."

"No chaperone. Yikes. We better move outside where the neighbors can see before I suggest things I'm not medically cleared to do."

I laughed and grabbed some plastic wineglasses out of the cabinet. "Cookies?"

"Hell yeah." He lifted the plate off the kitchen table,

grabbed the bottle of wine, and headed out the back door. I grabbed a corkscrew from the kitchen drawer and followed him out, an odd range of emotions coursing through me.

On the one hand, I was relieved that Ally's text had interrupted our moment in the kitchen. On the other hand, I was disappointed that we'd been interrupted. It seemed my entire relationship with Carter had been that way—one step forward, ten seconds jogging back. And that was all on me. Carter had been clear about his intentions from day one. Even when he was only flirting, I knew he was interested. I may be socially inept, but my female parts still worked fine, and they had a normal response to a sexy man putting out the signals.

The problem was the lie. The great, big, enormous honking lie that created the chasm between us that only I could see. I knew it wasn't fair to get involved with Carter without telling him the truth, but it was better for Carter's safety if he didn't know, at least not until the situation with Ahmad was resolved. Sometimes I worried that simply getting involved at all put him at risk. If Ahmad's men made me in Sinful, Carter would be perceived as a threat. Given Ida Belle and Gertie's age, and the fact that no one in Sinful knew the real story behind their military service, they would probably be safe.

Because she was currently living with me, I worried about Ally as well, but the construction company assured her the repairs to her house would only take three weeks. If they kept on schedule, she'd be back in her own space soon enough, leaving me the lone target. Well, and Merlin, but he seemed to have more than the requisite nine lives, so no matter what happened, I figured he'd come out fine.

Carter was dragging two lawn chairs over to the edge of the bayou when I walked outside. He grabbed a cooler from next to the hammock and put it over in front of the chairs to serve as a table. The sun was just starting to set, and it made pretty ripples of orange and yellow over the bayou. I sank into the lawn chair and Carter popped open the wine and poured.

Carter lifted his glass. "Here's to that one day of peace and quiet we got yesterday."

I tapped my glass against his. "If I'd known things were going to go south this quickly, I would have stayed awake for more of it."

"Ha! Can you believe that before you came to town, I actually used to get bored?"

"Correlation does not equal causation."

Carter smiled. "A lot of criminals use that same defense. But no, I'm not saying things happening around here are your fault. How could they be? Jeez, some of them have been going on for years or happened years ago. You appear to be a woman of many talents, but I don't think time travel is one of them."

"If it were, I'd have already won the lottery—twice." I looked out over the bayou and frowned. It seemed so peaceful, but I knew firsthand that awful, deadly things lurked beneath the surface. In that way, the entire town seemed to be mimicking the bayous that surrounded it. On the surface, everything appeared fine, but clearly, Sinful was brimming with problems.

"Gertie, Ida Belle, and I were talking about that earlier," I said.

"Time travel?"

"No. How things used to be quiet around here. Ida Belle seemed upset that so many bad things were happening right under her nose."

Carter nodded. "The law enforcement part of me wants to say that little old ladies shouldn't be crime fighters, but the practical, small-town boy in me knows that the little old ladies usually have the dirt on everyone. Ida Belle's had her finger on the pulse of this town since she returned from Vietnam, practically running it if people were to admit the truth of things. I can see where it would bother her to be caught by surprise on the depth of issues here. It certainly bothers me."

"I wish there were something I could do." I held my hand in the air to stop Carter from interrupting. "Not about the crime. Just about Ida Belle and Gertie feeling bad about it. They're not responsible, but I get the impression they feel that they are."

"They love this place. I can understand that." He turned a bit in his chair so that he could face me. "When I left here, I was thrilled and absolutely certain I never wanted to return. Then when I got to Iraq, I couldn't think of anything but coming home."

"You were fighting a war, Carter. It's not like you were vacationing. Wanting to come home sounds perfectly normal to me."

"When I got back stateside, I told myself the same thing. So I headed home for a visit with my mom, then I took off again. For three months, I traveled around the US. Sometimes, I went to visit friends. Other times, I went to a place just because I wanted to see it. One time, I threw darts at a map and the first three places I hit, I went to."

I stared at him for a moment, absorbing this information. It was a side of Carter I didn't know, and it was an interesting thing that he'd done. "I guess nowhere else compared?"

"No. And I saw some pretty amazing things—beautiful coastlines, majestic mountains, those enormous trees that you can drive a car through—but no matter how great it was, it wasn't home. So I came back. Sheriff Lee hired me on as a deputy and the rest is really boring history."

"Until a month ago."

He nodded.

"I have to ask, does Sinful still look as good now?"

His brow creased. "It's still home. I'm not sure what it would take to change that. But I see it differently than I did before. It's impossible not to."

"Yeah," I said. I knew exactly what he was saying. Every time I was on a mission, I thought about the end, when I'd go home to my quiet, safe apartment and decompress. Where I could relax with Harrison over a beer and a discussion of firearms. It was a pace so slow, sometimes it felt I was going in reverse, and a lot of the time I was bored and itching for that phone call from Morrow that would send me back into the field. But no matter what, I still looked forward to going home.

Except now, I had another basis for comparison. Living in Sinful had opened my eyes to what being part of a community was about. It had exposed me to true friendships and the sacrifices people were willing to make for them. Bottom line—it had shown me how hollow my life in DC was. When all of this was over and I went back to my old life, things would never be the same.

There was no way they could be.

"Have you heard anything from Dr. Stewart?" I asked, feeling the need for a change of subject. The current one was becoming too deep and far too depressing.

"You mean have I called Dr. Stewart to ask him about the thing I'm not supposed to mention and that you're not supposed to ask questions about?"

"Yeah, that would be the one."

He shook his head. "You never give up, do you?"

"In my defense, you never told me I couldn't ask questions. You told me to stay out of the investigation. Since I'm here with you drinking wine and waiting for explosives in the sky, I'd say I'm definitely meeting that criterion."

He raised one eyebrow.

"C'mon," I complained. "I'm going to find out one way or another. I'm sure Ida Belle and Gertie know a nurse, volunteer, or janitor who owes them a favor, or have somehow linked their home computers to the hospital's security feed, or maybe they'll just dress up like hospital staff, stroll right in, and read the file over a cup of coffee. Bottom line, it's just a matter of time."

Carter sighed. "Given that Gertie was impersonating hospital personnel a week ago, your list is more plausible than one would hope. Yes. Dr. Stewart called right before I left to come over here."

"And?"

"The leg tested positive for meth, both on the skin and in the bloodstream."

"Crap. I knew you were right. You're too good at your job not to be, but I still hoped…"

"Yeah. Me too."

"I don't suppose they had any way of identifying who the leg belonged to?"

"Unfortunately, no. No tattoos, no surgical implants with serial numbers, not even a unique scar."

"So you've got nothing."

"It was a white male, thirties to forties, approximately five foot ten to six foot two and fairly lean."

"That doesn't narrow it down much."

"No, it doesn't. And that's assuming he was a Sinful resident, which is something we can't be certain about. With the oil field work and all the construction after the hurricanes, plenty of people have come and gone around here. Any one of them could have scouted out a place for their operation and come back much later to fire it up."

"It would be nice if it turned out to be a stranger. Or mostly one. You know what I mean."

"Yeah. Well, we can hope."

The words said one thing, but the tone of his voice said another. Whether it was instinct or a hunch or whatever mojo made Carter good at his job, he already knew that the problem was homegrown. Which meant I was going to be forced to hang out with teens and probably steal a boat, but in the big scheme of things, those weren't the worst things I'd done since I'd arrived in Sinful.

A loud whistling sound disrupted my thinking and I looked up to see the first of the fireworks explode across the night sky. Carter reached over and took my hand in his, giving me a smile. I took a drink of my wine and relaxed. Tonight was all about enjoying the splendor of things that blew up.

Tomorrow I'd concentrate on the darker side of things going *boom*.

Chapter Four

I had just changed into my sleeping tee and pulled on shorts when I heard the front door open. I headed downstairs for my late-night snack and found Ally in the kitchen, dumping her purse on the table.

"You stayed out late," I said. The fireworks show had ended around an hour before. Right about that time, the breeze stopped and the mosquitoes moved in for the kill. I invited Carter in but he declined, saying he needed to get some rest as he was on Walter duty tomorrow, per Emmaline. I guess she figured having them in one place would make it easier to keep both of them from overexertion. I wished her all the luck in the world on that one.

I could tell Carter was tired, but the wistful expression he wore when I dropped him off in front of his house made me wonder if the real reason he left was because he knew Ally would be home soon and didn't want to tempt either of us into a compromising position. It was just as well. I knew I wanted Carter, but I still wasn't sold on it being a good idea. And even though I was rarely embarrassed, the thought of Ally sleeping across the hall with Carter and me only two walls away made me kinda squeamish. Since Emmaline had moved into Carter's spare room until Dr. Stewart gave him clearance, his house was even worse on the "hell no" scale.

"I was talking with a couple of the vendors after the show,"

Ally said. "I went to school with some of them, and people from other towns stopped by to comment on the festival and mostly on Francine's pies. Then the mosquitoes moved in and everyone cleared out." She began to yawn and threw her hand over her mouth. "I swear, I had all this energy just a little while ago, and now I'm about to fall asleep standing here."

I took a closer look at her. Her eyes were half closed and she was swaying slightly in place. "You've had a long day. Do you work tomorrow?"

"No. Francine changed the schedule to give me the day off since I worked at the café this morning and the pie booth at the festival."

"That's good. Maybe you can sleep in."

Ally smiled. "I always try to, but it never works. I finally accepted that I'm one of those awful morning people. But I do think I'm going to head up now. I hope I can stay awake long enough to shower the street dust off of me. See you tomorrow."

"Good night," I said and watched her trudge out of the kitchen and down the hallway. As I opened the refrigerator, I heard a crash in the living room and rushed down the hallway. Ally and one of the decorative tables in the living room had apparently had a run-in. The lamp was the big loser. Ally was struggling to get up from the floor and I grabbed her hand just before she got a fistful of drapes. As I hauled her to her feet, her knees started to buckle.

"Are you drunk?" I asked, trying to lock in on a logical explanation for her collapse. One that didn't involve anything serious.

"Someone sneaked champagne to the festival, but I only had one glass," she said, her voice slurred.

"That must have been one helluva glass. Let's get you into bed."

I half carried her up the stairs and let her drop onto the bed, then I swung her legs over onto the mattress and pulled off her tennis shoes. She was already snoring when I pulled the blanket over her. I shook my head and headed out of the room. Ally had always been a lightweight when it came to drinking, but this seemed extreme after only a glass.

I knew she'd been working a lot and worrying over her house construction. Sometimes I heard her moving around her bedroom in the middle of the night, so I knew her sleep wasn't all that great. Neither was mine, for that matter, since her restlessness always had me leaping out of bed and scrambling for my gun. Secretly, I was proud of myself for not having accidentally shot anything in one of my recent midnight grabs. I hadn't always been so lucky since I'd arrived in Sinful.

I tromped back to the kitchen and grabbed my usual bedtime snack of chocolate milk and cookies, then headed back upstairs to my bedroom, ready to crawl into bed myself. I was halfway through a thriller novel and it was a doozy. With any luck, I could get in a couple more chapters before my eyes started drooping.

I put the chocolate milk and cookies on the nightstand next to the book, turned on the lamp, and turned off the bedroom lights. Then I pulled off my shorts, propped the pillows up and slid into bed. Merlin hopped up next to me and curled himself into a tight, purring ball. I leaned back against the pillows for a bit, sighing as the cool sheets made my whole body tingle. I hadn't realized how tired I was until I'd gotten into bed.

Two chapters.

I opened my eyes and reached for the book and a cookie. The private investigator heroine had just chased a killer into a dark alleyway and was now sneaking among the Dumpsters and crates, ready to fire if necessary. I could easily picture the dim light from the yellow bulb at the top of the building and the chill she felt from the drizzling rain. As she inched closer to a Dumpster at the end of the alley, I clenched the pages. Just a couple more steps and she'd be there, looking behind the Dumpster.

I turned the page, ready for the big showdown…and heard a noise downstairs.

I froze. Merlin's head flew up and his ears went back. Damn it. That meant I hadn't imagined it. I dropped the book and slid out of bed, lifting my pistol from the nightstand as I went. I crept out of the bedroom and across the hall. Ally was still in the same position I'd left her in and I could hear her softly snoring. I reached for the door to close it, then hesitated. Sometimes, it squeaked. Best to leave it alone.

I looked over the stair railing into the living room. A sliver of light crept into the room from the hallway to the kitchen. I frowned, fairly certain I'd turned off all the kitchen lights. I held position for several seconds, listening for any sign of movement. I was just about to chalk it all up to something shifting in the refrigerator or falling in the pantry when I heard the sound of a chair sliding across the kitchen floor. A couple seconds later, I heard someone opening the refrigerator.

What the hell? What kind of intruder broke in to raid your food supply?

I considered my options. Conventional wisdom said I should call the police, and if Carter were at full capacity, I might have actually considered doing so. But with the options for response being Deputy Breaux or even worse, Nelson, I wasn't convinced that calling the police would result in anything more effective than crawling in bed and letting him eat me out of house and home would accomplish.

I sighed. Regardless of the current lack of ability of law

enforcement, I needed to try harder to stay off the radar, especially as long as Celia was running the show. She'd take any opportunity to make an example of me. I headed back into my bedroom to make the call, but my cell phone wasn't on my nightstand. Then I recalled seeing it on the kitchen counter as I'd poured my glass of milk…sitting right next to Ally's purse, which contained her cell phone. Great. The first time I'd actually intended to do the normal-person responsible thing, and the phones were right next to the bad guys.

Right next to the remainder of the chocolate chip cookies.

I gripped my gun, my resolve firm. No way was someone getting away with the last of my cookies, but I couldn't possibly catch the intruder if I used the stairs. They made too much noise. Before I could change my mind, I made my way over to my bedroom window and lifted it up. I eased over the ledge and onto the porch roof, then hurried to the edge of the porch and jumped off the side, rolling as I hit the ground. Dried leaves and twigs from the shrubs bordering the front of the house dug into my bare feet, but I didn't give them more than a second's thought as I set out around the side of the house for the back. I would be able to see inside the kitchen from the window. If I could manage to get up the steps without alerting the intruder to my presence, my plan was to burst in through the back door and take him by surprise.

When I reached the corner of the house, I peered around, looking for any sign of movement in the backyard. Moonlight provided decent illumination from the house all the way to the bayou, but the backyard and the waterfront were clear. Whoever it was hadn't arrived by boat, or hadn't docked behind my house. I slipped around the corner and skirted the back of the house behind the shrubs until I reached the kitchen window. I peered over the edge and held in a curse when I saw that the blinds were drawn.

I never closed the blinds.

I dropped back down and considered my options. I could knock on a neighbor's door and ask to use their phone, but then I'd have to explain how I got out of my house without the intruder hearing me and why I was prancing around my lawn in a T-shirt and underwear, packing a nine-millimeter. The T-shirt was long enough to cover my rear, but just barely, and more than likely, it was illegal to be outside without pants on Thursday nights. I couldn't believe I'd left the house without putting my shorts back on. This whole domestic living thing had completely ruined me.

I tapped my fingers on my pistol and considered my other limited options. I could jog to Gertie's, but then I risked being seen jogging in a T-shirt and underwear and packing a nine-millimeter, not to mention, the intruder might leave before I could get to Gertie's and get the police to my house. And that would still leave me explaining my state of undress and gun-toting to law enforcement and anyone else who happened to see me half streaking down the block. Besides, I couldn't leave Ally inside unprotected.

Crap.

Seemed as if only one option was available, and that was bursting into the kitchen with no knowledge of what awaited me on the other side of the door. It wasn't as though I hadn't done it before, and to people who were likely far more dangerous than the refrigerator raider. But then, crazy people were unpredictable, and breaking into someone's house to eat was decidedly crazy. Mind made up, I crept out of the bushes and up the back steps. I expected to find the back door jimmied, but neither the lock nor the door appeared damaged at all.

How the heck had he gotten inside?

I placed my shoulder against the door, then took a step back and leaped as hard as I could against it.

Sorta.

At least, it would have been against the door if someone hadn't opened it at the exact time I launched.

I flew into the kitchen, my bare feet not even connecting with the tile floor before I went sprawling down on it. I gripped my gun with both hands to avoid dropping it, rolled over to get my feet underneath me, and leaped up ready to fire. And found myself looking directly at Big and Little Hebert. I glanced over at the door and saw Mannie standing there still holding the knob.

Big, who was sitting across two of my kitchen chairs, lifted a chocolate chip cookie and took a bite. "You have an interesting way of welcoming guests into your home."

I lowered my gun and stared. "Have you lost your mind? You broke into my house, and for the record, this is exactly the way I deal with intruders."

Big looked over at Little, who smiled. "Interesting," Big said. "You have some odd habits for a librarian, Ms. Morrow. I find you fascinating."

Little nodded. "She's quite muscular as well. Hauling books around must be great for the physique."

Crap!

As I dashed to the laundry room, I heard Mannie chuckling behind me. I yanked on a pair of shorts, then stalked back to the kitchen and glared at the three of them. "How did you get in here?"

Mannie looked amused. "Are you kidding me? I could have picked that lock when I was three. You should get a dead bolt."

"It's at the top of my list," I said. "What are you doing in my house? You're lucky I didn't shoot you."

"We can see that now," Big said. "We thought taking your

roommate out of the equation meant you'd be easier to handle, but we didn't count on this much vigor and stealth, even though we've seen some of your work."

"What are you talking about?" I asked. "What did you do to Ally? Oh my God. I have to call the paramedics!"

"Your friend is fine," Big said. "She simply had a long day that ended with a lovely glass of champagne laced with a bit of a sleeping pill. She'll wake up in the morning feeling more rested than she has in ages."

I closed my eyes and clutched the top of my head. This had to be a dream, because none of it made a lick of sense. But when I lowered my hands and opened my eyes, they were all still there. "You drugged Ally? What in the world for?"

"Because we needed to talk to you in private," Big said.

"You couldn't just call? Or show up at a decent hour and ring the doorbell?"

Big cocked his head to one side. "We were unable to locate a telephone number for you, so that wasn't an option. Would it really have been a better choice for us to show up at your door in broad daylight...perhaps when that deputy boyfriend of yours was here?"

Just the thought had me cringing. No way could I have explained that one. "Okay, you've made your point, but you still could have sent a note or something and had me meet you somewhere."

"What we need to discuss couldn't wait. Time is always of the essence with such matters. Even a single day can make the difference between success and failure."

"What matters are you talking about? Can you just spit it out already?"

The smile vanished from Little's face, and Big looked somber. "We have a 'friend' at the hospital who told us about an interesting body part received for testing."

Holy crap! The meth lab belonged to Big and Little Hebert and they were going to kill me here in my kitchen. Whatever they gave Ally would probably kill her as well.

My face must have shown exactly what I was thinking, because Big raised one hand in the air. "Ms. Morrow, I assure you we are not here to harm you. And we certainly don't involve ourselves in such sordid business as the production of meth." He waved a hand at Mannie. "Step outside while we finish up. You make people nervous."

Mannie grinned and slipped outside, but I had no doubt he could be back inside, guns blazing, at the slightest call from Big. Not to mention that I didn't think for one minute that Big and Little couldn't be as deadly as Mannie if required. But I also knew how to read people, and everything about Big's demeanor and body positioning told me he wasn't a threat. My breath came out in a whoosh, and the tension began to evaporate from my back and neck. "Then what is your interest?"

"Before we get down to business," Little said, "can you please sit down? It's straining my neck to look up at you."

I pulled out the remaining kitchen chair and sat across from them.

"Meth is bad business," Big said. "It kills people and destroys towns."

I stared. Was he serious?

"I know what you're thinking," Big said. "Our business ventures aren't exactly the kind that you report to the IRS, but running books or acquiring the occasional odd object for a client doesn't bring the kind of issues that hard drugs do. We like Sinful, and we don't want to see anything like that moving through this town."

I nodded. I had a feeling their "business" extended a bit

beyond bookmaking and odd-object acquisition, but I wasn't about to say so.

"You have to understand," Little said, "we've got no beef with the moonshine trade. Heck, we have some interests ourselves, and even pot isn't an issue."

Big nodded. "But meth is insidious. It creeps in dark alleys and behind closed doors, silently reducing a town like this to ash. We've seen it before."

"Okay," I said. "You're a little more melodramatic than I would have expected, not that I don't agree with everything you said, but what does any of this have to do with me? Surely you don't think I'm involved with something like that."

"Of course not," Big said. "We never would have come here if I thought such a thing. But what I *do* think is that you're nosy, and I think you and those old broads like to get in the thick of police business and aren't afraid to break the law to do it. Most importantly, you're good at it. Your closure rate on recent crime is better than the New Orleans Police Department."

"Uh, thank you. I guess." He had called me nosy but it mostly seemed to be complimentary, so I was happy to roll with it.

Little cocked his head to one side. "Out of curiosity, what does your deputy boyfriend think about your side activities?"

I frowned a bit at the word "boyfriend." It sounded so juvenile, not to mention permanent. "If he finds out about my extracurricular activities, he's not happy, but I don't volunteer anything about this particular interest of mine."

Little laughed. "I just bet you don't."

"Anyway," Big said. "The bottom line is that Little and I would like to know who was manufacturing meth in Sinful, but it's not the sort of thing we can physically take on ourselves. We prefer to maintain a low profile."

Little nodded. "So if you were interested in poking around, we're offering you anonymous assistance."

I know I should have ended the conversation right there with a resounding "no," but the offer was so intriguing and unexpected that I couldn't help myself. "What kind of assistance?"

"You need a background check on someone, we can handle it," Big said. "Weapons, gear for night excursions, fake IDs, flash money…whatever gets us that information."

Fake IDs? Hmmmmm. I filed that one away for future thought. "What about a boat?"

"You don't have one?" Big asked.

"I'm sure you already know that I'm only visiting for the summer to settle up my aunt's affairs, and she didn't have one. Gertie and Ida Belle both did but we ran into some trouble with them, and they're sorta out of commission."

Big laughed. "I'm not even going to ask. But to answer your question, yes. I'm happy to provide a boat. For the obvious reasons, it won't be one from my personal stock, but I can arrange for something to be docked behind your house tomorrow morning."

This is the point where you politely decline.

I knew I should say, "Thank you, but no." Butting my nose into law enforcement matters was bad enough, but being bankrolled by the local mob to do it was a whole other level of insanity. "Let's say I happen to track down the people involved. What do you plan to do with them?"

Big raised one eyebrow. "Do you really want to know?"

I shook my head. It was a stupid question with an obvious answer. Besides, it's not as if I had a leg to stand on with a moral argument against what he had planned. My entire career involved eliminating threats to public safety that the vast majority of people in the world never even knew existed.

"It's a deal," I said. "On the condition that no one ever knows we're involved."

"Ha," Big said. "You think I want word getting back to my boss that I'm contracting with a deputy's girlfriend for family business?"

"Probably not."

Big extended his hand across the table. "Then it's a deal."

Against all my better judgment, I reached across the table and shook his hand, feeling every bit as though I'd just made a deal with the devil.

Little reached into his suit jacket and pulled out a business card. He handed the card to me and I saw it contained a single phone number.

"Consider that your personal hotline," Little said. "You need anything, you call that number. It can't be traced to Big or me, and when all this is over, it will be disconnected."

Big placed his hands on the table and lurched upward. I leaned on the table, putting all my weight on the other side to keep it from flipping over. Once he was upright, I rose from my chair as Little opened the back door. Mannie was standing outside, whistling as if this were a normal every-night activity—and for all I knew, it might be.

I held my breath as Big walked down the steps and into the backyard, wondering if the steps would hold him, and if he fell, would he crater the lawn. With Mannie and Little's help, he made it to safety without incident. As they walked away, Mannie turned around. "Get that lock changed."

"Then you might have to ring the doorbell," I said.

He grinned. "Doubt it."

I threw my hands in the air and went back inside, closing and locking the door behind me—for what good it did. The only kind of people I really wanted to keep out of my house were the kind that weren't deterred in the least by a lock.

I grabbed my gun off the kitchen table and headed upstairs, straight to Ally's room. I hovered over her, making sure she was breathing, and let out a sigh of relief when she appeared fine. I glanced across the hall at my room, but knew I wouldn't get a wink of decent sleep until I knew for certain that Ally was okay. I walked to the corner of the room and slumped into an overstuffed chair.

My really long day kept getting longer.

Chapter Five

"Fortune."

The voice sounded far away, and I struggled to identify it.

"Fortune."

Something shook me and I leaped up, gun in hand and ready for battle.

Ally stared. "It's just me. I didn't think I was going to wake you there for a minute."

I lowered my gun and rolled my head around, trying to loosen up my cramped neck. "I don't even remember falling asleep."

"It was a big day yesterday. I don't even remember coming upstairs." She looked down at my hand, still clenching the pistol. "Any particular reason you were sleeping in my room armed?"

Crap. I needed a plausible story, and I needed to come up with it on limited sleep and absolutely no coffee. "You don't remember coming upstairs because I sorta carried you after you assaulted a table in the living room and broke a lamp. It must have been the champagne combined with too much stress and not enough sleep."

Ally's eyes widened. "Seriously? Oh my God, I'm sorry. I'll replace the lamp."

I waved a hand in dismissal. "I don't care about the lamp. It was ugly anyway. But I was worried because you were so out of it, so I kept checking on you. Then I heard a noise outside shortly after I went to bed and took my pistol to check it out."

"Fortune! You're supposed to call the police. You know things never go well when you start checking them out yourself."

"I didn't shoot anything this time." Only because I fell into my kitchen. Otherwise, the refrigerator probably would have bought it. "Anyway, I was on edge when I came back upstairs so I sat in the chair for a minute, and I guess I fell asleep."

She shook her head. "I bet your neck is stiff all day. Anyway, I woke you up to tell you I'm leaving to meet the contractor at my house."

"Great. One of these days, I need to go by and see how the work's going."

Her eyes lit up. "It looks awesome. The kitchen of my dreams. After I meet with the contractor, I'm going to meet with a decorator in New Orleans to pick out fabric for the barstools and cornices. Do you want to come?"

My face must have conveyed my horror, because she laughed.

"If you could see your expression," Ally said. "You really don't have a domestic bone in your body, do you?"

"If I do, I haven't found it yet. I promised Ida Belle and Gertie I'd help them with some Sinful Ladies stuff today anyway."

"Well, have fun and stay out of trouble—if that's possible." She headed out of the room and paused as she entered the hallway and looked back at me. "Oh, and someone parked an airboat in the bayou behind your house. See you later!"

I waited until she was out of sight before rushing over to the window to peer outside. My pulse spiked when I saw the shiny new airboat parked in my backyard. Bass boats had been getting the job done, but that was totally friggin' awesome. Big and Little weren't playing around. I hurried downstairs and out to the backyard, anxious to check out the boat. I'd never ridden in one, but I'd seen them on television and it looked like a blast, and didn't appear to be nearly as bumpy as regular boats. Plus, these things were fast!

I jumped inside, admiring the bench across the middle and two captains' seats perched high on the back. Everything was pristine, and the aluminum hull shone like new money. Even the giant fan on the back was pretty. I checked the ignition for a key, but it didn't contain one. Frowning, I glanced back at my house, wondering for a second if it was on my kitchen table. I wouldn't put it past Mannie to make a point. Again.

I scanned the boat and realized the bench probably had storage beneath it. I lifted the seat and on top of a stack of life jackets, I saw an envelope with my name on it. I opened the envelope and pulled out the key and a couple of folded papers. The first was a handwritten note.

Ms. Morrow,

It was a pleasure chatting with you at the café last week. Attached you will find your summer lease for the airboat, as we talked about. Enjoy it and be safe!

Bob Hebert

Swamp City Airboats

Hebert, huh? Probably a relative. I couldn't help but grin. Not only had Big and Little delivered the goods, they'd given me a way to easily explain my acquisition. Salesmen stopped at the café all the time. It wouldn't be a stretch for one of them to talk to me. In fact, I'd been offered deals on a number of items, including salesmen themselves. And Hebert was so common in Louisiana. Unless Bob was a known crime lord, no one was going to put together him and my association with Big and Little.

I hopped out of the boat and headed for the house, eager to get Gertie and Ida Belle over here to see what we had to work with. With any luck, one of them knew how to drive the thing. With good luck, it would be Ida Belle.

My cell phone was signaling that I had a text message waiting and when I looked at the display, I saw it was from Carter. I picked up the phone to read the message, hoping he didn't want to hang out today. While I was happy that he seemed to actually be resting, as Dr. Stewart ordered, if he insisted on spending most of his resting time with me, it would seriously cramp our investigation. Not to mention that I wasn't comfortable with a full-time relationship. Hell, I wasn't comfortable with any relationship, but I could manage part-time. I just wasn't ready to have all my waking hours under scrutiny.

Going to watch movies at Walter's. Will call you this afternoon.

I smiled. Good. The two of them sitting in recliners was perfect. They'd get some rest, Emmaline would get a break from supervising, and Ida Belle, Gertie, and I could sneak out into the bayou without drawing attention to ourselves. With Ally off to New Orleans, that left no one to witness our complete disregard for the law.

I sent a text to Gertie and Ida Belle.

Get over here as soon as you can. Have solved the boat problem.

I slid my phone onto the counter and poured myself a glass of milk. I probably had time to polish off the last of the cookies before they got here. I sat down at the kitchen table and opened my laptop. The first thing I did was Google the boat retailer listed on the lease. A banner with a bass boat and a face that looked like a combination of Big and Little popped up. Good Lord, that was a strong family gene. I hoped the women didn't have it. The look wasn't all that great for men, but for women, it would be a cat-lady sentence.

I clicked on the list of boats for sale and scanned it until I found the one that looked like my lease. Holy crap! Sixty thousand dollars. That cost more than a really nice car. Big and Little weren't exaggerating their hatred for hard drugs. They probably made plenty of money, but given my track record—which they also knew plenty about—they couldn't really hope to get the boat back in the same condition it was delivered. Heck, given our history with boats, I'd be thrilled if it was still floating when we were done with it.

I closed the boat website and clicked over to email to see if I'd gotten a reply from Harrison. I was more than a little worried about the attack on Morrow. I still hadn't put my finger on what they thought it would accomplish. If someone was looking for me, then killing him wasn't the way to get an answer, but then if I assumed it was the CIA mole that ordered the hit, then maybe they thought killing Morrow would draw me out of hiding.

It was a sobering thought that someone I worked with—who received paychecks from the same office and made the same promises of service to the country that I did—could have allegiance with one of the worst people in the world. I knew money and power were a big draw, but to sell out not only your comrade but the safety of future generations was a scumbag move beyond the limits of my understanding.

I logged on to email and saw a message from Harrison. I grabbed a cookie and clicked to open the message.

To: farmgirl433@gmail.com

From: hotdudeinNE@gmail.com

Glad to hear things are going well at the farm. I know that could change at any minute, but it's nice to have a turn of good luck. Speaking of which, the forecast is calling for cooler weather this week. I'll believe it when I see it, but it's nice to have hope again. I do remember that trip. I thought we'd never find a nice place, and then we ended up finding it somewhere we never would have looked if we hadn't been exploring outside of the usual tourist lines. If things don't cool down here soon, I'm going to start checking into a vacation. I probably should start doing some research and see what looks good.

In other news, the auditors are here, so everything is a mess. They have a knack for asking for the one damned receipt that seems to be missing from the files. So far, we've been able to satisfy them on everything. They should be done by the end of next week.

Well, guess I better run and get back to work. My dad is getting better every day. He's started complaining—loudly—so I know he'll be fine. Talk to you later!

I took a bite of my cookie and read the message again. Harrison had gotten my hint about Ahmad changing his appearance and looked like he was going to move on that line of investigation, which was great. Also great was that the first part of his message seemed to indicate he had a lead on Ahmad's location. With any luck, that would pan out and I could go back to only looking over my shoulder every minute instead of every ten seconds.

The audit part confused me for a moment, but then it clicked—he was doing a sweep of the financial records of the other agents, which fit in line with my thinking earlier that someone was getting a hell of a payoff to try to find me. His message indicated no success so far, but that didn't surprise me. No agent was foolish enough to dump a bunch of money in a US bank account, but looking at everyone might expose some oddities that made him do a wider sweep. Everyone thought international bank accounts were private, but the reality was, nothing in the world was private if someone with technology and money didn't want it to be.

I swallowed the rest of the cookie, downed half my glass of milk, and hit Reply.

To: hotdudeinNE@gmail.com

From: farmgirl433@gmail.com

A vacation sounds like a wonderful idea. Let me know if you find anything interesting. I might want to try it out when things settle down here. Yuck on the auditors. That doesn't sound fun at all. Hopefully they'll finish up soon and you can move on to bigger and better things.

I'm glad your dad is improving. Complaining is usually a sign that someone is on the mend. Well, time to feed the animals. Good luck with the vacation hunt.

I hit Send and reached for another cookie. I knew Harrison was doing everything he could to locate Ahmad and the mole, but I couldn't help but wish I were there helping. Surely two of us working on it would be more efficient. On the other hand, a moving target was more of a hindrance than a help. But it still grated. This was my life and my career on the line.

I took another bite of the cookie and frowned, contemplating my own line of thought. At one time, the idea that my career could be in jeopardy would have sent me into a tailspin of anxiety and despair. I *was* only my career. Fortune Redding, the person, didn't exist other than to fill that role. But ever since I'd arrived in Sinful, I'd started to wonder just how much living I'd been missing out on. Granted, with the recent burst of criminal activity here, I hadn't really had time off the job, per se, but there was downtime in between emergency investigations that I enjoyed. I really liked eating breakfast at the café and chatting with Francine and the regulars. I liked hanging out with Gertie and Ida Belle watching television, even though Gertie had exposed me to things I might have to bleach my eyes to forget. I loved lying in my hammock in the backyard and reading a great book, and if two months ago, anyone had told me I'd think that, I would have shot them for being stupid.

I wanted the problem with Ahmad to be over. Wanted it more than anything. And I wanted the mole identified and put on trial for treason. But when I thought about returning to my quiet, organized condo in DC, I didn't feel the anticipation I thought I would. If I was being honest with myself, the thought felt kind of lonely.

I sighed and polished off the cookie. The frustrating reality was that coming to Sinful had changed it all. And while I wasn't even ready to consider ditching everything I'd spent a lifetime building, I wasn't eager to jump back in where I'd left off, either.

The doorbell rang and I slammed the laptop shut, then jumped up from the table, happy for the interruption. What I would do when the Ahmad threat was over was something I needed to spend some time thinking seriously about, but it didn't have to be now. Today, we had bigger fish to fry. I hurried to the front door and opened it to let Ida Belle and Gertie inside.

"I hope you have coffee," Gertie said. "I overslept and I can't seem to get moving."

"Actually," I said as I headed for the kitchen, "I haven't put any on yet, but what I have to show you might get your blood pumping."

I stopped short at the back door and looked back at them. "Are you ready for the surprise?"

"Oh for Christ's sake, get on with it," Ida Belle said. "I haven't had breakfast yet."

I flung open the door and stepped outside, the two of them

trailing behind me.

"Ta da!" I said and waved a hand at the bayou.

"Holy crap!" Ida Belle clutched her chest and for a minute, I was afraid she might have a heart attack. She shoved me out of the way and headed across the lawn. I grinned at Gertie and we hurried after her.

Ida Belle stopped short at the boat and gave it a long, lingering once-over, then she ran one hand gently across the side. I smiled. "Are you going to pray to it or ask it on a date?"

"Maybe both," Ida Belle said.

Gertie nodded. "Totally over the coffee thing. This is awesome."

"This is more than awesome," Ida Belle said. "This is glorious."

"I don't really care how you managed this," Gertie said, "but it wouldn't be right if I didn't ask—how the heck did you manage this?"

Ida Belle whipped around to stare at me. "You didn't steal it, did you?"

"What? Of course not," I said. "How would that help matters? It so happens I have a legitimate lease on this boat."

Ida Belle raised an eyebrow. "You leased a boat between last night and this morning? You wouldn't even know where to start with such a thing."

I handed her my lease papers and she glanced them over, her eyes widening when she got to the note. "Bob Hebert? As in—"

I nodded. "They paid me a visit last night. Broke into my house, helped themselves to my chocolate chip cookies, darned near broke my kitchen chairs, and proceeded to tell me how much they hated meth."

"But only a few people know that explosion was a meth

lab," Gertie said. "How did they find out?"

"They have a friend down at the hospital lab…or more likely, someone at the lab who owes them money. Whatever. I didn't ask and it doesn't matter. Whoever it was told Big and Little about the leg, and they got riled up over the thought of meth production in Sinful. They want the town to remain unspoiled, or relatively unspoiled."

"Or only as spoiled as they intend to make it," Ida Belle said. "Which, admittedly, hasn't really caused problems. The people they service would have been in trouble without their help, and some people actually bailed themselves out of the hole by borrowing from them and paying it back."

Gertie nodded. "Georgia Fontaine spent so much money on infomercials that she knew Wilfred would divorce her if he saw the credit card bills. The Heberts lent her the money and she paid off the credit cards before he ever saw them."

"How did she pay back the Heberts?" I asked.

"Well, for starters, she sold the stuff she bought, although that didn't bring enough to repay the loan. You know how resale value is, and Georgia has simply horrible taste, so nothing went for top dollar. So she took her engagement ring to New Orleans, had a fake made up to match, and hocked the real one."

I shook my head. "All that because she couldn't say no to the television?"

"Oh, well, Georgia's never been able to say no. How did you think she ended up married to Wilfred? The man has more hair on his body than bigfoot."

Ida Belle sighed. "Georgia and her bad hairy taste aside, how did the whole issue of the boat come about?"

I gave them a recap of the entire conversation with Big and Little, then finished off with Ally's announcement of the boat. "So I looked outside and darn if it wasn't parked here all pretty with the lease under the storage bench. It even had that note with it, so it looks legit."

Ida Belle nodded. "I have to admit, I'm impressed. I'm certain Big and Little are experts at running books and loan-sharking, but I never took them for big thinkers. You realize that makes doing business with them an even riskier proposition than before, when we thought they weren't as clever."

"I know," I said, "but so far, they've been straight with us. I don't pretend for a minute that things couldn't change. As soon as we serve no benefit to them—be it for delivering drug dealers or even just entertainment value—they could easily become a problem."

"But you're willing to gamble it?" Gertie asked.

"I think so," I said. "I'm pretty good at reading people, and I don't think they have an ulterior motive."

Ida Belle nodded. "If you're satisfied, then so am I. And I have to be honest, it would be foolish to look a gift boat in the mouth." She placed her hand on the boat as if she were afraid it was going to spirit away.

"I don't suppose either of you know how to drive this thing?" I asked.

Gertie opened her mouth to reply and Ida Belle slapped one hand over it. "Don't even think about it," she said. "This baby is all mine."

"Ally's meeting with her contractor and then heading to New Orleans for the day. Carter is parking at Walter's for a television coma marathon. I say we hatch a plan, put together supplies, and get a move on."

We all turned around and headed back toward the house.

"Can the plan include breakfast?" Gertie asked. "Because I'm starving."

"As long as you're cooking," I said. "Otherwise, I can offer you cereal and Pop-Tarts."

"You got bacon and cheese?" Gertie asked.

"I think so. Ally's been doing the shopping."

Gertie nodded. "Omelets it is."

I looked over at Ida Belle. Her expression looked like she'd won the lottery. Then a sudden flash of memory ripped through me—the Corvette, the motorcycle—Ida Belle and speed were a dangerous combination.

"Can we say grace before breakfast?" I asked as we walked inside.

Gertie looked confused. "Sure, but you've never asked to pray before."

I shrugged. "I guess I figured we could use all the help we can get."

Gertie opened the refrigerator and took out ingredients. I headed upstairs to put on jeans and tennis shoes. My rubber boots were in the laundry room. I'd grab those on the way out. You never knew what you might step in on the bayou islands around here. Sometimes even the mud smelled like poo and it clung like glue, making it almost impossible to clean off of anything but rubber. And I even had to use an ice scraper on the boots.

By the time I got back downstairs, Gertie was already serving up omelets. I slid into my spot at the table as Gertie placed the plate in front of me.

"Are you ready for grace?" she asked.

"Yes, but can you do it? It's not in my wheelhouse."

"Sure," Gertie said. "Bow your head."

I bowed my head and waited for Gertie to get on with the praying.

"Dear Lord, we thank you for this day, good food, better friends, and the fact that Ida Belle and I have outlived so many people we didn't like. We're hoping you give us a few more. Please help us track down the meth dealers and run them out of Dodge before Big and Little Hebert turn the town into showdown at the OK Corral. And if you have some spare time after handling all that, could you please see to it that Ida Belle doesn't injure anyone with the boat—including scaring people half to death—and that it doesn't sink before we're done addressing this issue. Amen."

I looked up and saw Ida Belle frowning. I held in a grin. Gertie might seem woolly-headed at times, but she clued right in on my prayer request.

"Let's eat," I said and grabbed the saltshaker. "Have you heard anything from Myrtle?" Myrtle was a card-carrying member of the Sinful Ladies Society and ran the office down at the sheriff's department, shifting from paperwork to dispatch when they were shorthanded. Carter was careful not to allow her access to things we were poking into, but others weren't as diligent. From everything I'd heard about Nelson, I couldn't imagine he had one careful bone in his body, which meant Myrtle could be a great source of information, assuming Nelson gathered any.

"Yeah," Ida Belle said. "She's fit to be tied with Nelson lording over the place. The idiot has already ordered new office furniture complete with a five-thousand-dollar chair covered in alligator skin. The taxpayers are going to have a stroke."

"Did he say anything about investigating the explosion?" I asked.

Ida Belle snorted. "Please. Myrtle asked him if he wanted her to get the sheriff's boat gassed up so he could take a look, and he told her he wasn't interested in hassling people over moonshine."

"But he can't be sure it was moonshine unless he looks," I

argued.

"You and I know that," Ida Belle said, "but Nelson is beyond lazy. Myrtle said he spent all day yesterday alternating between eating funnel cake and sleeping on a cot in the jail."

"Someone should have closed the door and locked him in," Gertie muttered.

"Well, if he spends all his time sleeping, he won't be in our way," I said. "Hopefully Marie's audit will be over soon, and Nelson will be following Celia out the door."

Gertie held up crossed fingers.

"So did you come up with a plan?" I asked.

"Yeah," Ida Belle said. "We're going to take the boat out to where the explosion happened and see if we can find a clue."

I'm not sure what I expected. Realistically, there wasn't anything else to do but poke around, which was the whole point of the boat. But I guess I was hoping they'd have something more. "That's it?"

Gertie put her plate on the table and took a seat. "We can stop and talk to any fishermen we see—ask them who they've seen in that area lately."

"That won't seem suspicious?" I asked. "What if it gets back to Carter that we were asking questions?"

"We won't ask them about the explosion," Ida Belle said. "We're not fools. We'll say we had some problems at the Sinful Ladies Society cough syrup manufacturing site and want to know if they saw anything that can help."

"Exactly," Gertie said. "And because it's moonshine, it falls under Sinful code of silence."

"Is that one of those weird Sinful laws?" I asked.

"No," Gertie said. "That's Southern law. You don't ever rat out a man's moonshine operation. You're better off sleeping with his wife."

Ida Belle stopped eating for a moment, her fork frozen in midair, a piece of omelet dangling from it. "You know what? Sheriff Lee's still is in the same area as the explosion."

"Does that make a difference?" I asked, not sure where she was going with that bit of information.

"Only in the sense that we can ask him who he's seen in the area," Ida Belle said.

"Do you really think we should question the sheriff?" I asked.

"He's not the sheriff anymore," Gertie said. "And besides, he'd have to remember we talked to him before he could cause us any trouble with it."

Hmmm. She had a point. Sheriff Lee's memory was longer than his brother's, who still couldn't remember who I was despite spending a good twenty minutes in a boat with me only days before, but the good sheriff was light years past his best time of mental acuity.

"He'd also have to remember if he saw anyone to be helpful," I pointed out the flaw in their argument.

Gertie sighed. "True."

"Then I guess we have a plan," I said. "Do you guys need to go home and grab rubber boots or something?"

They both stared.

"We keep rubber boots in the trunk of Gertie's car," Ida Belle said. "No good Southerner is caught without access to rubber boots."

"Or firearms," Gertie said. "Besides, your message said you'd solved the boat problem, so we dressed for the event, and I grabbed my emergency boating backpack."

"What exactly does an emergency boating backpack contain?" I asked.

"Bottled water, flare gun, hunting knife, tool kit, small

hatchet, protein bars, fishing line, rope, plastic cups, and a bottle of champagne."

"You lost me at champagne." And "small hatchet" was a bit concerning.

"For if your boat breaks down," Gertie said. "Do you want to wait for rescue drinking water or champagne?"

She had a point. "I have a box of Wheat Thins. Haven't even opened it yet."

"Oh, that would go nicely. We should throw it in."

"If you two are done with the grocery part of the morning," Ida Belle said, "I'd like to get going."

She looked entirely too energetic for this early and I was glad breakfast had been relatively light. I had a feeling the airboat ride was going to be more like a roller coaster and less like a pleasant drive in a Cadillac.

"Last potty break before we leave," Gertie said and headed for the downstairs bathroom. I put the plates in the dishwasher and five minutes later, we were headed for the boat.

Chapter Six

"I call shotgun," Gertie said.

"No way," I said. "Ida Belle needs a navigator with good vision, and don't even start with that lie about you not needing new glasses. Besides, it's my boat."

"She's got you on both counts," Ida Belle said. "Besides, the last thing we need is for you to fall off the seat and break a hip or something."

"Breaking hips is for old people," Gertie said. "I have decided that I am middle-aged."

"Ha!" Ida Belle said. "Middle-aged for what, a tortoise? Your walking speed would indicate that's the case."

"I don't know," I said. "Sheriff Lee and his brother probably owe Moses a trip charge, so it's not exactly impossible."

"Either that, or they're zombies," Gertie said. "Like real sophisticated ones. Not like those idiots in *The Walking Dead*."

"Even if Gertie's mind is middle-aged," Ida Belle said, "her hips are still ancient and she has a tendency to land on them, so my point still stands."

"But—" Gertie started.

I held up a hand to stop the argument. "Just get in the boat. Even if you have the hips of a twenty-year-old, what you will never have is your name on the boat lease. My boat. My seat."

"Fine," Gertie said as she climbed into the boat and flopped down on the bench in the middle. "But you could at least let me give it a whirl on the way back."

Ida Belle rolled her eyes and stepped into the boat.

"Tell you what," I said as I untied the boat from the docking post, "if you're good while we investigate, I'll let you sit in the big-girl seat on the way back."

Gertie shot me a dirty look.

"Hey, you're the one who wants to be thought of as young," I pointed out. "I just deducted a few more years."

I shoved the boat back and took a running leap inside, landing in a perfect crouch position in the front of the boat.

"Your hips can't do that," Ida Belle said.

Gertie sighed in grudging admiration. "True."

I made my way onto the high seat next to Ida Belle and adjusted my sunglasses. "Let's do this."

Ida Belle started the boat, and the giant fan whirled to life. "Hold on," she said, and pressed her foot down on the accelerator.

At that moment, I got a full education on what those bars on each side of my seat were for. The boat practically flew out of the water, pinning me back in my seat. Gertie, who hadn't been gripping anything, flew backward and landed in the bottom of the boat, directly on those hips Ida Belle had expressed concern about earlier. I looked over at Ida Belle, who shook her head but didn't reduce speed. Gertie tried to crawl back onto the bench, but we were going so fast, she couldn't manage it. Finally she gave up and gave Ida Belle the finger before sitting in the bottom of the boat.

I clenched the hand bars as if my life depended on it, and I was fairly certain it did. The boat moved so fast up the bayou that my cheeks flapped, even though my mouth was closed. My sunglasses pressed into the bridge of my nose, making it ache, but I thanked God I'd put them on. If I hadn't, my eyeballs probably would have leaked out my ears. The houses and trees along the bayou started to blur and tears squeezed out of the corners of my eyes.

Then we hit the lake and Ida Belle accelerated to something like warp speed on the *Millennium Falcon*. I swear, I could feel myself getting younger, maybe even thinner and taller. I saw boats flash in my peripheral vision but couldn't make out any details. If we were ever going to question people, we were going to have to slow down to at least the speed of sound.

"Hard right!" Ida Belle yelled and jammed the steering stick forward. The boat spun around so quickly, it was as if it were floating on air rather than water. I tried to appreciate that the ninety-degree turn had just been accomplished with no reduction in speed, but fear prevented me from giving it the props it deserved. When my vision cleared a bit and I could make out the terrain in front of me, all I saw was land.

"Holy crap!" I yelled as Gertie let out a shriek in the bottom of the boat.

Ida Belle lifted her foot from the gas pedal and the boat dropped into the water and slowed by two-thirds of its speed. I lurched forward, clutching the hand bars so tightly my knuckles ached. Gertie fell over and rolled into the bench. I felt my shoulders and arms tighten and then release as the boat glided onto the bank and to a full stop.

Gertie flopped around a bit and finally got upright. She glared up at me. "Still happy you let her drive?"

Ida Belle waved a hand in dismissal. "What are you complaining about? We got here in one piece and a quarter of the time it would have taken in a bass boat." She climbed down from the driver's seat. "Let's go find some evidence before someone sees us."

I jumped off my seat and blinked several times to put some

moisture back in my eyes, and followed Gertie off the boat. "Which way?"

Ida Belle pointed to the right. "There's a trail this way." She reached into the bottom of the boat and lifted her shotgun. "I don't have to tell you to be on alert. Even if the lab and its remaining live workers have cleared out, there could also be a still back here, and people are fiercely protective of their still locations."

I pulled out my pistol and followed Ida Belle onto the trail. "Could someone who already had a still on this island have been responsible for the explosion? You know, if they thought someone else was encroaching on their space?"

"Anything is possible," Ida Belle said, "but my understanding is that meth production is a risky proposition as far as explosions go."

"Definitely," I agreed as I pushed a tree branch to the side. "I'm just thinking out loud, wondering if we have a drug manufacturing issue only or manufacturing and murder."

"Let's hope it's just the first option. We don't need any more killers in Sinful. We could probably handle an idiot drug manufacturer who blew himself up."

"Except that the idiot would have associates," I said. "The cooker is never the distributor who is never the salesman."

Ida Belle sighed. "Then I'm going to keep hoping they were just opening up shop and the rest of the crew weren't from Sinful."

I completely understood her desire for the bad guys to be from anywhere else but Sinful, but someone picked the location for the lab, and that someone had to know the bayous and channels around Sinful. That didn't mean they were a full-time, card-carrying resident of Crazytown, but they probably had been at some point.

Ida Belle drew up short, and I slid a little in the loose dirt. I touched her on her shoulder and she pointed to the left where charred lumber peeked over a group of dense foliage. I turned around to Gertie and gestured to the lumber. She nodded and lifted her pistol up with both hands. I thought for a moment she had been watching too much *Law & Order* again, but then I got a good look at her gun and almost had a heart attack. It was a Desert Eagle .50 AE. Not only would a single shot blow a hole through a mountain, the gun weighed over four pounds. It was no wonder she needed two hands to lift it.

"Please tell me you don't have a round chambered," I whispered.

"What good would it do me if I didn't?" Gertie asked.

Clearly, I hadn't been aware of things that should have been included in grace. "If you shoot me, I swear I will come back and haunt you forever."

Gertie took one hand off the pistol to wave it at me, and the hand holding the gun dropped to her side. I reached out and grabbed the weapon from her. "Give me that. Take mine." I shoved my nine-millimeter into her palm. "If you fire this thing out here, you might create a hole that sucks up the entire town."

Ida Belle peered around me and saw the Desert Eagle. "Have you lost your mind? Good Lord, another ten steps and you probably would have fallen hands-first into the swamp. That thing is half your body weight."

"I was doing fine until bossy pants got involved," Gertie said.

"You'd have been yelling carpal tunnel tomorrow," I said.

"Or not guilty by reason of stupidity," Ida Belle said.

"Fine, fine, you've made your point." Gertie waved the nine-millimeter toward the burned timbers and Ida Belle and I both ducked. "Can we get on with it?"

We turned around and started down the trail again. When we got to the group of bushes right in front of the charred timbers, Ida Belle stopped and parted the seared shrubbery with her shotgun. She peered through the bushes, then looked back at us. "I don't see anything moving."

I nodded and moved into the primary position. Ida Belle was the swamp tracking expert, but when it came to entry into a potentially hostile environment, I wanted to take point. I crept down the line of shrubbery toward an opening I'd spotted about ten feet off the trail. When I got to the edge of the bushes, I lifted the Desert Eagle up to my shoulder and spun around the edge of the bushes to face what was left of the lab.

"It's clear," I said as I stepped toward what remained of the building.

Two charred four-by-fours stretched upward, crossed over each other and wedged between two huge cypress trees with blackened sides. Pieces of plywood and aluminum lay strewn over a twenty-feet-square radius. Glass glittered on the ground as the sunlight filtered through the trees. The tops and inside branches of the trees surrounding the clearing were completely gone, shards of wood hanging where huge branches had once stretched out over the building. When I looked up, it appeared as if I were in a round hole looking up at the sky.

"Wow," Gertie said. "This was some blast. Way worse than that incident with our still."

"You had a still incident?" I asked.

"That's the way Gertie tells it," Ida Belle said.

"How many times do I have to tell you I thought it was water in that bottle?" Gertie asked.

Ida Belle raised one eyebrow. "As opposed to 190 proof, like it said on the label? Gertie tried to put out a generator fire with the contents of that bottle."

Good. God.

"Let's see if we can find anything in this mess," I said.

We picked through the rubble of broken glass, burned wood, melted plastic, and torn aluminum, but didn't come across anything that would give us an indication of who might have been using the site. After thirty minutes of digging in soot and ash, I rose up and clapped my hands together, trying to remove some of the black goo that clung to them.

"Maybe we're not thinking about this right," I said.

"What do you mean?" Ida Belle asked.

"We're searching right in the site of the blast—ground zero," I said. "Everything here would have been blasted to bits, some of it falling back down here and the rest scattered out."

Ida Belle nodded. "And everything that fell back down here continued to burn while things flung outside of the clearing might have retained more of their original properties."

"Exactly," I said. "The side we entered from had thick foliage that probably prevented things from getting through, but the other sides of the clearing only have trees and low brush. I say we each take a side and start looking from the edge of the clearing to ten feet out."

We all tromped off into our section of the swamp and I started scanning the foliage and the ground for anything that might give us a clue as to who had built the lab. "Remember to look up. Things could be caught in limbs."

I spent thirty minutes scouring every inch of my area and was just about to call it a bust when I caught sight of something under a clump of weeds. The color didn't match anything in the surrounding area, so I squatted to get a closer look, then smiled.

It was a finger!

"I found something!" Gertie yelled.

"Me too," I said and made my way back to the clearing.

Gertie held out her hand, and Ida Belle and I looked down at the black matchbook she held.

"It's not weathered," Gertie said, "so it couldn't have been here very long."

"So could be he's a smoker," Ida Belle said, "which still keeps a good portion of the men in Sinful in the running. Or he could have been using the matches for the meth cooking. Either way, I don't see how that helps."

Gertie smiled and flipped the matchbook over to show the Swamp Bar logo in bright yellow. "And we know he hangs out at the Swamp Bar, which narrows things down a bit more."

A wrinkle formed across Ida Belle's brow. "I wonder if we could get a good print off of it?"

"No need," I said and held up the finger. "I've got the print thing covered."

They both made a face like they'd smelled something bad, then brightened.

"That's a great find!" Ida Belle said.

"Do you think it belonged to the cooker?" Gertie asked.

Ida Belle stared at her. "No. It probably belonged to some other guy who happened to have his finger blown off in the swamp."

Gertie put her hands on her hips. "Lots of people in Sinful are missing fingers, and they weren't running meth labs."

"Yeah, but those fingers are either at the bottom of the bayou or inside a gator," Ida Belle said.

"I think it's reasonable to assume only one person lost a finger here," I said.

"You're probably right," Gertie said. "Besides, if it had been here a while, something would have already eaten it."

"With a little Tabasco, it might not be so bad," I said. "Isn't that what you guys say about everything?"

Ida Belle laughed.

Gertie made a face. "Ick. I'm glad I found the matchbook and don't have to carry that thing back. How are you planning on securing it?"

I slipped it in my jeans pocket. "All secure."

Gertie frowned.

"What?" I asked. "It's not like I can do more damage than has already been done."

"If we're done here," Ida Belle said, "we should probably clear out before someone catches us."

"I don't think there's anything else to find," I said.

Gertie nodded and we headed out of the clearing and back down the trail. I paused at the end of the path and scanned the bayou. "Coast is clear," I said.

We hurried over to the airboat and hopped inside. I started toward the back and Gertie grabbed my arm. "You said I could ride shotgun on the way back."

I knew what I'd said, and I would never go back on my word, but given Ida Belle's love of speed, I was positive that Gertie could last longer on a bull than in that seat. "Fine," I said, "but we do it my way."

Gertie narrowed her eyes at me. "What way is that?"

"Give me your shirt," I said, pointing at the long-sleeved pink plaid print that she was wearing.

"I'm not taking off my shirt," Gertie said.

"I know you're wearing a tank underneath it," I said. "It's not like I'm asking you to go back to Sinful naked."

"Thank God," Ida Belle muttered.

Gertie unbuttoned her shirt and pulled it off, but still didn't look convinced. "I don't see what good this is going to do. Not like air is going to catch in the thing and haul me away like a parachute."

"Not with those hips," Ida Belle said.

"I've lost three pounds," Gertie said.

"No you haven't," Ida Belle said. "Your vision has just gotten worse and you can't see it."

I pointed to the seat. "Just climb up there before all of Sinful parades by and sees us here."

Gertie climbed up into the seat and plopped down, looking smug and happy. "This is great!"

"Uh-huh," I said as I climbed onto the platform next to her. "Just wait until your eyeballs turn inside out."

I draped the shirt across her chest and pulled the sleeves behind the seat, then tied them in a knot.

Gertie struggled to release herself from the restricting fabric. "What the heck are you doing?"

"Ensuring you don't pitch out into the bayou," I said. "You'll thank me when it's over."

"Wanna bet?" Gertie asked.

Ida Belle grinned. "If you're done strapping in Junior, let's get out of here."

I hopped off the platform and gave the bench a once-over. No way was I sitting there without a roll cage. I pulled two life vests out from the bench storage and placed one on the bottom of the boat and one against the side of the bench to make a cushioned seat. Then I took a seat and gave Ida Belle a thumbs-up.

"Pansy," Ida Belle said and fired up the engine.

The name-calling rankled a bit, but it was better to be rankled than tossed about like salad. If experience had taught me anything, I knew I'd need to be in tip-top shape for whatever came next. Our excursions into private detective territory always involved something insanely physical before it was over.

Ida Belle stomped on the gas pedal and my head jerked

back as the boat leaped out of the water. I grabbed the back of my neck and pulled my head back into place as the boat leveled out at two million miles per hour. As soon as I got home, I was *so* ordering one of those neck thingies that race car drivers wore.

I heard Gertie squeal and turned around. Her face looked as though she'd gone through five hundred facelifts, and none of them good. Her skin was pulled back so tight, her mouth was a solid line across her face, and despite the fact that I was positive she had her eyes as wide open as a hoot owl, they formed narrow slits that matched her lips. Her white hair stood straight up and back, and I wondered if it would make it all the way back home, or simply give up and let go. If she'd had a beard, she would have doubled for post-op Kenny Rogers, or with a mustache, Albert Einstein.

"Whoohoo!" Ida Belle hooted and pushed the steering rod forward for one of those 12-G turns.

I braced my legs on the hull in front of me and grabbed the side of the boat to try to keep myself from being flung down into the bottom. I heard Gertie yelling behind me, and she didn't sound nearly as enthused as Ida Belle. I managed to stay mostly upright and pulled myself back to a sitting position as the boat straightened out again.

I didn't think it was possible, but Ida Belle pressed the accelerator harder and the boat jumped forward again. Buoys, land masses, and clouds began to pass before my eyes, or maybe it was my life. It was so blurry, I couldn't be sure. What concerned me even more was how Ida Belle could see to drive at this speed.

That thought had no sooner entered my mind when Ida Belle entirely cut her speed and the boat slammed down on top of the water. My knees gave and I pitched forward, rolling into the hull. "What the hell?" I cried as I pushed myself upright.

"We got trouble," Ida Belle said and pointed to the channel opening that led back to Sinful.

I peered over the hull and saw a bass boat at the opening of the channel, but not just any bass boat. That particular boat belonged to Walter, and he wasn't lending it out. "What are they doing out here? They're supposed to be lounging in recliners watching television."

"Apparently, they lied," Ida Belle said.

"Well, it's not like we can bitch about it," Gertie said. "Not with our track record."

"I didn't lie about anything today," I said.

"Only because you haven't talked to Carter today," Ida Belle said.

"That's beside the point." I blinked a couple of times to put some moisture in my eyes and took another look, then sighed. "Might as well head in. Carter's got a pair of binoculars trained on us."

"What's our cover story?" Gertie said.

"Simple," Ida Belle said. "Fortune leased an airboat and we're trying it out. They don't have a line of sight to the island where the lab was located. For all they know, we've been cruising back and forth across the lake."

"Sounds good to me," I said.

Ida Belle pressed the gas pedal down again and we lurched forward, hurtling across the lake toward Walter's boat. When we were about twenty yards away, Ida Belle cut the speed and we coasted to a stop beside them.

"What the hell is this?" Carter asked, pointing at the boat.

"It's an airboat," Gertie said.

Carter looked up at her and did a double take when he saw her long-sleeved shirt straitjacket. "I know what it is. Why do you have it?"

"Fortune leased it for the summer," Ida Belle said. "Isn't it great?"

Carter's eyes widened and he pinned his gaze on me. "You leased an airboat? Why in the name of all that is holy would you do such a thing?"

I shrugged. "I don't know. I was talking to this boat salesman a week or so ago in the café. I asked him about airboats since I'd seen one going by my house one day, and he told me they were the most fun ever and said he'd make me a deal. When I explained I was only here for the summer, he offered to do a lease."

Carter shook his head in disbelief. "You leased an airboat? Oh my God."

I heard a chuckle and looked behind him to see Walter wiping his eyes with the back of his hand.

"You're not helping matters," Carter said. "The three of them will kill themselves in this thing. They've already tied Gertie up, for Christ's sake."

"That was Fortune's idea," Gertie said. "I was mad about it, but she swore I'd thank her when it was over. I have to admit, she was right on that one."

"Told you so," I said.

Gertie nodded. "I'd be swimming for shore if it wasn't for this shirt. Good thing I bought the one made out of the sturdy material and not that cheap stuff."

"Stop all your worrying," Ida Belle said. "This isn't my first rodeo. I can handle this thing just fine."

"Like you handled the Corvette?" Carter asked. "Or the motorcycle?"

Ida Belle glared at him. "You seen any police reports with my name on them? Call my insurance agent and check my record. I'm clean."

Carter threw his arms in the air. "Only because they don't know about things. I have a farmer missing a chicken coop that would disagree on the motorcycle record."

Ida Belle sighed. "I still have no idea what you're talking about."

Walter started choking and then coughing. "Give it up, son," he said. "You'd get a confession out of a Cold War spy before you would any of those three."

"Yeah," I said, "and let's talk about what you two are doing here. The text you sent me said you were going to sit in recliners and watch television. So not only are both of you out doing things the doctor has forbidden, you lied to me."

"Damn straight," Gertie said.

The righteous indignation fled from Carter's expression. "That was the original plan," he hurried to explain, "but then we thought a relaxing morning of fishing would be better for us. Dr. Stewart didn't say anything about fishing."

"And if you had your fishing rods in the boat," Ida Belle said, "that story would work just fine."

I crossed my arms over my chest and tapped my fingers on my biceps. I had to admit, it felt good to watch Carter squirm. It was usually the other way around, and a dose of his own medicine was good for him. "Admit it. You're poking into police business—against doctor's orders and definitely without Nelson's okay."

"*And* you're using a civilian to help," Gertie pointed out. "Is this where you tell us to do as you say and not as you do?"

"Fine," Carter said. "I'm doing my job because no one else is going to. And if Dr. Stewart wants me to sit around in a bed all day, then he's going to have to chain me to it or drug me. But I'm not going to sit around and watch this town fall apart."

I looked over at Walter, who raised his hands in defense.

"Don't look at me," he said. "I'm only in it for the free beer he promised me."

I rolled my eyes. "No one would ever know you two are related, would they?"

Carter shot Walter a dirty look, then turned back around. "If you are done watching me squirm, I'd like to get on with this so we can get back to Walter's house before my mom gets home from shopping."

I grinned. "Go on with your bad self. We're going to park this baby and run some errands."

He narrowed his eyes at me. "What kind of errands?"

"We're chaperoning the dance tonight, remember?" I said. "I figure a bulletproof vest, Mace, and a couple pairs of handcuffs will do."

Ida Belle fired up the boat and I dropped down on the bench just in time for her to take off. The look of dismay on Carter's face was priceless.

"You really got him!" Gertie yelled. "Holy crap! I ate a bug. Jeez, someone get some mouthwash. Gah! I ate another one."

I put one hand over my mouth and kept grinning.

Chapter Seven

While Gertie gargled with half a bottle of mouthwash, I pulled out a ziplock bag for the finger and the fixings for ham sandwiches, then placed it all on the counter. Ida Belle looked at the finger and shook her head as she took a seat at the kitchen table.

"How are we going to get that print run?" I asked. "Even if Carter were on the job, we couldn't ask him, and I don't trust Deputy Breaux to keep silent about it."

"I've been thinking about that," Ida Belle said, and pulled out her cell phone. "I figure I'll ask Myrtle to do it."

"Can you do something like that?"

"I don't see why not. It's not like Nelson is going to be paying attention."

"True."

Ida Belle dialed Myrtle, who must have had the phone in her hand.

"I need a favor," Ida Belle said. "A sheriff's department kind of favor."

I heard loud talking on the other end but I couldn't make out what she was saying.

"I'm at Fortune's house," Ida Belle said. "What's wrong?"

A second later, Ida Belle lowered the phone. "She said she was on her way over and hung up. I haven't heard her sound that stressed since the last time we were in hot water."

"So a couple of days ago?"

"About that."

I slid the sandwiches onto the table and took a seat.

"Spit that crap out and come eat!" Ida Belle yelled.

A couple seconds later, Gertie came shuffling into the kitchen and plopped into her chair. "I swear I still taste those bugs."

"It's your imagination," Ida Belle said, "and you ought to know better than having your mouth open in a boat."

"I think that first one scarred my trachea." Gertie rubbed her throat.

"It hasn't slowed down your talking," Ida Belle said.

Gertie shot her a dirty look. "I think that bug flew out of my mouth and crawled up your butt."

"Something's up with Myrtle," I said, "and she wouldn't tell Ida Belle what."

"She's on her way here now," Ida Belle said.

Gertie frowned. "You know it's that idiot Nelson."

"I'm sure," Ida Belle said. "What I'm worried about is the extent of his stupidity."

The doorbell rang, and I jumped up and hurried to let Myrtle in. Her face was bright red, and I thought she was going to pass out. "This way," I said, and hurried back to the kitchen.

Myrtle dropped into a chair and began to wail. I grabbed a bottle of water out of the refrigerator and put it in front of her. Gertie dug in her purse and pulled out a box of tissues. Myrtle snatched a tissue out of the box and blotted her face, then grabbed the bottle of water and held it against her forehead.

"What happened?" Ida Belle asked.

"That butthole Nelson is what happened," Myrtle said, her voice catching. "I'm so darn mad. I always cry when I'm mad, and I *hate* crying!"

Ida Belle shot us a knowing glance. "What did he do?"

"He *fired* me!"

"What?"

"He can't do that!"

"I'm happy to shoot him for you."

We all spit out our outrage at once.

Myrtle gave us a sad smile and patted my hand. "I might take you up on the shooting offer, dear." She blew her nose, then shook her head. "That's not even the worst part."

Gertie's eyes widened. "What's worse than that?"

"He replaced me with a hooker."

We all sucked in a breath.

"Not a real hooker," I said, thinking it was probably just some sleazy, trashy woman—basically, the kind that would date Nelson.

Myrtle nodded. "A real, honest-to-God, has a record and a pimp, hooker. I ran a background on her as I was cleaning out my desk. Not that I needed one. She'd practically bathed in cheap perfume, and her skirt was so short I could see the Milky Way up there even when she was standing up straight. I don't even want to think about what would happen if she bent over. Probably suck the whole town in like a giant black hole."

I grimaced. "And Celia allowed this? I know she's a nut and a flaming bitch, but I can't see her being okay with a hooker."

"I don't think she knows," Myrtle said. "She's been closed up in the church with her posse all day, probably plotting things to do to make all our lives miserable."

"I hope that election audit happens soon," Gertie said. "This has gotten out of control faster than I thought it would."

"Was Deputy Breaux there when Nelson brought in his new employee?" Ida Belle asked.

Myrtle nodded. "He spit an entire mouthful of soda right

on Nelson. That was the only good part of the morning. Then when Nelson left to get a towel, the hooker hit on him. He turned white as a sheet and completely lost the ability to talk. The poor boy couldn't even look at me when he ran out of the building. He's probably halfway to New Orleans to find a shrink."

Ida Belle shook her head. "When all this is over, you're going to have to fumigate the entire building."

"And maybe spread some penicillin around," Gertie said.

"I know," Myrtle said. "I used antibacterial gel on my hands twice on the way over here, and I don't even know how many times before I could get out of the sheriff's department. My hands are starting to chafe."

"Maybe when this is all over," I said, "we can cover the whole building with one of those termite tents and hose down the entire place with Lysol."

"So anyway," Myrtle said, "it looks like I'm out of the sheriff's department favor business until further notice. I'm really sorry, Ida Belle."

Ida Belle waved a hand in dismissal. "None of this is your fault. You're just caught in the middle of a nasty turf war. Hopefully, the audit will get everything straightened out and this town can get back to normal. I know that's not saying a lot to outsiders, but I'll take Sinful normal over Celia normal any day."

"Got that right." Myrtle rose from her chair. "If you guys don't mind, I'd like to go home and shower until next Tuesday."

"Hang in there," Gertie said as Myrtle headed down the hallway. "We're going to get this fixed. You just wait and see."

Myrtle held her hand in the air, one thumb up.

"Okay, this sucks," I said as soon as the door closed. "We are now completely closed off from information at the sheriff's department."

"I know," Ida Belle said, her expression grim. "Deputy Breaux is a good sort, and I'm sure he'd do anything within his power to get Nelson out and Sheriff Lee back in, but I don't think he's got the smarts or the fortitude to handle being a double agent."

Gertie shook her head. "He'd fold like a cheap towel."

"And he's got no game," I said. "Everything he's thinking is right there on his face. I don't think he has a sneaky bone in his body."

"He doesn't," Ida Belle agreed. "His momma raised him right, which is great for whatever woman realizes he's a safe and decent catch, but not good at all for us. We're going to have to figure out a plan B."

I hopped out of my chair, opened the kitchen drawer, and pulled out the card Little had given me the night before. "I have a plan B. Assuming it's something they can handle."

"The Heberts?" Gertie asked.

I nodded. "If that's okay with you guys. I know I accepted the boat, but I don't want us to get in too deep with them if you have some concerns."

"Of course we have concerns," Ida Belle said. "We're not idiots, but at this point, it's the lesser of two evils. And if we're being honest, Big and Little have been pretty straight with us. They could have handed us over to the ATF over that last hiccup."

"Do you trust them?" Gertie asked me.

"Hell no!" I said. "No further than I can throw them on most everything, but on this…yeah, I do."

I grabbed my cell phone and dialed the number on the card. He answered on the first ring.

"You got Little," he said.

"Hi. I have something I need help with." I was intentionally vague because I wasn't sure about the security of the line.

"Give it to me."

"I'd love to, but I have to do it in person. Is there somewhere we can meet?"

"Now?"

"If that's possible."

"Sure. Meet me at Swamp City Airboats in forty-five minutes."

I did a quick mental calculation based on the location I'd seen for the boat store on the website. It was probably a thirty-minute drive. "Great."

I slid back into my seat and grabbed my sandwich. "We're meeting him at the boat store in forty-five minutes. That means we've got fifteen to eat and get on the road."

Gertie reached for her sandwich and squirmed in her chair. "My ribs are killing me. I need a hot shower."

"No time for that," I said. "Don't you have some muscle rub or something in that purse of yours?"

"You're thinking of vapor rub," Ida Belle said. "Old ladies always carry vapor rub."

"I'm not an old lady," Gertie said.

"Do you have vapor rub in your purse?" Ida Belle asked.

"Shut up," Gertie said and lifted her bag into her lap. "I think I put a tube of sports cream in here. Yep, here it is. And my heating pad. I'll plug this baby in and it will be nice and hot for the ride to the boat shop."

"You're falling apart," Ida Belle said as Gertie plugged her heating pad in and laid it on the kitchen counter. "I'm putting you on a workout routine starting Monday."

"The hell you are," Gertie said as she sat back down. "I just need my kidney belt for any future boat excursions. And maybe my girdle, support hose, and some well-placed Ace bandages, then I'll be good to go."

Ida Belle shook her head. "You'll be wound up so tight, if you fart, you'll blow a leg off."

"I have Gas-X in my purse, too."

I grimaced. "Ten minutes. More eating. Less talking."

We made quick work of the sandwiches, Gertie gargled one more time, and we were on the road. After the boat ride, seventy miles per hour in my Jeep almost seemed like running in reverse.

"Have either of you ever met this Bob?" I asked as we headed down the highway.

"No," Ida Belle said. "He has a reputation for building some of the best airboats around. After today, I'd definitely agree with that."

"I hope he wasn't strong-armed into giving me the boat," I said. "I don't want any problems with an Hebert, even if he's not part of the family business."

"Oh, I'm sure he's in it up to his neck," Ida Belle said. "In their line of work, money laundering always comes in handy, and boats are high-dollar items. And remember, Bob builds his own boats, so no inventory straight from the factory to trace. Easier to run cash through the bank for fake sales without getting caught."

I nodded. That made sense and lowered my chances of coming face-to-face with a resentful business owner who had to give away his product. "So what are we going to do about this Nelson problem?"

We spent the rest of the drive discussing the possibilities, but unraveling the mare's nest of Celia, Nelson, and the newly introduced hooker was currently out of our reach. We were still trying to come up with something other than "wait for the audit" when I turned off the highway and onto the road that led to the boat store.

After about twenty yards, I decided that "road" might have been a stretch. This was more like the path to the Swamp Bar—no shoulder, constructed of rocks over dirt, and potholes you could lose a small child or large dog in. Cattails and weeds grew right up to the edge of the road, and occasionally slapped the side of the Jeep. I was thrilled when the boat shop came into view around a corner about a half mile onto the path.

While the condition of the road was expected, the shop was a surprise. Fairly new construction, all brick, with stained brown trim. Behind it stretched a wide channel with a bunch of airboats docked right behind the store. I parked next to a shiny new black Cadillac, figuring it belonged to Little. I peered into the car as I exited the Jeep, but it was empty.

"He must be inside," I said.

"You go in first," Ida Belle said. "He'll probably want to keep things looking casual, especially as it looks like there's some customers inside." She gestured to the trucks littering the parking area.

I nodded and headed inside the shop. A beefy man with the same face I'd seen on the website looked up as the door chimed and smiled as he made his way over.

Forty-five years old. Six feet two. Three hundred ten pounds. High blood pressure. Bad knees. Threat level low except for the Hebert part of the equation.

"Fortune," he said as he extended his hand. "It's good to see you again." He winked at me, and I knew the show was for the other patrons. "Are you enjoying your new boat?"

"I love it," I said. No show required on my part. Despite the fact that Ida Belle did her best to take years off my life, I still thought the boat was one of the coolest things ever. "I took it out this morning for a spin with some friends. It is seriously fast. You build a great product."

His smile extended and this time, it was genuine. "Thank you. We pride ourselves on building the best boats in southeast Louisiana. I'm glad it's working out for you."

A much older man working behind the counter yelled and Bob held up one finger. "Sorry, we're a little busy right now. I need to go handle this, but let me know if there's anything I can do for you."

"Thanks," I said.

As he walked away, I scanned the store and spotted Little at a table in a sitting area at the back of the building, drinking coffee and reading a hunting magazine. I headed his direction and he looked up and gestured toward the chair across from him.

"Is hunting a hobby of yours?" I asked as I sat.

"It used to be."

"What did you hunt?"

He smiled. "Nothing you can talk about in magazines."

"Oh." Stupid question.

The door chimed and Little looked over as Ida Belle and Gertie walked inside. "I see your soldiers are accompanying you."

I nodded. "We headed out first thing this morning to the site where the lab exploded, which was possible thanks to you and the awesome airboat you supplied."

"So you like the boat?"

"The boat is incredible. I don't think I've had that much fun since, well, I can't remember when."

"I'm glad you like it. Airboats are particularly suited for the terrain here, and we didn't know what kind of obstacles you might run up against. You seem to get yourself in situations of pursuit. We wanted to give you the best advantage we could."

"You definitely did that." If the bad guys wanted to chase me on water, bring it on. The only thing beating that boat was a bullet.

"So you three got right on things, huh? And you already need my help with something. That's encouraging. Tell me what you've found."

"A way to identify the cooker."

His eyes widened. "So quickly? That *is* impressive. What do you need from me?"

"Help with the actual identification part." I pulled the ziplock bag out of my pocket and stretched my hand under the table toward Little.

He took the bag and opened his hand, keeping it below the table line. He raised one eyebrow and looked at me. "You've just been carrying it around in your pocket like that?"

"Sure. It's not like I'm going to rub the ridges off of it or something."

He gave me a respectful nod. "You're one unflappable broad. You know it?"

"Thanks."

"You ever want to ditch the ole card catalog and take on some work that gets a little more risky than overdue books and pays a hell of a lot more, you let me know. Our organization could use a woman with the smarts and skills you got."

I held in a smile. If he only knew exactly how overqualified I was for the position he had in mind, he probably wouldn't be smiling at me. "If I'm ever looking for that kind of career change, you'll be the first person I call."

He nodded. "I take it you need me to run the print?"

"Yeah, with the whole Nelson deal, we lost our contact at the sheriff's department."

"You had a contact who would have run the print, even though you're dating the deputy?"

"She's a good friend of Ida Belle and Gertie's."

He laughed. "So they've had a mole inside the sheriff's department? Beautiful."

"Until today."

"What happened to her?"

"Nelson replaced her with a hooker."

He stared at me for a moment, probably waiting for the punch line, but when none was forthcoming, he shook his head. "You're not joking."

"I couldn't make that up if I wanted to."

"This whole issue with Nelson and the new mayor could present a lot of problems for Big and me. We're watching the situation very closely. Rest assured, if that election audit doesn't change things, we will."

I nodded. I had a really good idea how the Heberts would go about enacting change, and it would probably involve a ceremony at the graveyard. I thought Celia was a bitch and a complete nutter who couldn't have a consistent feeling or thought from minute to minute, but that didn't mean I wanted her dead. If Marie knew just how much was riding on her audit, she'd probably have a heart attack.

"I have someone that can handle this," Little said and stuck the finger in his suit pocket.

"And you'll let me know what he finds?"

"Of course. This is a promising start, but it's not the end. That cooker wasn't working alone. We need to know who he was in business with before they fill the vacancy and rebuild."

"Great. Do you need an email or something? I can set up a fake one."

"I don't like to leave an electronic trail. I'll have someone deliver the paperwork to you when I receive it."

"Your delivery boy isn't going to drug my roommate and break into my kitchen, is he?"

Little grinned. "If I told him how you dressed to confront intruders, he'd insist on it. But the answer is no. The drop will be during normal waking hours but unnoticeable as anything suspect. You have my word on that."

"Great."

"Are you working any other angles?"

"We found a matchbook from the Swamp Bar at the explosion site."

Little grimaced. "That place. I keep telling Big we should open a competing bar—one with a little more class. The place is full of petty criminals and scumbags."

"Mostly your clients?"

"Touché."

"Well, I'm hoping the print trace will narrow down the scope a bit. Investigating everyone who goes to the bar would take a lifetime and manpower we don't have."

"Good. Anything else going on?"

"Sorta. I mean, it's a real long shot, but we're chaperoning the dance tonight."

He frowned. "The teen dance? I don't think I get the connection."

"We figured if someone's dealing in Sinful, teens would know."

"Because they're targeted buyers for dealers. I see. Well, in that case, I'm hoping you come up empty."

"Me too. Honestly, the three of us are hoping this problem was just getting started, and that we can stop it from gaining traction."

"You get me the information I need. I'll make sure there's no traction."

"Then I best get going. Thanks again for the boat."

"Enjoy. And be careful. Big and I aren't the only ones

who've noticed your strange choice of pastimes. There's talk in certain circles."

"I'll be careful," I said as I rose from my chair. "Thanks."

Great. I came to Sinful to hide from the giant target on my back only to whip up a brand-new target with a different group of shooters. Not that it surprised me. Sinful wasn't exactly New York City. My actions were bound to make rounds in the criminal gossip circles, especially now that it was fairly common knowledge that I was seeing Carter on a personal basis.

Ida Belle and Gertie were at the cashier when I crossed the store. Gertie took a receipt from the older clerk and dragged a large plastic bag off the counter. "What did you buy?" I asked.

"A diving mask," Gertie said. "It will keep my eyes from drying out the next time Ida Belle tries to kill us in the boat."

"That's actually not a bad idea," I said.

"Tell her what else is in the bag," Ida Belle said.

I looked down at the bag, which was far too large and saggy to hold only a dive mask. "Do I want to know?"

Gertie opened the bag and I peered inside at the large cardboard box with a huge inflatable alligator on the side.

"It's one of those that you tow behind a boat," Gertie said, her eyes lighting up. "I've always wanted to ride one of these."

"Let me get this straight," I said. "You're convinced that Ida Belle is trying to kill us with the boat, but you want to sit on a piece of plastic filled with air and let her pull you down the bayou…where the real alligators are also floating?"

Ida Belle lifted her hands, palms up. "That's what I said."

"If we're not investigating," Gertie said, "then there's no need to drive like we're being shot at. And if there's one thing the three of us could use, it's a break from crap and a little fun."

"I'm not riding on that thing," I said.

"Don't worry," Ida Belle said. "Watching Gertie attempt it

will cover the fun part."

She had a point, and we had the afternoon open. "It's a while before we have to get ready for the dance. What do you say we head back and try that thing out?"

"Really?" Gertie asked.

"Absolutely," I said. "But I'm warning you, the footage is going straight onto YouTube."

"Awesome!" Gertie said. "I'll be famous."

Ida Belle closed her eyes and sighed. "God help us."

Chapter Eight

I intended to drive straight home, blow up that alligator, and commence with the entertainment part of the afternoon, but when we drove into downtown Sinful, it was clear that something was wrong. A crowd was gathered on Main Street in front of the sheriff's department, yelling and shaking their fists.

"This doesn't look good," I said.

"Better stop and see what's going on," Ida Belle said.

I parked at the end of Main Street and we headed toward the crowd.

"Ida Belle!" Marie broke out from the crowd and hurried toward us. "Thank God you're here. I tried to reach your cell, but you didn't answer."

Ida Belle pulled her cell phone from her pocket. "I put the darn thing on silent earlier and forgot to change it back. What the heck is going on?"

"Celia and Nelson are what's going on," Marie said. "Word circulated quickly about Myrtle being replaced by the hooker, which was bad enough, but people figured even Celia would be decent enough to handle that one. Then she had Nelson trot out her new law."

"I'm afraid to ask," I said.

"You should be," Marie said. "The new law states that the Catholic church gets to let out at five 'til."

"What?"

"That's an outrage!"

"She's not going to get away with this!"

"He can't just change the law," Ida Belle said.

Marie nodded. "That's why all these people are here protesting. But that idiot Nelson won't come out of the building. Coward."

"The door's opening!" a man in the crowd shouted.

We hurried forward and watched as Nelson walked out of the sheriff's department and stood on a park bench on the sidewalk. "I'm going to have to ask you to disband," Nelson said. "You don't have a permit to occupy this street, so you're all breaking the law."

"You rewriting everything," one man shouted, "or just the things that benefit you and Celia?"

Nelson gave the man a condescending look. "I assume your comment is concerning the recent change to church hours. That law has been temporarily amended for the safety of the community."

"What the hell are you talking about?" a woman yelled.

Nelson glanced over at us and smiled. "Due to the recent assault on our mayor by a member of the Baptist church, I've decided that the safety of the community is protected by ensuring the two groups do not occupy the sidewalk at the same time. If you want to blame someone, blame her."

He pointed directly at me and I felt the target forming on my back.

"That's what you get for cavorting with Yankees," Nelson said.

"I'd rather cavort with a Yankee than a snake," another man shouted.

The crowd nodded and Nelson's smile fell a bit.

"It's pretty bad when your hometown prefers a Yankee over

you," Gertie yelled.

Nelson's expression hardened. "I don't care what any of you prefer. The fact of the matter is, I'm the sheriff, and what I say goes."

"But it only goes so far." Francine's voice sounded behind us, and everyone turned around.

She stood outside the café, hands on her hips and mad as a hornet. If she'd been holding a weapon, I would have hit the pavement. She walked through the crowd and looked up at Nelson. "You can make all the laws you want about church closing time. Hell, you can let them have Mass on Saturday if you want to, but the one thing you can't do is make me cook."

There was a collective intake of breath.

Francine turned around and faced the crowd. "Until further notice, the café will not serve banana pudding." She shot Nelson one final look of disgust and stomped through the crowd and back into the café.

As soon as the café door swung shut, the crowd exploded.

"See what you've done!"

"You and that mayor bitch are going down!"

"You're ruining the entire town!"

"I swear to God, I'll shoot you on sight at the next opportunity!"

Nelson wasn't completely stupid. His expression changed from indignant to fear as he jumped off the park bench and practically ran inside the sheriff's department. I heard the dead bolt slide into place and seconds later, all the blinds dropped.

"You can't hide in there forever!" a man shouted. "There's more of us than you."

I heard the sound of glass breaking and looked over to see a hole in one of the front windows of the sheriff's department.

"We've got to do something," Marie said, "before they burn

the place down."

Ida Belle climbed up on the park bench, stuck her fingers in her mouth, and let out a whistle that should have shattered glass. Everyone threw their hands over their ears and stared up at her.

"Good residents of Sinful," Ida Belle said. "I know you're all upset and so am I, but when this is all over, Sheriff Lee and Deputy LeBlanc will need a place to work for our protection. I know how frustrating this is, but I need you to believe that it won't last. And when the tide turns—"

"It's open season on Nelson!" a man shouted and people around him nodded in agreement.

"I can't tell you what to do," Ida Belle said. "I can only suggest that you don't do anything that causes damages to this town that we have to pay for later."

A low grumbling passed through the crowd, and they started to disperse. Marie sank onto the bench, clutching the sides of her face. "It hasn't even been a week since Celia got voted in, and things are already going to hell in a handbasket. I knew that woman would ruin this town, but I thought it would take longer."

Ida Belle stepped down off the bench and patted Marie on the shoulder. "Things are escalating quicker than I thought they would, but we're going to fix this."

Marie looked up at her. "What if the auditors find that the election wasn't fixed? What if Celia actually won?"

"That's not going to happen," Ida Belle said, her expression grim.

I nodded my agreement, saying a quick prayer that Ida Belle was right. Because if Celia was still mayor after that audit, she was a walking target for Big and Little Hebert, and she'd have no idea they were coming.

"I hope you're right," Marie said. "This town has suffered

enough lately. I don't think it can take Celia as mayor without imploding." She rose from the bench. "I need to get home to shower and change. I'm meeting the auditors in an hour and all this brouhaha has made me a complete mess."

"Let us know if we can do anything," Gertie said.

Marie gave her a sad nod and shuffled off down the street. As we walked to the Jeep, I told Ida Belle and Gertie what Little had said about Celia and Nelson.

"Do you really think they'd kill her?" Gertie asked.

"Of course they would," Ida Belle said. "They're criminals. Do you think they haven't killed people before?"

"I'm sure," Gertie said, "but I always figured they were killing other criminals. I would give my good dentures to see her run out of town, but not in a casket."

I nodded. "I would like to think that a threat would precede action, but Celia is so stubborn…"

"She would ignore the threat," Ida Belle said, and sighed. "Crap."

"Well, there's nothing we can do about it," Gertie said. "Little is not likely to give us a heads-up before he has someone put a bullet in Celia, and even if he did and we warned her, she wouldn't believe us, either."

"Probably not," Ida Belle agreed. "And the last thing I'm interested in is getting in the middle of that. I don't want to see anyone die, but that includes myself. If I'm going to take a bullet for someone, it's not going to be Celia Arceneaux."

We climbed into the Jeep and I pulled away up Main Street. "Let's just pray that the audit overturns the election results."

"And if it doesn't?" Gertie asked.

"Then we'll figure something else out," I said.

I glanced over at Ida Belle, who nodded, but I knew she didn't have any better ideas than I did.

"Anyway," Ida Belle said. "We have bigger fish to fry with our own investigation and an afternoon of relaxation and entertainment ahead of us. Let's just try to enjoy ourselves for a couple of hours. We'll be back in the thick of things soon enough."

"We're still going boating?" Gertie asked, her voice tracking up like a child.

"Of course," I said, forcing all thoughts of Celia and cement shoes out of my head. Instead, I replaced it with a mental image of Gertie on the floating alligator, except in my vision, Ida Belle was driving the airboat so fast, the gator hung in midair as Gertie clung on for dear life.

"Yippee!" Gertie cheered and pulled the box out of her shopping bag. A couple seconds later, she was huffing into the air valve as if she were in labor. About five seconds in, she dropped the float and started wheezing. "I can't breathe. Need oxygen."

"Then stop putting it in the float, you old fool." Ida Belle took the float from her. "Drop by my house," she told me. "We'll fill it up with my air compressor."

Gertie glared. "Why didn't you say that to begin with?"

"I wanted to see how long you'd last," Ida Belle said. "Are you sure you want to ride this thing? I'm seriously worried about your health."

"I have asthma," Gertie said.

"You don't have asthma," Ida Belle said. "What you have is no aerobic conditioning."

"I'm retired," Gertie complained. "I'm not supposed to need aerobic conditioning anymore."

"The way things are going in this town," Ida Belle said, "we need you to be a superhero, so do me a favor and start walking. Anything to get your heart rate up a bit."

I grinned. "I think we're about to take care of that."

We stopped to fill the alligator up with air at Ida Belle's, then made a pass by Gertie's house for her to grab a bathing suit and her water shoes. We got more than a few stares from residents as we drove to my house with the alligator tied to the top of the roll bars on my Jeep.

Since we weren't going to be tromping around weedy, mosquito-infested landmasses, I changed into shorts and a tank top and hurried outside where Ida Belle was attaching the alligator to the airboat with a towrope. Gertie was still inside changing.

"You sure this is a good idea?" I asked.

"Are you kidding me? It's a horrible idea," Ida Belle said as she tugged on the towrope. "If she doesn't break something, it will be a damned miracle."

"Then why are we doing it?"

"Because she's a grown woman and I am not going to listen to her bitch for the next forty years."

"Maybe you could take it easy," I suggested.

Ida Belle stood up straight and glared at me. "Of course I'll take it easy. I'm not trying to break the woman. We need her tonight."

"Maybe a ride up the bayou and back will be enough for her."

Ida Belle snorted. "We'll be lucky if she can stay on long enough to pull away from the dock. Don't worry, Fortune. This will all be over soon, then we can ditch the float and go have some real fun in this baby."

I cringed a little. Gertie on the float was starting to look like the safer option for everyone.

I heard my back door slam and looked over to see Gertie strolling across the lawn. "What in the name of all that is holy?"

The bathing suit was one piece, but that's where anything nice I could say about it ended.

It was made of red sparkly material that couldn't possibly be comfortable for the skin, especially when a good bit of a bathing suit usually wound up shoved up your butt crack. The straps were gold chains, and a matching gold chain encircled the waist, two little bits of it dangling down the front of the suit. The water shoes were the same shade of red and had sparkly gold hearts stamped on them.

A purple boa completed the ensemble.

Ida Belle climbed out of the boat and shook her head. "Someone is going to mistake you for Nelson's hooker."

"Please," Gertie said and flung one end of the boa around her neck. "That hooker can't possibly look this good."

I wrinkled my nose. "I'm no fashion expert, but is a feather boa a good choice for marine sports?"

Gertie lifted the end of the boa and held it out to me. "The feathers are plastic. Isn't that cool?"

"A plastic feather boa?" I couldn't begin to process the horror.

Gertie nodded. "I got it from one of those Mardi Gras costume shops in New Orleans."

Things started to make more sense. "Well, Madame of the Bayou, if you're done with your wardrobe change, let's get this show on the road."

"That looks more like a wardrobe malfunction than a change to me," Ida Belle grumbled.

Gertie waved a hand in dismissal. "How are we going to do this?"

I took stock and considered the options. "I think it will be easier for you to get on the alligator here in shallow water. Then I'll launch the boat and Ida Belle can inch forward until the towline is straight and tight. Then we can take off." I looked over at Ida Belle. "Is that okay?"

"Works for me," she said, and hopped into the boat.

I handed Gertie a life vest and she pulled it on, securing it tightly around her.

"Okay," I said, "let's get you on that alligator."

Gertie pulled on her dive mask and tromped into the water, pushing the alligator with her. When she was about thigh-deep, she stopped, then put both hands on the alligator and shoved down while launching herself upward. But instead of landing on the alligator, in a surprising show of strength, she launched over the float altogether and sank into the bayou. I hurried into the water and a second later, she was back up sputtering water everywhere.

"What happened?" she asked.

"You overshot the float," I said, "and you have a crab hanging off your strap."

"They like dead things," Ida Belle said.

Gertie shot her a dirty look and pulled the crab off her suit, then flung it into the bayou.

"Try again," I said, "and this time with less muscle, She-Hulk."

Gertie moved to the side of the alligator again and this time I held the tail. She jumped up with a little less enthusiasm and landed flat in the middle of the float. She reached for the handles and squirmed around, trying to get herself into an upright position. I clutched the tail to keep the entire thing from tipping over. Finally, she managed to get seated and waved a hand at me.

"Get going," she said. "I'm ready to get my ride on."

I slogged back onto the bank, my tennis shoes now caked in

mud, and headed for the boat.

"You're not wearing those dirty shoes in here," Ida Belle said. "It would take a sandblaster to get it off this aluminum. You don't need shoes anyway, and besides, you're getting tan lines around your ankles. It looks silly."

I pulled off the tennis shoes and socks, then dragged my hands across the grass to get the mud off them. A final rinse in the bayou and a good bit of it wiped onto my shirt, and I was good as new. I untied the boat from the docking post, shoved it back with one of my bare feet, and hopped inside.

"Ouch!" I yelled as my bare feet landed in the bottom of the hot aluminum hull. I practically ran on my tiptoes to the passenger seat and jumped into it, then gently placed my sore feet on the rubber footrest. It was warm, but it wasn't going to melt my heels off.

The boat drifted backward and slowly started to turn with the tide, heading up the bayou. The alligator turned with the tide as well until both were more or less facing the same direction. Ida Belle started up the boat and inched forward until the towline was taut. I looked back at Gertie, who gave me a thumbs-up, then clutched the handles.

"She's good," I said and turned on the video on my cell phone.

Ida Belle pressed the accelerator down and I wondered if I'd spoken too soon. The towline snapped taut and the alligator dropped down for a split second, then launched out of the water before crashing back down on the surface. Even though she was wearing the mask, I could see Gertie's eyes widen and I hoped her shoulders could take the strain. She bobbled from side to side for a bit and I thought she was going to pitch off into the bayou, but finally she steadied and let out a hoot. The purple boa trailed behind her like Snoopy's scarf when he was doing the Red

Baron routine on top of his doghouse.

Ida Belle glanced back and grinned. "That woman is never going to grow up. It's one of the things I love most about her."

I looked at Gertie, who was yelling like a child on a roller coaster, and had to admit, it did look like fun. Maybe if we had some time left over when she was done, I'd give it a whirl. It couldn't possibly be any more dangerous than the other things I'd gotten myself into.

"How far are you going to go?" I asked.

"To the end of the bayou," Ida Belle said. "It will be safer if I make a big sweeping turn in the lake than a tight one in the channel."

"Sounds good."

She continued up the bayou toward the lake as Gertie yelled at fishermen and people suntanning as we passed. They all stared at her as if she'd lost her mind, and I could about imagine what kind of spectacle we looked like. Fortunately for Gertie, I was getting it recorded, so she'd get to see herself in all her alligator-riding glory once we got back to my house.

"The lake's coming up," Ida Belle said. "Signal to her that I'm going to turn."

I stopped recording and slipped the cell phone back in my pocket, then stuck my hand in the air and waved it in a circle with one finger extended. Gertie nodded.

"She's good," I said as the boat shot out of the end of the channel and into the wide-open waters of the lake. Ida Belle started a big sweeping turn to the right, easing the boat over a little at a time, but careful to stay far enough away from the bank to avoid stumps and sunken wreckage. I saw a couple of boats crossing the lake for the channel and pointed at one. "That's Carter and Walter."

Ida Belle nodded. "For men with no fishing gear, they've

been out here a long time."

"I wonder if they found anything."

"Unless they got a tip from a fisherman, I doubt it. We combed that site well. I don't think there was anything else left to find."

I watched as Walter guided his boat into the channel, feeling a little guilty about scooping Carter on the evidence run.

"Don't even go there," Ida Belle said as she slowly turned the boat to the left, making a giant sweeping arc across the lake.

"What?"

"You had no way of knowing that Carter was going to ignore Dr. Stewart's orders and go searching that site, so don't go feeling bad because we beat him to the punch."

"We could have turned the evidence over when we ran into them."

"So he could do what? Give it to Nelson? What would that have accomplished?"

"He could have run the finger himself."

"Sure he could have, and then he'd have been smack in the middle of an investigation that he has no business involving himself in until all that swelling is gone from his brain. Hell, we're doing him a favor by handling this ourselves."

Her theory wasn't without some holes—some of them the kind you could drive a bus through—but I was willing to go along with it, especially if the alternative meant fessing up to Carter that we'd turned evidence of a crime over to a criminal. I wasn't certain there were enough words in the English language to talk my way out of that one.

"You're right," I said, feeling better about the entire situation. "As long as Carter doesn't have a line on the bad guys, he can't get himself into a situation that threatens his health."

Ida Belle grinned. "You're getting the hang of this."

We had completed the turn without incident and Ida Belle straightened the boat out and headed back for the channel. Gertie was still hanging on, but her face was starting to show signs of fatigue.

"We better get her in before she drops," I said.

"I'll take it up a notch," Ida Belle said. "A bit of an increase won't make a difference in the pull on her arms, but it will get us back quicker."

"Sounds good." I lifted my thumb up in the air several times, indicating we were going to pick up speed. Gertie nodded. "It's a go."

Ida Belle pressed the gas pedal down a little harder and we entered the channel. Another couple of minutes and it would all be over but the aspirin and heating pad. The alligator bounced on top of the wake left by the bass boats and I could tell Gertie was straining to hold on. Just a little bit longer.

Then Ida Belle yelled.

I whipped around in time to see hornets buzz by Ida Belle's face, then circle back. She waved her left arm in the air, trying to get the angry insects to take off, and I started flapping my arms as well. One landed on her right hand and she yelled again, simultaneously shoving the steering rod forward and pressing harder on the accelerator.

The airboat made a hard, fast turn and I heard Gertie scream. I clutched the seat and looked back to see the alligator swing around the side of the boat, skipping on top of the water like a stone. When it was parallel to the boat, the towline snapped and it shot off across the lake, right toward Walter's boat. Gertie let out another shriek as the plastic boa whipped around her head, completely covering her face.

Ida Belle let off the gas and the airboat dropped to a crawl as Carter stood up in the bow of Walter's boat, staring in horror at the oncoming alligator. I yelled at Gertie to let go, but she couldn't hear me, and she was running blind. Realizing they were about to crash, Carter shouted at Walter to stop just as the alligator ran in front of his boat. Walter cut the engine and swung the boat hard to the right, pitching Carter out into the bayou.

The alligator continued to speed across the bayou, then hit the bank and slid right up it and in between two men fishing. Then it hit an ice chest and flipped it over, sending the fish it contained onto the lawn. Gertie finally lost her grip and flew off the gator and right into the pile of flopping fish. The gator came to a stop on top of a fish and started to deflate.

Chapter Nine

Ida Belle punched the accelerator again and drove the airboat right up the bank behind the alligator. We both jumped out and rushed over to Gertie, who was lying immobile in a fish-and-ice pile. The two stunned fishermen inched over and peered down at her.

"I killed her," Ida Belle wailed.

I dropped down and put my fingers on her neck. "She's got a pulse." I unwrapped the boa from her head and yanked off the diving mask, then leaned over and put my ear next to her mouth.

And that's the moment Gertie decided to regain consciousness…and yell.

I sprang backward, clutching my ear, and sat right on a fish. As quickly as I sat down, I rolled off it and jumped up, my bare feet squishing in the slimy fish-covered grass. Gertie popped up into a sitting position, gazing wildly around, her eyes wide.

"What happened?" she asked.

"You took a side trip into Stumpy Duhon's backyard," Ida Belle said.

Gertie frowned and looked around at the fish, then her expression switched from confused to mad and she glared at Ida Belle. "You tried to kill me."

"It was an accident," Ida Belle said. "A bunch of hornets flew at me and one stung my hand. Can you move? Is anything broken?"

"Hornets? You expect me to believe that nonsense?"

Ida Belle thrust her hand in Gertie's face. A huge red bump was already forming on the back of it. "Look. There's a stinger hole right in the middle."

Gertie leaned forward and made a show of inspecting the hand. "Doesn't look like a hornet sting."

"Oh hell," I said. "Put your hand down. You know she can't see that bump, much less the stinger hole."

"I see the bump," Gertie said.

"Then you're going to have to trust that it was a hornet," I said. "I saw them myself."

Gertie gave Ida Belle a begrudging nod. "I guess I can see where that might cause a problem, especially as that is your driving hand. Okay, I forgive you."

"About time, you old coot," Ida Belle said. "Now, can you move?"

"I think so." Gertie put her hands on the ground and tried to push herself up, but her arms buckled. "I think it took the last of my muscles to ride that baby up the lawn."

"Well, don't just stand there," Ida Belle said to the two men. "Help a lady up."

The two men hurried over and each put a hand under Gertie's arms and lifted her to an upright position. "How's your legs?" one of the men asked.

"They feel like I've been riding a horse for a week," Gertie said, "but I think they'll keep me upright."

The two men removed their hands, still standing close in case she had overestimated the leg thing. She wobbled for a couple of seconds, but ultimately stabilized.

"What the heck were you thinking?" Carter's voice sounded behind us.

I turned to see him dripping wet and stomping up the bank.

Walter was a couple steps behind him, laughing so hard he was stumbling as he walked.

"Here we go again," I said.

Ida Belle put up a hand to stop Carter before he got started. "I got attacked by hornets. One stung my driving hand and I accidentally sent the airboat into a hard turn, slinging the alligator float around the boat. The towline broke and Gertie took a ride into Stumpy's backyard, where she collided with his ice chest of fish. Nothing is broken and the fish are probably still good to eat."

The guy Ida Belle had indicated as Stumpy looked around and nodded. "Looks fine to me. Was gonna have to clean them anyway."

Carter stared at us in disbelief. "You have no business doing things like this."

Gertie put her hands on her hips. "Like you have no business pretending to fish when we all know you conned Walter into helping you work? Last I checked only one of us was under doctor's orders to stay inside and rest, and it wasn't me."

"Actually, two of them are under doctor's orders," I said.

Carter shot me a dirty look. "You're not helping."

"I wasn't trying to," I said. "At least, I wasn't trying to help you."

"Why the hell not?" he demanded.

"Because you're being rude," I said. "You're implying that Gertie is too old to be having fun, and that's wrong. If Gertie wants to dress like a hooker and ride an alligator float down the bayou when she's a hundred and two, she should do it."

"Darn straight!" Gertie said. "Would you prefer I sit in a chair and wait to die?"

"That's not... I didn't..." Carter stammered, looking more than a little uncomfortable.

Carter glanced back at Walter. "You wanna jump in this?"

"No way," Walter said. "You're on your own."

"Smart man," Stumpy said, and gave Walter an approving nod.

Carter looked back at Gertie. "I just mean that it's dangerous and you could have been hurt."

"Well, of course I could have been hurt," Gertie said. "Bernadine Stansbury broke her ankle getting off the toilet yesterday. Do you want me to stop using the toilet?"

Ida Belle nodded. "And last week, Archie Bradford fell in the shower and broke his hip."

"Yeah," Gertie said. "Should I stop showering as well?"

"I…uh." Carter threw his hands in the air. "I quit. Ride flying alligators down the bayou towed by an insane woman with a penchant for fast engines and questionable driving. Live it up."

"That's what I was doing," Gertie said. "Hey, Stumpy, how about you give us a couple of those trout? You can't eat them all anyway."

"Sure," Stumpy said. "The show was worth a couple of fish." He reached down and grabbed two of the trout. He righted the ice chest, laid them on top of it, and pulled out a hunting knife. "If you give me a couple minutes, I can fillet these for you."

"Great," Gertie said, and looked at me. "Maybe we can build a bonfire behind your house and cook them up."

"No!" Ida Belle and I spoke at once.

Fire and Gertie didn't sound like a good combination at all.

Carter shook his head. "Sure, listen to them, but when I say it, I'm the bad guy." He waved his hand at Walter. "Let's get out of here. These jeans are sticking to me."

"In all the right places," I said.

A slight blush rose up his neck. His lips quivered and I

could tell he was trying not to smile. "You're going to be the death of me," he said.

"Helluva way to go," Stumpy said.

Carter grinned and motioned to Walter. "Let's get going before I say more things I shouldn't. I'll call you later."

"Remember, we're chaperoning the dance tonight," I said.

"I remember," he said. "I've been praying for those kids all morning."

"Hhmmpff," Gertie said. "What does he know? I've been praying for *us* since I knew we were chaperoning those kids."

I nodded. I had to admit that the thought of running herd over a bunch of teenagers put fear into me in a way my job never did. "Maybe it will be fine," I said.

Ida Belle shook her head. "Maybe you shouldn't go armed."

"Will you get a move on?" Ida Belle said. "We're going to be late."

I dashed on a bit of lip gloss and hurried downstairs where Gertie and Ida Belle were waiting for me. They both took in my outfit and nodded. Earlier that afternoon, while we were eating fish and packing ice for Gertie's arms, we'd discussed wardrobe for the dance—specifically, my wardrobe.

Gertie had suggested that I was attractive and young enough to catch the interest of high school boys, which would make it easier to get information out of them. The whole suggestion of underage boys looking at me that way was totally ick—hell, I hadn't completely come to grips yet with a very grown Carter being interested in me—but I figured she was probably right. At least if all those teen movies she'd had me watch were to be believed.

Dress for the event was casual, so I'd donned my tightest

pair of jeans and a black tank top with a glittery skull on it. Gertie had furnished the tank top. Ida Belle and I had wisely stayed away from any questions like "where did you get this?" and the even worse "who did you buy it for?" A pair of new Nikes completed the outfit and I had to admit, I did look considerably younger.

"You look great," Gertie said. "You could pass for a teenager."

"Let's not get carried away," Ida Belle said. "Just because she looks a hundred years younger than you do, that still doesn't make her a teen."

Gertie shot her a dirty look. "I beg your pardon. I look hot."

"Your arms are wrapped in bandages and you reek of Bengay," Ida Belle said. "And one of those bandages is coming loose. You look like an extra in a zombie movie."

Gertie lifted her arm and frowned at the dangling bandage.

"And you," Ida Belle said. "You look fine except for the accessory."

"What accessory?" I wasn't even wearing a watch, and I didn't think lip gloss counted.

Ida Belle pointed to my right foot. "Your sock is sagging. Lose the gun."

"You were serious about me not going armed?" I asked.

"What's the worst that can happen?" Gertie asked. "Some kid tries to feel her up and finds her gun?"

"If some kid tries to feel me up and starts with my ankles, there's bigger problems afoot than my being armed," I said.

"No weapons," Ida Belle said. "We can barely deal with adults. This is a herd of hormone-driven, drama-laden half humans who think they know everything and don't think they can die. It's a recipe for disaster."

"Fine," I said, and pulled the ankle holster off. "Are you going to frisk Gertie's purse? Because what she's hauling could probably put the US military out of business."

Gertie clutched her purse close to her side. "Traitor."

"No way am I going unprotected with you packing an arsenal," I said. "That's more dangerous than the kids, unless you have a bulletproof vest in there."

"I've got one on order," Gertie said.

"Of course you do," Ida Belle said. "Did you order one for everyone else you come in contact with?" She stuck her hand out. "Hand it over."

Gertie clenched harder and shook her head.

"We're not leaving here until you do," Ida Belle said.

"Bunch of Nazis," Gertie said and thrust her purse at Ida Belle.

Ida Belle grabbed the purse, her arms dropping a bit, then set it on the coffee table. I leaned over as she pulled out a small retail store. Nine-millimeter, handcuffs, rope, Mace, rape whistle, duct tape, box of tissues, aspirin, sports rub, bandages, bottle of peroxide, roll of antacids, earplugs, matches, panty hose, Sinful Ladies cough syrup, two protein bars, and a can of ravioli.

I stared down at the collection, trying to make some sense of it. "Okay, the weapons I understand, and I'd include the duct tape and rope in that description. The first aid supplies are probably a good idea, as are the earplugs. I sorta get food although the ravioli is a strange choice, and I suppose the matches could be for lighting a fire to heat the ravioli, but I'm at a loss on the panty hose. You're not even wearing hose."

"That's in case we need a disguise," Gertie said.

"You've been watching too much television," Ida Belle said, and started repacking the purse. The first aid, food, and cough syrup went back inside, along with the earplugs.

"That's it?" Gertie asked. "We're solely responsible for wrangling a group of teenagers, who are already plotting on how to spike the punch, and you're giving me a first aid kit and earplugs?"

"Fine," Ida Belle said and tossed the rope and Mace in the purse.

"Mace?" I asked.

"Have you ever tried to restrain a drunk teenager?" Ida Belle asked. "The last thing we need is someone yelling that we tried to molest little Johnny. Mace won't kill anyone, but it will definitely stop whatever undesirable behavior they're currently engaged in."

"You're right," I said. "Distance is better."

Gertie grabbed her purse and slung the strap over her shoulder, grunting as she bent her arm. "Now that you're done robbing me, can we go?"

I headed out of the house, locking the door behind me. Not that it did any good. I figured if Mannie wanted in, he'd find a way. It was why I hadn't gotten in any hurry to change the locks. What I really needed was a better set of acquaintances.

The park was only a couple of blocks away, but we drove over in my Jeep anyway, in case we had an emergency that required transportation faster than feet. Besides, after her fateful alligator ride, Gertie was even less energetic than usual. She'd be lucky to make the entire event without slouching under a tree to sleep.

A group of about twenty teens were already standing around a pile of lumber in the middle of a sandbox. One of them held a milk jug with a brown liquid in it that I suspected was gasoline. Another jug sat on the ground next to his feet.

I pointed. "This is either the beginning of a horror movie or a comedy special."

Ida Belle jumped out of the Jeep as I rolled to a stop, hurrying toward the arsonists.

"Isn't it illegal to have gasoline in milk jugs?" I asked.

"Sure, but if they enforced that, half of Sinful would be sitting in jail," Gertie said.

Frightening. I watched as Ida Belle stepped in front of the jug holder and wrestled the container from his hands. Then she pointed to the second jug on the ground and the teen picked it up and walked away, looking more than a little agitated.

"I guess the party's over before it begins," I said.

"Oh, she's not going to stop the bonfire," Gertie said. "She wants to do it herself. Ida Belle is *that* person. You know, the one who thinks no one can fire up a grill correctly?"

I watched as Ida Belle popped the top off the milk jug and started dousing the pile of wood. Then she waved her hands around like a crazy woman until all the teens had stepped back a good ten feet, and she pulled a box of matches from her pocket.

"Isn't that your matches?" I asked Gertie.

"Yes," Gertie said. "Bitch."

She lit one of the matches, then stuck it inside the entire pack and threw the whole flaming mess onto the lumber before leaping backward. And it's a good thing she moved so quickly. The flames shot out and upward in a giant ball, and I wondered if she hadn't lost a bit of hair, or maybe an eyebrow. The kids cheered and Ida Belle took a bow before turning around to wave at us.

"What are you waiting for?" she yelled.

"For you to finish setting the place on fire," I grumbled as I climbed out of the Jeep.

"Told you," Gertie said. "And you thought I was the dangerous one."

I was starting to wonder.

We headed over to Ida Belle, who still looked entirely too gleeful for my taste. Her face was flushed with excitement, or maybe a flash burn. Only time would tell.

"Did you see that flame?" she asked.

"People in Montana saw that flame," I said. "It probably singed Pluto."

Ida Belle nodded. "I think it was better than the Big One of '84."

"Was anyone injured in that one?" I asked.

"Of course not," Ida Belle said. "I'm careful when I do things. But you should ask Gertie about the Big One of '73."

I looked at Gertie. "Did you burn the park down or something?"

"Ha," Ida Belle said. "We were attending a candlelight wedding."

"I don't want to talk about it," Gertie said and stomped off toward a group of teens spiking their sodas with Sinful Ladies cough syrup.

"I'm not sure I want to hear about it," I said.

Ida Belle patted my arm. "Just make sure if you and Carter ever get married, you do it in broad daylight."

I squirmed. The thought of marrying Carter was even more uncomfortable than the thought of Gertie probably burning a church down. "I think we're safe."

Ida Belle laughed. "For now."

"So what are our official duties, anyway?" I asked, desperate to change the subject.

"Not much, really," Ida Belle said. "Just mill around, confiscate alcohol, and if you come across a student who's had too much to drink, signal me, and I'll call his parents."

"No police?"

Ida Belle shook her head. "Even if Nelson weren't honking

up the department, we never involve law enforcement unless there's a brawl. Parents can lower the boom on drunken teens better than the sheriff's department, anyway."

I wiped my brow. "I hope the sun sets soon. Between that and the fire, it's hot as hell out here."

"All the sun setting is going to do is bring mosquitoes."

"All kinds of things to look forward to." I pointed to a group of boys standing near the merry-go-round. "I'm going to head over there and see if I can work my wiles on them." I shook my head. "That sounded all kinds of wrong."

"It's for a good cause," Ida Belle said. "The teen you tempt may be a life saved from meth addiction."

"There is that."

I headed off for the merry-go-round, assessing the group as I approached.

Five males. All around eighteen years of age. Ranging in height from five feet ten to six feet one. Weight one-thirty to two-twenty, and that was the shortest one. Decent physical conditioning on two of them. Three looked like they played video games all day. Threat level—likely to annoy me to death.

"What's up?" I asked as I stepped up to the group.

Their eyes widened and they glanced at one another, their uncertainty clear. Finally, they all looked at the tallest one, who must have been the leader.

"Uh," tall one said. "Nothing."

I held in a sigh. If it had taken that long to get such a simple response, I didn't hold out much hope for real information. "I'm Fortune. I'm visiting for the summer."

"Dale," the tall one said. "This is Kenny, Mark, Adam, and T-Boy."

"Hi." I waved a hand at them, feeling more idiotic every second.

"You in high school?" Kenny asked.

"No. I've already finished."

Kenny nodded, looking pleased with himself. "I didn't think so. College girl. Cool."

The rest of them smiled.

"Hmmm." Technically, I was a college girl, just not in recent years.

"What are you majoring in?" Adam asked.

I paused for a second, trying to think of a major that would get me the most mileage. "Chemistry."

"Wow," Kenny said. "You must be smart."

"Nah, I just like to mix things together and see what happens. I'll probably end up working in a lab somewhere or maybe teaching. I don't know."

"Like Heisenberg," Adam said.

"Who?" I asked.

"That science teacher from *Breaking Bad*," Adam said. "He was awesome."

"I haven't seen it," I said.

Adam's eyes widened. "Dude, you should totally watch it."

Mark nodded. "He's this teacher who gets cancer and starts cooking meth in a motor home to pay for the treatment."

"Yeah," Kenny said, "and his shit is like, the best stuff ever and he's making bank."

"Really?" I said, pleased that my degree choice had led straight into a meth discussion. "A motor home, huh? I guess that's one way to stay off the cops' radar."

"It works at first," Kenny said, "but I don't want to spoil the show. You should watch it."

"I will. Thanks for the tip." I glanced around at them. They all seemed relaxed and comfortable, so I went for it. "Hey, nothing like that goes on around here, does it? I mean, with all these bayous and stuff…plenty of places to hide."

They all looked at one another again, some silent form of communication passing among them.

"Meth, you mean?" Kenny asked finally. "I don't think so."

"Nothing interesting ever happens in Sinful," Adam said.

"Really?" I asked. "Because I got here a month ago and it seems like a whole bunch of stuff has happened for such a small place."

"Yeah," Kenny said, "but that's like murders and stuff. That's not meth."

"Got it," I said. Meth manufacturing was interesting. Murder was not. "I don't suppose you can tell me the best spot to catch speckled trout."

They all brightened and started talking at once. As I suspected, fishing was even more interesting than meth manufacturing. I pretended to listen as they pointed and gave descriptions of channels and markers, but my work was done here. These kids didn't know anything about meth in Sinful.

When they started to argue over which bait to use, I made my getaway and headed toward the bonfire. The sun was finally starting to set, but without a breeze, I didn't hold out hope of it getting much cooler. I spotted Ida Belle and Gertie at a picnic table near the fire and walked over to them. Gertie was sitting at the table, rubbing sports cream on her arms.

"What's wrong?" I asked.

"It's getting worse," Gertie says. "Feels like they're on fire."

Ida Belle shook her head. "I bet she hyperextended them. They're going to feel a lot worse before they get better."

"Good thing I still have the medical supplies," Gertie said and pulled aspirin and Sinful Ladies cough syrup from her bag. She tossed back three aspirin and took a gulp of the cough syrup. "That should hold me until I get home."

I wasn't about to ask what she had at home. "Did you guys

find out anything?"

They both shook their heads. "What about you?" Ida Belle asked.

"I found out those kids don't know anything about meth in Sinful," I said.

"Same here," Gertie said. "When I brought up the topic, the kids I was talking to looked at me like I was crazy."

Ida Belle nodded. "And they're no good at lying. If there's meth here, I don't think it's hit the high school…not if these kids are any indication."

"That's a good thing," I said. "I know it doesn't give us anything to go on, but maybe that means this was their first lab."

"It was definitely recent construction," Ida Belle said. "The lumber was charred, but the inside hadn't cured completely. It hadn't been out there for long."

"So maybe they were just getting started in Sinful," I said. "Maybe they'll take the explosion as a sign to move on, especially if they think it may have drawn attention to them."

"Normally, I would agree with you," Ida Belle said, "but whoever built that lab knew the bayous well enough to find a good hiding place, which means they're local or have strong local connections."

"Which means they'll know about the Nelson situation and Carter being on medical leave," I said.

Gertie nodded. "Which means it's low risk to have another go at it."

"Crap," I said. "I hope that finger narrows things down."

"Me too," Ida Belle said.

"So do we keep checking the kids?" Gertie asked.

Ida Belle nodded. "We've got to be here anyway, so might as well nose around. You never know what we might turn up that's useful."

The sound of whooping had me looking toward the street. Another wave of teens was arriving in the bed of a pickup truck.

"Football team," Gertie said.

"The popular kids," I said. "Looks like I have work to do."

Chapter Ten

I trailed a bit behind the new group of teens as they carried an ice chest and lawn chairs toward the bonfire, assessing them as I went.

Seven guys, three girls. The guys were the typical stocky jock types. The girls all had on cheerleader skirts. No threat to me, but they were probably hell on the other students.

As they arranged the chairs and passed out sodas, I sauntered up. "Mind if I have one of those?" I asked, and pointed to the ice chest.

One of the guys gave me a look up and down. He must have liked what he saw, because he gestured for one of the girls to hand me a can. She gave me a look up and down too, but I got the impression she wasn't as impressed as he was.

"Who are you?" she asked.

"Fortune. I'm visiting for the summer."

"I know you," one of the other guys said. "Didn't you kill some dude?"

The girl rolled her eyes. "If she'd killed someone she would be in jail, not hanging out in the park bumming a soda. God, you're so stupid sometimes." She whirled around and stomped off to where the other two girls were standing, then the three of them huddled close to one another, alternating whispering and glaring.

"She didn't kill him," another guy said. "They found some

dead dude in her yard, right?"

"Sort of," I said. "The house belonged to my aunt, and the bone was in the bayou behind the house."

"Oh." The first guy looked slightly disappointed. "That's something I guess, but not as cool as killing him yourself."

"So you've killed someone?" I asked.

"Me? What—no!"

"Then how do you know it's cool?"

"I, uh, it's not cool for me to kill someone. I mean, unless he's hurting my dog or using my duck blind without permission…you know, serious shit."

"Of course," I said. I could get on board with the dog part. Jury was out on the duck blind. I might have to live in Sinful longer before that one kicked in.

I motioned to the cooler. "I don't suppose you have some beer hidden in there."

"Nah, we're not much for drinking."

"Oh, you go for the harder stuff then?"

He stared at me for a moment, his brow wrinkling, then he finally got it and his expression shifted to one of slight disgust. "Drugs? No way!"

I checked out his biceps. "Not even steroids?"

"That crap will shrink your balls. And get you banned. A college scholarship to play football is the only chance we have to get the hell out of this town. We're not about to blow it on something stupid."

"Good for you," I said, and meant it. "A lot of players aren't nearly as smart."

"A lot of players aren't trying to get out of Sinful."

"Hey, look!" One of the other players pointed to the street. The food vendors that had been at the Fourth of July celebration the day before were unloading their trailers at the curb and setting up shop. Hot dogs, pretzels, funnel cakes, and snow cones. Yum!

"Oh!" One of the cheerleaders ran over to grab the arm of the player I'd been talking to. "I want a snow cone."

"Sure, baby." He gave me a nod. "Nice talking to you."

The popular kid crowd, along with half of the other teens, made their way over to the food vendors. I headed back for the picnic table to regroup with Ida Belle and Gertie.

"Anything?" Ida Belle asked as I slid onto the bench.

"No. Apparently, they don't even do steroids because they could lose their chance at a scholarship, also known as 'getting the hell out of Sinful.'"

Gertie frowned. "That's completely logical and a little surprising coming from them, but hey, who am I to question one's motivation for getting out of here. If I had been a normal teen, that might have been my goal as well."

"You did get out of here," Ida Belle said. "We went to war, remember?"

"What about after the war?" Gertie argued. "We could have gone anywhere, but the three of us parked ourselves right back in Sinful."

I knew the "three of us" referred to Ida Belle, Gertie, and Marge Boudreaux, the woman whose niece I was pretending to be. They'd served together in Vietnam in a capacity that no one but me and their commanding officers knew about. Assuming their commanding officers were still alive, which might be a stretch.

"Where else could we be in control?" Ida Belle said.

Gertie shook her head. "How's that working out for you?"

"Right now, it's a bit troubling," Ida Belle agreed, "but we're going to get it all straightened out."

"I hope so," Gertie said. "Retirement wasn't supposed to

require this much energy."

I pointed to the food vendors. "You didn't tell me there would be fat snacks."

"That's because there never have been," Gertie said. "At least, not of the professional sort. Used to, it was limited to whatever you brought in yourself."

"Well, then I think our hard work here deserves funnel cake," I said.

"Darn straight," Gertie said.

"I'll stick around here," Ida Belle said. "There's a couple kids near the bonfire I want to chat with. Get me a bubble gum snow cone. Maybe it will cool me down."

Gertie hopped up from the bench…well, maybe "hop" was a little strong. She sort of rolled off of it and into a standing position, then we set out for food. The girl I'd met at the festival was serving up funnel cakes and her husband was working the snow cone end of things.

"Kayla, right?" I asked when it was our turn.

She brightened. "Yes. I met you yesterday. And hello again, Gertie. I didn't expect to see you guys here."

"We're chaperoning," I said.

"It's good of you to volunteer," Kayla said. "When I was in high school, we wondered every year if the dance would be canceled because no one would volunteer to chaperone."

"It was our time in rotation," Gertie said. "We dragged Fortune along for the ride. We're surprised to see you here as well. I figured you'd be halfway to your next gig."

Kayla nodded. "We have a couple days before it starts. Normally we would have cleared out this morning. But Celia asked all the food vendors if they would work the dance, and get this, she's paying us a flat fee to do it on top of what we'll make from selling."

Gertie's expression shifted from pleasant to annoyance. "That woman. After the debacle she made of the sheriff's department and Francine's menu, she's trying to get brownie points by doing something for the kids."

"Will it work?" I asked.

"Not a chance," Gertie said. "Some funnel cake and snow cones can't make up for the mess she's made. No offense to your food, dear."

"None taken," Kayla said. "The whole mayor thing has been the buzz since we've been here. It doesn't sound like anyone's happy."

"No," Gertie said. "At this point, I'm pretty sure the people who voted for her are unhappy, and the people who didn't vote for her are ready to kill her."

"Let's hope it doesn't go that far," Kayla said. "What can I get you ladies?"

"Two funnel cakes and a bubble gum snow cone," I said.

"Coming right up." She turned around and doctored up two fresh funnel cakes with a load of powdered sugar and put them on the counter just as her husband handed Gertie the snow cone and gave her a wink.

"On the house," Kayla said.

"No," Gertie started to protest.

"I insist," Kayla said. "You're working. It's the least we can do."

"Thanks," I said and lifted the funnel cakes from the counter.

"I can't believe Celia," Gertie said as we walked back to the picnic table. "Trying to buy people off."

"And doing a really poor job of it," I said. "She's not overly bright, is she?"

"No. Never has been. She's in charge of her group because

there's no end to her mouth, and she's a bully. Always was."

"If people know that, then why did they vote for her?"

"Some did only because Marie is Baptist and Celia is Catholic. Others, I don't know. Probably, they don't know her like we do, or maybe since she hasn't ever set the world on fire with anything, they thought she'd leave things well enough alone."

"I wonder what they think now?"

"That mob downtown this morning is a good indication. At least half were good Catholics. I think Celia got too big for her britches."

I set the funnel cakes on the picnic table and took a seat next to Gertie as Ida Belle plopped down on the other side and reached for her snow cone. Gertie filled Ida Belle in on Celia and the vendor deal as we ate.

Ida Belle shook her head. "She's out of her mind if she thinks this will fix anything."

Gertie nodded. "That's what I said. The banana pudding thing is bad enough, but Nelson is going to be the far bigger problem."

"Speak of the devil," I said and pointed to Nelson, who had parked in front of the funnel cake trailer and was climbing out of a new Mercedes.

"Where did he get the money for a car like that?" Gertie asked.

"Probably one of those high-interest leases," Ida Belle said. "He'll have it for a couple months until they repossess it for nonpayment."

"You're probably right," Gertie said. "The man can barely tie his shoelaces. No way is he making that kind of bank at a job. Janitorial work is about all he's qualified for, and it doesn't score people a Mercedes."

We watched as he walked over to the funnel cake trailer, cutting in front of the kids. Several of them shot the finger at him, but he ignored them all and scooped up the funnel cake that Kayla had just placed on the counter for the next customer. She frowned as he smiled at her and made off with the cake.

"What a douche," I said.

"And a coward," Gertie said. "Notice he stepped in front of the geeky kid. If one of those football jocks would have been standing there, he wouldn't have been so gutsy."

"I would have paid money to see that," I said.

"So would a lot of other people," Gertie said.

"Don't look now," Ida Belle said, "but he's headed this way."

I glanced over without turning my head and saw Nelson making a beeline for our picnic table.

Gertie sighed. "Why does it have to be when we're eating? The man turns my stomach."

I nodded and stuffed a huge piece of funnel cake in my mouth, trying to get it all in before he reached us. I made it three-quarters of the way through before he stepped up to the table, lips and chin dripping with powdered sugar and wearing a fake smile.

"And just what are you fine citizens of Sinful doing here?" he asked.

"Chaperoning," Ida Belle said.

He glanced around. "Looks like you're eating to me. You can't keep things in line sitting here by yourselves."

"Really?" Gertie asked. "That's exactly what you do at the sheriff's department, and you get *paid* to leave the building and work."

Nelson's smile vanished and he sneered. "Don't think Celia hasn't filled me in on all the meddling you two have done in this town." He looked at me. "And you…a Yankee trying to take over, causing trouble when it was such a nice place before."

"Oh," I said, "you mean trouble like saving Celia's life before she died of poisoning and finding out who killed her daughter? That kind of trouble?"

"For all I know," Nelson said, "you could have been in cahoots with that woman who poisoned Celia."

"You are so stupid," Gertie said. "Fortune almost died from poisoning herself."

"Maybe," he said. "Or maybe that's just what she claimed."

"Yeah, that's it," Ida Belle said. "She poisoned herself to look like a hero. What do you want?"

"What do you mean?" he asked.

"You don't like us," Ida Belle said, "and we can't stand you. Because we're human and you're not, we have nothing in common so therefore nothing to talk about. So tell us what you want and then go away."

His expression hardened. "What I want is for you three to slip silently into the wind. Stop causing trouble. Stop poking your nose in where it doesn't belong."

"And if we don't?" Gertie asked.

"Then I can make it really difficult for you, especially wearing a badge." He looked at me. "And I can make things really difficult for your boyfriend."

"I wouldn't bet on that," I said.

His expression wavered for a moment, then he recovered. "We'll just see, won't we?" He spun around and strode back across the park.

"What was that about?" I asked.

Gertie smirked. "He thinks he's putting us on notice. Like that fool could scare us."

"If he even knew the half of it," I said, "he'd be running for

Canada."

Ida Belle nodded. "But that's the good part—he's totally underestimated his opponents."

"He's definitely got our abilities all wrong," Gertie said, "but he knows enough to watch us, and that alone could be a problem."

"He's watching us because Celia whined about us to him and probably made it his job to keep us out of her hair," Ida Belle said. "That man has never had an original thought in his life. I doubt he's starting now."

"He wouldn't have to be original to get in our way," Gertie said.

"Hopefully, he'll be too busy avoiding work to notice," I said.

"Hopefully," Ida Belle said, but she didn't sound convinced.

I looked at the street as Nelson climbed into his car and pulled away. A teen with a black hoodie on watched as he pulled away from the curb, then headed into the park and walked behind the bonfire where no other teens were congregated. The fact that he stood alone wasn't necessarily suspicious—hell, I wasn't a big fan of people either—but no one had forced him to come. The hoodie, however, in the heat and humidity was a bit of a stretch.

"I'll be back in a minute," I said and hopped up from the picnic table.

"Is something wrong?" Ida Belle asked.

"I'm not sure. Wait here. If you see anything strange, then move in."

"Like we'd know strange from every day," Gertie grumbled as I took off for the back side of the bonfire.

I paused about two-thirds of the way there near a crowd of kids sharing a funnel cake. The boy hadn't shifted in position and no one had moved to join him. He stood stock still, hands in his pockets and staring at the bonfire. No other teens or structures were nearby, so I had no choice but to approach him in the open. If he had a weapon in his pocket that he intended to use, no way could I reach him before he got a shot off.

Ida Belle had missed my pocketknife during her wardrobe search, but unless I took an offensive approach, it was of little use against a bullet. And it probably wasn't a good idea to make a running leap at a teenager in a public park, especially holding a knife. Of course, it was Sinful, so maybe it wasn't as big a deal as I thought.

I finally decided what the hell and set off directly for him. When I was about five feet from him, he lifted his head and looked directly at me. Something about his eyes was very familiar.

"You're Fortune," he said, but it was more of a statement than a question.

"Do I know you?" I asked.

He smiled. "Nah, but the description I got was a good one, although I think you're even hotter than he said."

"Than who said?"

"My uncle."

And then it clicked where I'd seen those same piercing brown eyes. "You're an Hebert."

He nodded. "People call me Vapor."

"That's a strange name."

"Nickname. Because I have a talent for disappearing."

"Depending on what your line of work is, that's a good ability to have."

He laughed. "My line of work is being an Hebert."

"How old are you?"

"Old enough. You interested?"

I stared at him, unable to prevent my look of dismay. "Right now, I'm as involved with the Hebert family as I'm ever going to be."

"Uncle Little said you were smart. Anyway, I got some papers for you." He pulled some papers folded into a square out of his hoodie pocket. "Little says to tell you he didn't know this guy or his people, so he ain't got no chains to rattle, if you know what I'm saying."

I took the papers and stuffed them into my back pocket. "Tell him not to worry. I'll find him a chain."

Vapor smiled. "I just bet you will. You ever change your mind about your proximity to the Hebert family, you give me a call." He glanced past me, then gave me a wink and turned to walk away.

"You already exchanging me for a younger model?" Carter's voice sounded to my right.

I turned around and saw him walking toward me and understood Vapor's hasty retreat. I hoped he'd retreated before Carter had seen me stuffing the papers in my pocket. I glanced back to make sure Vapor was far enough away that Carter couldn't get a good look at him and frowned.

The boy was nowhere to be seen.

No way. I hadn't looked away but a second. How could he vanish in an open area?

But as I scanned the park grounds and the clusters of teens, I didn't see him anywhere. Impressive. If he hadn't opted for the criminal route, he could have had a hell of a career at the CIA. They didn't call us spooks for nothing.

Carter stepped up beside me. "I saw Ida Belle and Gertie over at the picnic table. How come you're separated from your herd?"

"We're taking turns making the rounds. You know, making

sure no one is falling down drunk or using the Lord's name in vain…whatever happens to be illegal on a Friday night in July."

He grinned. "It's a long list. Probably a dozen violations going on right under our noses."

"Well, it's a good thing Nelson left before he noticed any of them."

The grin vanished. "Nelson was here?"

"Yeah, but I have no idea what for. He pulled up, swiped a funnel cake without paying, then made a beeline for Ida Belle, Gertie, and me and threatened us."

"Threatened you? How?"

"He said we'd be in trouble if we didn't keep our noses out of anything going on in Sinful, and since that didn't appear to move us, his next threat was directed at you. He said he could make things difficult for you."

Carter scowled. "That worthless son of a bitch."

"I told him not to bet on it."

The grin returned. "That's what I love about you."

"*And* what you hate."

"Maybe I just don't like your friends."

"Water seeks its own level."

"Ha. You may think you know them, but I guarantee you, no one is on the same level as Ida Belle and Gertie. It would take a combination of a criminal and magician to even come close."

I laughed. "They'd take that as a compliment."

"I know. That's why neither of us is going to repeat it."

There was a pause in the conversation and Carter glanced around the park, looking as though he wasn't quite certain what he was supposed to do. "What are you doing here anyway?" I asked. It didn't seem like the kind of thing he'd voluntarily show up for.

He gave me a fake surprised look. "What? You're not happy

to see me?"

My radar went off. He wasn't here out of any personal interest at all. He was here because he didn't trust Ida Belle, Gertie, and me. "If I thought your motive didn't include checking up on me," I said, "I'd be happier. What I can't figure out is exactly what you think we could be up to among a bunch of high school students. Do you think they're hiding a meth lab under the merry-go-round?"

A flash of guilt passed over his face, but he quickly recovered. "No. But I don't think Ida Belle and Gertie volunteered you for this job out of the goodness of their hearts, either."

"Well, if they have an ulterior motive, I'm not in on it. I'm just here to level the playing field. Two old ladies against a bunch of teens didn't seem balanced."

"A lot of people might argue with you given that the two old ladies in question are Ida Belle and Gertie."

"Maybe, but I don't see how this gets them anything but sore feet and a monumental dose of boredom." Time to turn the tables. "In fact, the only people in this town I've seen today who were doing things they weren't supposed to are you and Walter."

"The doctor didn't say anything about fishing."

"And if you were really fishing, no one would have a problem." I stared at him for several seconds. "You went to look at the explosion site, didn't you?"

"So what if I did?"

"Look, I got no problem with you going against Nelson or whoever and doing what you think is right, because I trust your judgment. But the reality is that you were lying in a hospital bed a couple days ago, damned near dead. And I don't care what kind of shape you're in. Your body still needs a reasonable amount of time to recover from trauma, and your brain is worse than any other part. It's running the whole show. You're literally messing around with your microprocessor."

He looked a tiny bit guilty, but still wasn't willing to give up the ghost. "You sound as if you care."

"I do care," I said, my voice stronger than I intended for it to be.

To hell with it. I turned to look him straight in the face. "Do you have any idea what it felt like to see the top of your boat disappearing beneath the water and knowing that by the time we got there, you'd be long gone? Do you have any idea what it felt like to dive into that inky black, nothing to go on and desperately hoping for a miracle? Do you have any idea how hard it was to watch you airlifted away and have no idea if you'd be alive when I got to the hospital?"

My voice choked a little on the last sentence and it made me even angrier. I'd never meant to blurt all that out, but I couldn't take it back now.

Carter stared at me, his expression a mixture of surprise and guilt. "I'm sorry," he said. "I never thought about it from your perspective. The truth is, I've been trying to forget about it from mine. I really am sorry. I didn't think…"

"You don't think I worry?"

"No. That's not it. I guess I didn't think about how much it took out of you." He shoved his hands in his pockets and blew out a breath. "What are we doing here, Fortune? Me and you?"

The old me would have quipped "standing in front of a bonfire," but the current me wasn't feeling sarcastic. Current me only felt scared. "I don't know."

"If you don't know, should we even bother?"

"Do *you* know?"

His eyes widened. "I, uh."

"That's what I thought. The reality is you haven't thought it out any further than I have, and when you try, you get to the same roadblocks."

"There's only one roadblock that I can see, and that's what you plan to do at the end of the summer."

Chapter Eleven

The honest answer was that I didn't know, but if I said it, I was afraid Carter would think he was the reason I wasn't sure. The reality was I didn't know what I would do at the end of the summer because I didn't know if I would be cleared to return to DC or have to go into hiding somewhere else. Either way, at that point, the gig was up and Carter, along with everyone else in Sinful, would meet the real Sandy-Sue and know that I'd lied.

"Are you going back home?" he asked.

"That's where my life is. What would you have me do? Throw it all away and move down here? And for what? I'm not rich, and I don't have a job here. There's not even a job in this town that fits my skill set."

Except working for the Heberts, and that wasn't a viable option.

"And while I'll be the first to admit that I'm insanely attracted to you," I said, "we're barely in the beginning of a relationship, if you could even call it that. It's nowhere near the stage where you start changing your life for someone. And the truth is, we don't know that it ever will be."

"I…when you put it that way…." He sighed. "I know it's completely unreasonable to ask you to pick up and move, and honestly, that's not what I meant."

"You asked me my plans for the end of summer. What else could you have meant?"

"I guess I wondered if at the end of August you would get on a bus and leave and that was it."

How could I possibly answer him when I didn't know the answer myself? I couldn't explain the real me, and even if it didn't put me, Carter, and everyone else in Sinful at risk, I still wasn't sure I could answer the question. I'd been struggling for a while now with my life, my choices, my definition of friends, family, and happiness. And the only thing I knew for certain is that I'd gotten it all wrong before Sinful. That didn't mean I was ready to leave everything behind for something new. I wasn't even sure I was capable of doing so. But what it did mean is that I was taking a hard look at my life for the first time, and it was coming up short.

"I don't think that would be 'it,'" I said finally. "I can't picture my life without the people I've met here, but I can't picture my life here, either." I shook my head. "My trip here has me questioning a lot of things, but I'm afraid I don't have any answers."

He took my hand and squeezed it. "I understand. You know that I do. I reassessed everything about my life when I came home from the Middle East, and it took a long time to settle on what I thought I needed."

I nodded, remembering Carter telling me about his life evaluation after his military career. "But you found your answer here in Sinful. Now that everything you wanted is under fire, what are you going to do?"

"If I lose my job, Sinful is in a lot more trouble than me. I refuse to have my happiness owned by my career. There's plenty of places I can be a deputy, and I'm sure they've all got good fishing and nosy old women."

"What about Emmaline?"

"I can visit. Or she can move. Whatever. My point is, I'm

not willing to let one thing have that much control over me. The military required a hundred percent of me, every second of every day. I'll never let something have that big a piece of me again."

"Know thyself."

"Yeah, something like that."

I took in a breath and blew it out. "This is what I know. I have a career I love, but I'm beginning to realize that I need more. I like spending time with you, and I don't want it to stop. Beyond that, I don't know anything else."

He lowered his lips to mine and gave me a soft kiss. "Then that's good enough for now."

"And the end of summer?"

"I'm sure by then, we'll have it figured out."

He sounded confident, which should have made me feel better, but he didn't have all the facts. Carter thought I was dedicated to filing books and chasing down overdue fees. If he knew that the career that had such a hold on me was being a CIA assassin, would he be as confident of those answers? Would he even feel the same way about me at all?

I forced a smile and we started walking, hand in hand, toward the picnic table. No matter how many times I asked myself those questions, I knew the only way to get the answer was to lay it all on the line. And that was something I couldn't do. Not yet. And if I was being truthful with myself, I was worried about what the answers would be.

"How's Walter feeling?" I asked, trying to change the subject to something that wouldn't jack my anxiety level up.

"Stubborn and ornery as ever."

"In other words, fine?"

"Exactly. My mom was over at his place when I left, cleaning his house and rearranging his pantry. He had this pained look—like he had gas and had just been shot, you know?"

I smiled. "I'm sure he'll survive it."

"I don't know. Walter's lived a quiet, long life without a woman interfering. He loves Mom, but every man has his limits."

"And those limits include rearranging a pantry?"

"She'd just finished ironing his underwear, and she took all his beer because of the pain meds."

"Hmmmm. I didn't see you hustling her out of your house."

"Hell, I'm not that crazy. Besides, I'm her son. There are all sorts of Southern rules about things like allowing your mother to take over your house and your life when you've been injured."

"What if you're married?"

"Most wives are happy to get out of the way of an injured or sick husband."

"Good point." I'd spent a particularly long weekend hiding out in Turkey with Harrison, who'd broken his thumb during our mission. You would have thought he'd been placed under a steamroller for an afternoon with all that whining. If our extraction had taken any longer, I would have broken something else on him just to hear a different complaint.

I knew Carter was stubborn about being less than a hundred percent, but I didn't think that was necessarily a male thing. I was the same way. Admitting that I was too injured or ill to perform at full capacity was something I'd do right after I voluntarily went to a nail salon. I'd gone once, but since Harrison had been armed and instructed not to let me leave, I didn't figure that counted.

"Aren't you going to ask *me* how I'm feeling?" he asked.

"No. I'm afraid you'll ask me to cook for you."

He laughed. "I haven't seen a domesticated thing about you since you stepped off the bus and tossed your shoes in the bayou. The closest I'd come is asking you to pick up takeout."

"I could get to Francine's and back in a second with that airboat."

Carter studied my face for a moment, then shook his head. "You're really having fun with that thing, aren't you?"

"Of course! It skims so smoothly across the top of the bayou, it's almost like flying. And even though I'm sure Ida Belle has a death wish, I have to admit that she knows how to handle fast engines."

Carter stopped and turned to face me. "I'm sorry I came off so harsh this afternoon at Stumpy's house. I'm not trying to get in your way of a good time, or Gertie's, for that matter. But when she flew across the bow of Walter's boat, I thought she was a goner."

"You were really worried about her." It was a little surprising and yet at the same time, it wasn't surprising at all.

"Yeah. She reminds me a lot of my grandma." He smiled and we started walking again. "You would have loved her. She was a real pistol, like Ida Belle, but had that try-anything spirit like Gertie. I thought she was the greatest ever, and she's also probably the reason my mom started going gray in her thirties. Anyway, I went a little overboard and I'm sorry."

"That's okay. I think it's sweet. And honestly, I wasn't wild about the idea from the beginning, but if you could have seen the look on her face riding that gator down the bayou. I mean, before it set off on its death mission."

"I can imagine. How is she feeling?"

"She darn near pulled her arms out of their sockets and Bengay's second-quarter profit is going to shoot up by a mile, but she'll be fine."

The words had no sooner left my mouth when I heard a whoop from a group of teens, then a boom box fired up, blasting MC Hammer's "U Can't Touch This." Ten or so teens wearing absurdly large, sparkly gold pants ran in front of the bonfire and started synchronized dancing.

Gertie jumped up from the picnic table, clapping her hands. "It's a flash mob. Darn it, if I'd have known, I would have brought my Hammer pants."

"You have some of those?" I asked.

"You don't?" Gertie set out toward the dancers. "I'm joining in anyway."

Ida Belle shook her head. "She won't make it five seconds before her arms give out."

I looked at the dancers and decided five seconds was generous. They looked like they were standing on hot coals while simultaneously shooting basketball. It was rather frantic, and not all that together. Gertie ran into the middle of the mix and started flailing around.

Carter climbed on top of the picnic table and took a seat.

"I've got to get this on video." I pulled my phone from my pocket and headed in front of the dancers, making sure I had a clear view of Gertie.

"That woman isn't going to be happy until she's a YouTube fiasco," Ida Belle said.

"If I'd been able to record the alligator float escape, she'd already be there," I said.

I zoomed in a bit on Gertie as she did some hip-thrusting thing. And that's when I noticed something white rolling through the dancers. I lowered the phone and looked at Ida Belle. "Did you use all the gas when you were starting the fire earlier?"

"No. Only about half of the jug."

I zoomed in on the jug and saw brown liquid splashing around in it as it rolled. I zoomed in again, and saw another flash of white farther back. "Uh, Ida Belle, where did that kid put the other jug of gas?"

"I don't know. I just told him to move it."

"Yeah, well, I think someone moved it afterward because it's sitting about ten feet in front of the fire, and it looks empty."

Ida Belle frowned. "If someone had added it to the fire, we would have noticed. The flames would have shot up to the moon. I'll go check."

She worked her way around the back of the dancers and lifted the milk jug. She frowned and felt the bottom of it, then looked at the ground. When she looked back up at me, she looked panicked.

Before I could figure out what was wrong, she rushed into the midst of the dancers and started yelling, "Everyone get away from the fire! There's gasoline on the ground!"

Holy crap! The jug had a leak, which meant that the ground around the bonfire was soaked with gasoline. I checked the other jug that was still rolling around among the dancers, basically a rolling explosive if that bonfire spread.

"Gertie," I yelled. "Grab that jug!"

She looked confused for a moment, then looked down at her feet where I was pointing and lifted the jug. I waved my arms, gesturing for her to get the jug away from the fire, and she started trotting out of the crowd. I hurried over to the dancers, yelling at them to move, but they looked at me as though I was crazy just as they had Ida Belle.

I grabbed the arm of the nearest dancer and pulled them out of the way. "There's gasoline on the ground. Get away from the fire."

The teen's eyes widened and she grabbed her friend and pulled her away with her. Some of the other dancers noticed others moving away and stopped dancing.

"You guys suck!" a teen yelled and tossed a full water bottle at the group. Clearly, he wasn't the quarterback because he overshot the group completely and the bottle landed in the bonfire. The bonfire wood, weak from burning, snapped in half and a long piece pitched forward toward the remaining dancers. Fortunately, they'd all heard the snap and turned to look, so now they all scrambled to get out of the way.

As soon as the flaming wood hit the ground, flames shot up, snaking across the grass. Gertie took one look at the approaching flames and set off running, still clutching the other jug.

And that's when I realized that jug had a leak, too.

As she ran, a steady trail of gasoline spilled out of the bottom of the jug and on the ground behind her, leading the flames away from the bonfire and straight down the slope of the park toward the street.

"Throw it!" I yelled at Gertie.

She turned to look at me and I pointed to the jug. "It's leaking! Throw it away."

Gertie glanced back and saw the fire chasing her, and her eyes got as wide as saucers. She was about twenty feet from the street when she reached back with her arm and did a shot put move, hurling the jug away from her.

Right on top of a car that had just pulled up to the curb.

The jug made a loud *thump* as it dented the car hood, then exploded, sending the remaining gas in different directions. Gertie leaped to the side as the flames shot by her, hit the ground, and didn't move. The car's driver jumped out and I groaned when I saw it was Celia Arceneaux.

I ran toward the street, shouting for her to get out of the way as the flames moved across the sidewalk. She paused for a second, then took off across the street as the flames ran up the side of her car. The entire thing caught fire. And that's when I realized the car was rolling forward.

I changed directions and ran for the food vendors, waving my arms like a madman for them to flee the scene. They'd come out of their trailers to watch the fray. I saw Kayla grab her husband's arm and they took off across the park away from the fire. A couple seconds later, Celia's car hit their trailer and the entire mess went up in flames. The pretzel vendor, who'd been parked in front of them, had left his truck attached. He fired up his vehicle and floored it. His tires squealed as he yanked the food trailer away from the curb, leaving a trail of pretzels and sodas as he went.

As soon as I was certain everyone was out of harm's way, I ran over to Gertie, who had pushed herself up into a sitting position. She looked around at the giant burning disaster and her mouth dropped. "What happened?"

"It's a long story," I said. "I can tell you while the fire department is putting it out. Let's get you farther away." I helped her up from the ground and hurried over to the sidewalk, some distance from the fire, where a lot of the teens were gathered. I looked back toward the bonfire and saw Ida Belle and Carter coming toward us, each helping a limping teen. Sirens were already sounding in the distance. I looked back at the park where the fire was still raging out of control. I hoped the fire trucks got here before it spread into the neighborhood.

Carter helped a teen sit down, then hurried over to us, Ida Belle right on his heels. "Are you all right?" he asked. "Did you get burned?"

We both shook our heads.

"Thank God," he said, his relief apparent.

The sirens grew louder and a couple seconds later, a fire truck squealed around the corner. The firemen jumped out and ran into the park with the hose, dousing the flames. Steam rose from the ground everywhere the fire used to be, leaving dark ashy patches behind. A second truck pulled up behind them and went to work on the car and food trailer.

"That was close," Ida Belle said.

"Too close," I said. "Are all the kids okay?"

"Yeah," Ida Belle said. "A few of them fell trying to get out of the fray, but I don't think there's anything more serious than a twisted ankle or two."

Relief coursed through me. "This could have been so much worse."

"Hold that thought," Gertie said and rolled her eyes to the right.

We looked over and saw Celia Arceneaux stomping toward us, her face flushed red, and I was pretty sure it wasn't from the heat.

"You three are responsible for this," she said.

"The hell we are," Ida Belle said. "This is unfortunate, but it was an accident. The gas jugs the kids brought to start the fire were leaking."

Celia glared. "And you were supposed to be supervising those brats to prevent them from doing something stupid like burning the town down."

"You're doing a fine job of that on your own," I said.

She whirled around to face me. "I bet it was you that threw that jug on my car, and I'm going to have a front-row seat when Nelson hauls you away."

"Good luck with that," I said and held up my hands. "Take a big whiff. Not one ounce of gasoline."

Celia wrinkled her nose and took a step back from my hands. "I don't care what you say. The bottom line is you were supervising this event and you're going to pay for the repairs."

"And you're going to pay for our trailer." Colby stepped up and glared at Celia. Kayla hovered behind him, clearly uneasy.

"What kind of idiot jumps out of their car without putting it in park?"

Celia's eyes widened. "It was on fire."

"Still doesn't make it my problem," Colby said. "Not only was it your car that just put us out of business, you paid us to work this venue. I'd say you and the city of Sinful are on the hook for the cost of our trailer and the revenue we lose while we're waiting for a new one."

"But…but it's their fault!" Celia flung her hands in our direction.

Colby pointed his finger at her. "Lady, I don't care what position you hold in this town. The bottom line for me is only one person jumped out of a moving car and that was you. I expect to hear from your insurance company tomorrow morning. Don't make me come looking for you."

"Colby, don't," Kayla pleaded and tugged on his arm. "I'm sure everything will be taken care of."

Colby turned to look at her. "Don't even start. You're the reason we're in this one-horse town to begin with."

He whirled around and went stomping off. Kayla lingered for just a second, looking as if she wanted to say something, then turned and hurried off behind him. Celia whipped around to glare at us.

"Before you say a word," Carter said, "they didn't bring the gasoline and you can't hold volunteers responsible for anything. You can try, but it won't hold water. So unless you can figure out which of those kids brought that gasoline and which one set it that close to the fire, a judge will laugh you out of court."

"We'll just see about that," Celia said. She gave us all a murderous look before stomping off across the park in the direction of her house.

"She's just leaving her car there?" Gertie said. "Flaming up the whole parish?"

"Let her go," Ida Belle said. "Her presence makes matters worse."

"I feel bad about Colby and Kayla's food trailer," I said.

"Me too," Gertie said. "Hopefully they have insurance to cover the trailer and the business loss."

"I'm sure they have something," Ida Belle said, "but Colby's right—the town will foot the bill for whatever his losses are."

"That doesn't pay his bills tomorrow," Gertie said. "And we all know how long insurance companies take to do anything. Maybe we could take up a collection at church on Sunday."

"That's a good idea," Ida Belle said. "I'll talk to the pastor about it."

"Count me in for a donation," Carter said, "but not the churchgoing part."

"Heathen," I said.

He snorted. "Please. You only go because Ida Belle and Gertie need you to win the banana pudding race."

"Not anymore," Gertie said, frowning.

"That's right," I said. "As long as Francine's not serving banana pudding, there's no race. Not having to go to church might be the only positive thing about all of this."

"Heathen," Gertie said.

"I was sleeping anyway, and you know it," I said.

"Why do you think I'm in the choir?" Ida Belle said. "If I didn't have to stand and sing periodically, I'd be snoring up there. Pastor Don is a nice man, but he can make any topic at all a snooze fest."

I heard one of the firemen yell and saw them head back to the truck with the hose. "Looks like the fire's out," I said.

With the flames extinguished, the only light left in the park came from the streetlights on the sidewalk. I could see a trail of burned grass leading away from the sidewalk in front of Celia's car. The car and trailer were a smoldering mass of twisted black metal.

"Cleanup isn't going to be fun," I said.

"No," Gertie agreed, "and there's going to be some angry toddlers tomorrow when their mothers tell them they can't go to the park."

"The cavalry's arrived," I said and pointed to Nelson, who was climbing out of his car.

He stopped to speak to some of the kids, who were filtering down the street, apparently deciding all the cool stuff was over. He waved his hands around like a madman, and I could tell he was yelling. The teens just looked at him as if he were crazy, shook their heads, and kept walking.

Then he caught sight of us and came stomping over. "What the hell happened here?" he demanded.

"Aliens landed," Gertie said, "and set the whole damned place on fire. I think they were after the kids."

A flush crept up Nelson's face and he opened his mouth to speak, but Ida Belle cut him off.

"Tell him the truth," Ida Belle said, and I saw her wink at Gertie.

"Okay," Gertie said. "The truth is we were burning crosses and it got out of control. You know how we Baptists are."

Nelson's entire body stiffened to the point that a good wind would have broken him in two. "I know you're up to something. If I was equipped, I'd arrest you."

Carter, Gertie, and I all pulled out a set of handcuffs and held them out toward Nelson.

Chapter Twelve

"This isn't over!" Nelson spun around and strode across the park, yelling at one of the firemen.

The four of us looked at one another and burst out laughing. Gertie clutched my arm, laughing so hard she was sobbing, and we both sank onto the ground in a delirious pile. "That couldn't have been more perfect if we planned it," I said.

"I know," Gertie said. "I'll never forget the look on his face."

"Yes," Carter said. "He's probably as confused as I am. Why exactly do the two of you have handcuffs?"

Gertie and I looked at each other and started laughing again. Gertie waved a hand in dismissal. "Shouldn't you be asking Ida Belle why she doesn't?"

Ida Belle wiped the tears from her eyes. "I thought I took your handcuffs away," she said to Gertie.

Gertie nodded. "You did, but I had a spare set stuffed in my bra."

Carter looked pained. "This conversation has gotten really uncomfortable. And since I know I'll never get a straight answer out of any of you, I'm going to call it a night."

"Me too," Ida Belle said. "It's going to take a whole tank of hot water to get the smell of ash off of me."

"Another advantage of burning the place down," Gertie said. "We get to go home a good two hours early."

Carter leaned over to give me a quick kiss. "I'll see you tomorrow."

I watched for a couple of seconds as he walked away, then turned around to find Ida Belle and Gertie grinning at me. "Stop it," I said.

"C'mon," Gertie said. "We're allowed a vicarious thrill."

"And if there were anything thrilling going on," I said, "you'd be in line to hear about it right behind Ally. She's already threatened me."

Gertie nodded. "It stands to reason. She's young and still holds out hope that she'll get lucky."

"Oh hell," Ida Belle said, "you're old and still hold out hope you'll get lucky."

"Wait a minute." I looked at Gertie. "I thought you two were committed to the single life."

Gertie patted me on the shoulder. "Getting lucky and being single are not mutually exclusive."

I wrinkled my nose. "Okay, but for the record, my life is complete without any vicarious thrills of the sexual kind."

Ida Belle laughed. "No doubt. Let's get out of here before Gertie sets another car on fire."

"That was an accident," Gertie said as we started toward my Jeep. "I was trying to throw it to the side, but with my sore arms, I couldn't hold on long enough to get it all the way around."

Ida Belle clapped her on the back. "Look at it this way—after this, everyone will probably forget about that candlelight wedding thing."

I reached into my pocket for my keys and suddenly remembered Vapor and the papers. "I'm an idiot!"

"About what?" Gertie asked.

"That kid I went to the back of the bonfire to check out—the one with the hoodie—he was Little Hebert's nephew. He gave me the results of the fingerprint trace."

"Jesus, woman!" Gertie said. "Talk about burying the lead. What do they say?"

"I don't know," I said. "Right after he gave them to me, Carter showed up and then you ran off to dance, and you know the rest."

"Emergency meeting time," Ida Belle said. "Either my house or Gertie's, since Ally will be at Fortune's."

"Who has food?" I asked. "I'm starving."

"I've got pot roast and brownies," Gertie said.

"You win," I said and jumped into the Jeep.

The crowd that had formed at the park was slowly making its way back home, most of them walking down the middle of the street rather than on the sidewalk. I weaved around them and made the couple blocks' drive to Gertie's house. As I parked at the curb, I heard my phone signal a text and pulled it out to look. It was from Ally.

Which one of you burned the park down?

I smiled.

Guess.

Gertie?

Actually, the park burning was an accident, but Gertie did take out Celia's car.

OMG Tell me!

We're stopping off at Gertie's house for a bit. Will fill you in when I get home.

"What's the matter?" Gertie asked. "Does Carter miss you already?"

"That was Ally wanting to know which one of us burned the park down."

"What did you tell her?" Gertie asked.

"I told her it was you, of course."

"Keep talking that way," Gertie said, "and I won't feed you."

"Yes, you will, because you want to know what the fingerprint search turned up as much as I do."

Ida Belle waved her hand at us. "Why don't both of you stop yapping and get inside."

We headed straight for the kitchen and Gertie pulled a stewpot out of her refrigerator and stuck it on the stove. "This will take about five minutes, but it doesn't taste the same if I use the microwave." She grabbed three beers from the refrigerator and slid them onto the table before taking a seat across from Ida Belle and me.

I pulled the papers from my pocket and started to read. "Dewey Parnell. Thirty-one years old. Lists his address as New Orleans."

Ida Belle and Gertie looked at each other.

"Did you know him?" I asked.

"Oh yeah," Ida Belle said. "Dewey was a real problem child. Before he even started school, he threw a rock through every window of the schoolhouse. Two weeks after he started kindergarten, his teacher filed for short-term disability, claiming severe mental anguish…and she got it."

Gertie nodded. "Week three, he used a pocketknife to shave three students' heads during nap time. The substitute teacher needed counseling."

"And an attorney," Ida Belle threw in. "By the time he hit first grade, the parish had had enough of Dewey and he was expelled when he duct-taped a student to his desk and set his tennis shoes on fire."

"That's about the same time he was asked to leave the

Catholic church for peeing in the holy water. His mother finally admitted there might be something wrong with him, and got him a shrink. He worked with Dewey for a couple of years, and Dewey finally returned to school in the third grade. His mother had kept him up by homeschooling him.

"And he was better?" I asked.

"Well," Gertie said, "'better' is a relative term. I suppose most of us thought he had improved over how he used to be, but he was still light years away from where he needed to be. But at that point, he'd learned to pretend just enough to keep from getting kicked out."

"If he wasn't cured, why didn't he keep seeing the shrink?" I asked.

"The shrink had a heart attack," Ida Belle said.

"Of course he did," I said. "What kind of trouble did this guy cause in high school—terrorist threats, drowning puppies?"

"No, that was the odd thing," Gertie said. "It was like one day, someone let the air out of him. He wasn't a different person, per se, it was more like he wasn't any person at all."

Ida Belle nodded. "He just went through the motions, graduated, then disappeared. I asked his mother about him once and she avoided the question. I figured he'd come to no good."

"Too bad he didn't have the big showdown moment in New Orleans instead of bringing it back here," I said.

"Well," Gertie said, "we figured from the beginning that someone from Sinful was involved. Maybe with Dewey dead, they'll relocate."

"Unless there was more than one from Sinful," I said.

"Any employment history?" Ida Belle asked.

"Dishwasher at a couple of restaurants, bartender, most recently employed with one of those traveling carnivals."

"A carny?" Gertie asked. "Now there's a good fit."

"Let's see what else is here." I scanned the papers. "Looks like a laundry list of arrests, mostly for stupid stuff—petty theft, pickpocketing, drug possession, but nothing about distribution."

"If he's the cooker, he wouldn't be distributing," Ida Belle said. "Whoever is in charge always keeps the cooker separate from the distributors. Otherwise, the distributors would cut out the middleman."

"Did Little know anything about Dewey?" Gertie asked.

"Not according to Vapor," I said.

"Vapor?" Ida Belle asked.

"Apparently, that's his nickname due to his ability to disappear. Since he managed to get out of my sight in about two seconds, it seems pretty accurate."

"Did he say anything else?" Ida Belle asked.

"Only that the Heberts didn't have information on the cooker or any known associates."

"Do you think they're telling the truth?" Gertie asked.

I shrugged. "Hard to say, but I'm going to guess they are. If the trace had produced the answer they wanted, why would they give me the information?"

"True," Ida Belle said. "Who are the known associates?"

I looked back at the papers. "Known associates include Rip Salazar, Conrad Fredericks, Lynne Fontenot, and Benedict Granger."

Ida Belle and Gertie both perked up. "You recognize any of those?"

"Benedict Granger is from Sinful," Gertie said. "Still lives here."

"Really?" I said. "I didn't see that one coming. Benedict is sorta an odd name for these parts, isn't it?"

Ida Belle rolled her eyes. "His mother was stuck on the whole British thing. Even flew a British flag outside of her house."

"South of the Mason-Dixon line?" I asked. "Did she have a death wish?"

"People kept shooting holes in the flags," Gertie said. "After she went through ten or so, she gave up."

"And he still lives here?" I asked.

"Yeah. He's not exactly a model citizen," Ida Belle said. "He works as a roughneck, but I think he only does jobs long enough to accumulate drinking money. From what I hear, he spends more time in the Swamp Bar than he does on an oil rig."

I sighed. "And we're back to the Swamp Bar. You know, Gertie, if you wanted to do the whole town a favor, the next time you're in pyromaniac mode, why don't you pay them a visit?"

"I'm not even going to be offended at that statement," Gertie said, "because you've got a good point."

"That matchbook Gertie found at the lab site seems to fit with this Benedict character," I said.

"You know what this means?" Ida Belle said.

I flopped back in my chair. "That we have to go to the Swamp Bar and see if we catch this Benedict doing something suspicious." I pointed a finger at them. "But I'm not dressing like a hooker again, and I'm definitely not doing a wet T-shirt contest."

"Oh!" Gertie sat upright. "I just remembered. At the festival yesterday, some of the usual Swamp Bar crew were talking about a crawfish boil that the bar was hosting tomorrow. It starts at noon."

"That might not be too bad," Ida Belle said. "And all of the regulars will come out for a free meal."

"Do we really want to see the Swamp Bar in daylight?" I asked. "Because it looks pretty seedy in dim light."

"The regulars probably look even worse," Gertie said.

"Something else to look forward to," I said. "It's one thing for me to dress like a hoochie and show up there after dark and sit in the dim light of that bar, but if the three of us show up in broad daylight, won't it look strange? I mean, I can't imagine those people would volunteer information to any of us."

"That is a problem," Ida Belle agreed.

"Sure," Gertie said, "the way we look now it wouldn't work, but we can rough it up."

Ida Belle and I stared at her.

"Okay," she said, "so maybe it would be easier if all three of us didn't go."

"I'm really tired of being the token bar slut," I said.

"I'll go with you," Gertie said. "Ida Belle can drive us over in the airboat. That way, if we need a quick escape, we have one."

I wasn't convinced that Gertie could pull off Swamp Bar attire and even less excited about the prospect of needing to get away quickly, but I knew it was the best option for getting information. Unfortunately, the men at the Swamp Bar seemed to respond to my bar slut persona. I wasn't sure whether to be flattered or dismayed.

"Hey," I said, "if the guy lives here, why don't we just watch his house?"

"Last I heard," Ida Belle said, "he lived on his boat."

I stared. "Seriously? That must be some boat."

"No. It's complete crap," Ida Belle said, "but when you don't pay your rent or utilities, you run short on options. I doubt anyone in Sinful will do business with him."

"Great," I said. "So when he's not drinking, or working a couple of days to pay for the next round, he's floating in a drunken stupor around the bayous of Sinful."

"That's pretty much it," Ida Belle said.

"Well, he's perfect for a middleman," I said. "No one's going to question him lounging around in the bayou all day when he lives there." I sighed. "Okay, so Gertie and I will go to this crawfish boil—but I'm not eating anything—and we watch for this Benedict and see if he appears in cahoots with anyone else, right?"

Ida Belle nodded.

"That doesn't sound like we're doing much," I said.

"I know," Ida Belle agreed, "but that's what we have to work with."

"At least the kids were clean," Gertie said as she rose from the table and started serving up the stew.

"That part is encouraging," Ida Belle said. "It would be nice to put a stop to this before it ever gets started."

I nodded, also happy that it appeared the meth hadn't made its way to the teen market, but my conscience was weighing heavily on me. So many lies. Even though the current ones were by omission, that didn't make me feel any better.

"What's wrong?" Gertie asked as she put a bowl of stew in front of me.

"Nothing," I said. "Everything."

"There's a bit of a gap between those two words," Ida Belle said.

"You want to tell us about it?" Gertie asked.

"Yes," I said. "And no."

"Well, at least you're consistent," Ida Belle said, and smiled.

Gertie placed two more bowls of stew onto the table and slid into her seat. "Eat, and talk. You'll feel better after you do both."

I took a bite of the stew and I had to admit, I did feel a little better. It had a rich, slightly spicy broth with chunks of beef, potatoes, and carrots and went perfectly with my beer. "The stew is great, but I don't think talking can fix anything."

"We may not have a solution for whatever is bothering you," Ida Belle said, "but Gertie's right that sometimes just talking about it brings some level of peace."

I took another bite and nodded. "Okay. It's getting harder to lie to everyone. And I know that sounds incredibly stupid, especially to you guys since you know who and what I really am. I mean, my entire career hinges on my ability to lie often and well and without conscience."

"Certainly," Ida Belle agreed, "but those lies aren't told to people you care about."

I sighed. "Yeah."

"Is there any lie in particular that's bothering you at the moment?" Gertie asked.

"It's a bunch of them," I said. "Take tomorrow for example. I'm pretty sure Ally is working at the café, so I don't have to make an excuse to get off without her to do this Swamp Bar thing, but I will probably have to come up with some excuse to avoid Carter."

Ida Belle nodded. "Our side projects were a lot easier when he was working."

"And there's the whole finger thing," I said. "What if we don't come up with something? How long do we wait before we turn the evidence over to the cops? Two days? Until Carter goes back to work?"

Gertie and Ida Belle frowned.

"I'm embarrassed to say," Ida Belle said, "that I hadn't gotten that far in my thinking, but you're right. Due to Nelson's incompetence, law enforcement is unaware of the presence of the meth lab. And no one but us and the Heberts know the identity of the cooker. If Carter gets back to work, we have to tell him about the print."

"How do you think that's going to go over?" I asked.

"Like a turd in a punch bowl," Gertie said. "Jesus, we've made a mess of this."

"Let's not get ahead of ourselves," Ida Belle said. "If we can run down the rest of Dewey's partners, then the easy answer is we turn it all over to the Heberts and rest well in the knowledge that it won't be a problem going forward. Then no one has to know anything beyond what they know now."

"But will you really rest well?" I asked, leaning forward to look at them. "I know you guys had your run in Vietnam. We haven't discussed the details and don't need to, but I'm sure you did things then that you wouldn't think of doing as a regular civilian. I made peace a long time ago with what I do. I know it's for the greater good, and to protect the innocent, even if no one else could understand that. But if we turn the Heberts loose on people…"

The kitchen was so quiet, all I could hear was the clock ticking on the wall. Ida Belle's and Gertie's expressions were both contemplative, and I knew they were thinking about their service and trying to put what we were doing now into perspective—weighing their own moral code against the safety of Sinful. It was a difficult thing to do, even when the target in question was clearly the bad guy.

Even when you weren't the one to pull the trigger.

"I think," Ida Belle said, finally breaking the silence, "that if it comes down to the Heberts settling the score, I wouldn't have a problem with it because it would have eventually come around to that regardless of whether we provided them information or not."

Gertie nodded. "I agree. They were already onto the meth problem because of their hospital snitch. All they had to do was wait for business to start up and go after them then. They have enough ears to the ground that they could have ferreted them out without our help."

"And the result would have been the same," I said.

They both nodded.

"Okay," I said. "I can accept that."

"Good," Gertie said. "So do you feel better now?"

I did to some degree, but my biggest problem still lurked in the back of my mind, pricking at me like damaged nerves in an old wound.

"Carter asked me what my plans were for the end of the summer," I said.

Gertie's eyes widened and she looked over at Ida Belle.

"What did you say?" Ida Belle asked.

I shrugged. "What could I say? I don't know what my plans are. Ahmad is off-grid and there's still a price on my head. I don't know what will happen by the end of summer. I don't know what will happen by the end of next week."

Gertie gave me a sympathetic look. "It's a lot for you to deal with. I think sometimes Ida Belle and I get so wrapped up in what's going on in Sinful that we forget why you're here in the first place."

"And that no one else knows the truth," Ida Belle said. "I mean, we know no one else knows who you really are, but I don't think we give much thought as to how difficult it must be for you to live a completely duplicitous life."

I nodded. "With you guys, I get to be myself, but with everyone else I have to live the lie. And it gets harder and harder not to slip."

"The more comfortable you get with people," Gertie said, "the harder it is to maintain the facade. I can see that."

"What did Carter say about your noncommittal answer?" Ida Belle asked.

"He didn't like it," I said, "but then I pointed out that he could hardly expect me to change my entire life after being here a month."

"Which would be a perfectly reasonable statement," Ida Belle said, "even if you were the real Sandy-Sue."

"I know," I said, "and he agreed."

"So how did you leave things?" Ida Belle asked.

"The same as they were before, I guess. He seems to think that if we're still together at the end of the summer, the answer will be apparent."

"But he doesn't know the truth," Gertie said.

"Exactly." I slumped back in my chair. "This is the very reason I avoided seeing Carter that way. Sure, I've been attracted to him since the beginning, but look at what a mess it is. And continuing on this path until the end of summer is only likely to make things worse."

"You could always tell him the truth now," Gertie said.

"No," I said. "Assuming the truth didn't make him run for the hills, he'd try to protect me, and that would be worse."

"She's right," Ida Belle said. "He's already invested in her, and if Carter is anything, he's the hero type. Despite her real identity, he'd take it as his personal mission to save her."

I nodded. "And he has no idea what that entails. Even if I tried to describe just how horrible the man is who's after me, I don't think there's good enough words."

"And if you tried to explain that he needed to stay out of it because he's not qualified, then you'd insult him." Gertie sighed. "Being single is so much easier."

"Men *are* a bit of a handful," Ida Belle agreed.

"Well, anyway," I said, "I told you that you wouldn't have answers because there aren't any. So that's what has been on my mind—some of it for a while, but it's gotten worse the last couple of days." I gave them both a small smile. "But I do feel better for telling you."

Gertie reached over and patted my hand. "It always feels better when someone understands that you're standing in a shit storm holding a broken umbrella."

That pretty much summed it up.

Chapter Thirteen

I awakened early the next morning, or maybe I just never quite went to sleep. I heard Ally milling around her bedroom around 5:00 a.m. getting ready for work, but I stayed in bed, hoping I could finally get some shut-eye. I finally gave up at seven and made my way down to the kitchen.

Ally had been waiting for me the night before, about to explode if I didn't tell her everything that had happened. Between Gertie and her ride on the alligator and Celia's flaming car, we spent an hour in the kitchen alternating between laughing and eating cookies. Sometime after midnight, Ally declared that if she didn't get to bed she'd never make it through work the next day and headed upstairs. I followed shortly after, but even a long, hot shower didn't bring on the sleep I'd really hoped for.

Quite simply, I had too much on my mind. So much that it raced from one problem to another, in a vicious cycle that had me tossing and turning in between small bouts of sleep with vivid, strange dreams. I awakened feeling more tired than I had when I'd gone to bed, and that was saying a lot given the day I'd had before.

As I scrambled some eggs, I tried to force everything out of my mind except for today's agenda. If there was one thing I'd learned, trips to the Swamp Bar required all of my concentration if I planned on getting out in decent shape. So far, I hadn't managed that, but I was determined that this time I was going to walk in and walk out. No running for my life. No wearing trash bags and nothing else. No clinging for life on the back of a motorcycle.

I'd just sat down at the table with eggs and toast when my phone went off. I picked it up and saw it was a text from Carter. Looks like everyone was up early.

Forgot I have MRI repeat at hospital this morning. See you this afternoon.

I felt some of the tension ease out of my neck. That solved one of the morning's problems. With Ally at work and Carter at the hospital, we were clear for our Swamp Bar excursion. With any luck, we could collect the information we needed and get back home before anyone was the wiser.

And I was going to keep telling myself that.

The festivities at the Swamp Bar were supposed to kick off around eleven, so Gertie and Ida Belle planned to be at my house at nine-thirty for Gertie and me to get in costume. I still had no idea what Gertie thought our costumes should consist of, and was more than a bit worried at the prospect, but she'd assured me I wouldn't have to wear anything that exposed body parts I wanted covered or made it impossible to run. That should have made me feel better, but I was afraid that in that description, too much leeway existed that I just didn't have the imagination to come up with. Gertie, on the other hand, was 90 percent imagination, 5 percent reality, and 5 percent alien.

I polished off my breakfast and opened my laptop to see if Harrison had sent me an email. I didn't expect anything so soon, and if anything big had happened, he would have risked a text, but I couldn't help myself from checking. I was a little disappointed when I saw the empty in-box, but then shifted to work mode and decided to do an Internet search on Dewey.

The search brought up several hits, all of them but one

news reports listing recent arrests in which Dewey was listed. All of the news articles matched items listed on the information I'd gotten from Little Hebert. The last hit was a short blurb about the carnival and had a pic of Dewey and two other workers standing in front of a Ferris wheel. His name was listed in the photo caption. The names of the other two men didn't match any of those listed on the information from Little.

Nothing.

I did another search, this time on the known associates. Rip Salazar didn't produce any results, but that wasn't surprising. I figured Rip was a nickname and not a legal one. I found one listing for Conrad Fredericks and it was an obituary. Thirty-two years old, former employee of the same carnival Dewey had worked for, and died of a drug overdose. Sounded like our guy. The obituary was dated a year before. One name off our suspect list.

A search on Lynne Fontenot produced so many results that I couldn't sort them out. I read through the first twenty or so, but couldn't find enough details to tie any of the search results to Dewey. The name was too common. Maybe not anywhere else in the world, but in Louisiana, it was the equivalent of Mary Smith. I typed in the last name—the subject of today's adventure—and a couple hits popped up. The first was a warrant listing and Benedict's name was on it for outstanding speeding tickets. The second hit was an article from a New Orleans newspaper talking about arrests made in a bar fight. Benedict was one of the participants.

Sounded like a really great dude. I couldn't wait to spend lunch with him.

I closed the laptop and headed upstairs. First, I was taking a cold shower to try to wake up. Then I was going to pick out jeans, a tank top, and tennis shoes. That was as bar-slutty as I was getting for a lunch event. And despite my commitment to strolling in and out, it never hurt to wear something I could sprint in.

Whatever Gertie had in mind, she could keep it to herself.

I opened my front door and blinked, then rubbed my eyes.

"Don't bother," Ida Belle said. "It's not going to get any better."

Gertie stood on my porch next to Ida Belle and if I hadn't been a trained operative, and expecting her, I wouldn't have recognized her at all. She'd matched my outfit of jeans and tank top, but that's where the similarity ended. Her bright pink tank was covered with a black leather vest. Her jeans sported black leather riding chaps. Around her neck was a black leather collar with silver studs. Her hair was tied up in a red bandanna and she wore huge polarized sunglasses accessorized with purple lipstick.

And that wasn't even the scary part.

Up and down both of her arms and peeking out of the tank and vest were tattoos. Tons of tattoos. Swirls of red, green, blue, black, and yellow surrounded her arms all the way from shoulder to wrist. The end of a bunch of red roses came out of her tank and splayed across her chest like someone had fired a paint gun at her.

"What the hell?" I asked and waved her inside before someone saw her and started a turf war.

"Looks good, right?" Gertie said, grinning as she pulled off her sunglasses.

I cringed at the dark black eyeliner and bright blue eye shadow she wore. I knew next to nothing about fashion, but I'd always heard black matched everything. Whoever said it was wrong. Nothing on Gertie fit. It was like those tests you did when you were a kid—you were shown a bunch of objects and had to pick the one that didn't belong. In Gertie's case, the correct answer would have been "all of the above."

"I don't know where to start," I said.

"No place to finish either," Ida Belle said. "It's probably best to skip starting altogether."

"Like you don't wear leather," Gertie said.

"I wear motorcycle gear, oddly enough, when I'm riding my motorcycle," Ida Belle said. "I don't wear it as a fashion statement."

"You two are such stick-in-the-muds," Gertie said. "This is the perfect disguise for the Swamp Bar. No one will recognize me, and I should fit right in."

It was more than a little over the top, and fantastically disturbing, but I had to admit she had a point. Definitely, no one would recognize her, and the look was one I'd seen sported by men and women at the Swamp Bar. Not the makeup part on the men, but leather and tattoos were popular.

Gertie lifted her handbag. "I brought stuff to fix you up." She opened the handbag and pulled out sheets of temporary tattoos, a blue bandanna, and black leather gloves with no fingers. "I didn't figure you for the vest and chaps type. Besides, you'll get more from the men if they can see your cleavage, and I didn't want the competition with the chaps. I'm betting everyone there takes one look at this leather-bound heinie and thinks, 'I hope I look that good when I'm her age.'"

Ida Belle shook her head. "People will take one look at you and hope they make it to your age."

"Say what you want," Gertie said, "but that Kim Kardashian doesn't have anything on these cheeks."

"Mother of God," Ida Belle mumbled.

I lifted one of the tattoo sheets and studied the red and

black swirls that looked like some sort of tribal art. "I'm not putting this on my body."

"It's temporary," Gertie said. "A little soap and it comes right off."

"You're sure?" I said. I'd had my share of run-ins with Swamp Bar patrons, and had to admit that the tattoos might be enough to throw them off my scent, but no way was I walking around the rest of the summer looking like an eighties headbanger or a rapper. I'd take my own self out before I let that happen.

"Positive," Gertie said. "I tested a small one myself last night on my leg. It came right off in the shower."

I looked at Ida Belle. "It might keep me from being recognized from my previous visits."

Ida Belle shrugged. "It's your skin. You want to walk around with arms looking like an angry hornet, who am I to say anything?"

"How long will this take?" I asked.

"The hardest part is getting everything lined up," Gertie said. "Thirty minutes, at least."

"Then we better get moving," I said.

"We should probably do them in the bathroom. You can hang your arm over the tub. That way, there's not a big mess."

"Cool." The last thing I wanted to do was clean. "My bathroom is set up best for two people standing over the tub."

Gertie pulled a tank top from her purse and handed it to me. "Once we get the tattoos done, change into this. It's a better fit."

I unfolded the black tank and was relieved when I saw the Metallica logo in the center. "I can roll with this."

"And you'll need to take off the sports bra," Gertie said. "I want to see cleavage."

Ida Belle grimaced and reached for the television remote. "I'm just going to sit here with the TV on really loud and try to cleanse my ears."

"You still have to look at us," I pointed out.

Ida Belle flopped down in the recliner. "I'm going to bleach my eyes when I get home."

Gertie and I headed upstairs, where she pulled off her black hiking boots, rolled up her jeans, and stepped into the bathtub. I draped a towel over the side and stuck my arm over. She turned on the water and wet my arm with a towel, then began to apply the first set of tattoos.

Thirty minutes later, I had on a push-up bra, the black Metallica tank, and more decoration on my arms than I had in my entire condo back in DC. I pulled my hair back in a ponytail and tied the bandanna around it, then pulled on my sunglasses. I took a look at myself in the mirror and blinked.

"You look great," Gertie said, grinning at me. "It would have been even better if we could have dyed your hair, but with it being extensions, I was afraid to suggest it."

"Yeah, that would have been a big no." I wasn't particularly attached to the hair that had been forced on me before I made my trip to Sinful, but I'd be lying if I said I hated it. Sometimes it bothered me because I looked like my mother with all that blond, but I'd finally decided that wasn't a bad thing. When I was a kid, I'd always thought my mom was the most beautiful woman in the world. It was sometimes hard for me to reconcile that fact with the thought that I looked so much like her.

"I don't think anyone will recognize you from before," Gertie said.

"Let's hope not. Getting a rash of trouble for showing up would make it hard to spy on Benedict."

"I just hope he's there to spy on."

"Well, if he doesn't work much, surely he'd be where free food and cheap beer are located."

Gertie nodded. "Unless he's in jail."

"True."

"Hurry up!" Ida Belle yelled. "We need to get this costume party on the road."

We hurried downstairs where Ida Belle was waiting. She took one look at me and blinked.

"What do you think?" Gertie asked.

"I think you two look like those sad mother-and-daughter combinations at the mall in New Orleans where the mother is trying to look like her daughter's sister."

"Yeah, yeah," Gertie said. "But do you think people at the Swamp Bar will recognize her from before?"

"I may not recognize her by the time we get to the boat," Ida Belle said.

"Told you," Gertie said and gave me a wink. She pulled her cell phone out of a vest pocket and handed it to Ida Belle. "Get a couple pics of us."

"I don't think that's a good idea," I said.

"Come on," Gertie said. "In a couple of hours, all this glorious art will be gone and we won't have any proof of how great we looked."

"The police wouldn't have any proof either," Ida Belle said, and snapped some pictures.

"You always think we're going to run into trouble," Gertie said. "I don't understand why you have to be so negative."

Ida Belle shook her head and traipsed off down the hall. We followed her out to the boat, where Gertie climbed in and promptly sat on the bench without my even having to argue with her. Maybe her gator ride had taken some of her enthusiasm for speed racing out of her.

"Take off your bandanna," Gertie told me, "and put it in your jeans pocket for the ride."

"Got it," I said and pulled the scrap of material off my head. I hoped my ponytail held during the ride over, but worse-case scenario, I arrived looking like I'd been sleeping on it for a day and didn't own a brush. In other words, I'd probably blend better.

Once I took my seat, Ida Belle started the boat and the thrill ride was on. I had to admit, though, this arrival at the Swamp Bar was going to beat any of my departures hands down. If my lucky streak continued once our little investigation was over, I was playing the lotto this weekend.

Boats lined the bank at the Swamp Bar when we pulled up, and from all the hooting and hollering, the party was going strong, even though it was barely 11:00 a.m. Ida Belle docked against the bank back a bit from the other boats, leaving enough room for a quick getaway, in case one was necessary. That was something I kept telling myself—"in case." I figured if I forced myself to think it wouldn't be the norm, then nothing bad would happen. So far, I was mostly glad that I'd worn jeans with spandex and my good running shoes, which didn't say much about my confidence in a clean getaway.

Gertie and I climbed out of the boat and I tied it off on an old post, leaving the knot loose so that it could be removed in a second. I pulled my cell phone out and checked. "No service, as usual."

"I figured as much," Ida Belle said. "No worries. Sitting here, I can see a good thirty yards up the bank. If you come running, I have plenty of time to untie us and be ready to haul by the time you jump in."

She pulled a baseball cap out of her back pocket and put it on, then dug out a copy of *Hot Rod* magazine.

"What's that for?" Gertie asked and pointed to the magazine. "You sold your car."

"I know," Ida Belle said, "but I'm thinking the motorcycle isn't practical for a lot of things."

Gertie snorted. "You mean things like being a hundred years old?"

"No. I meant things like getting away quickly with passengers. We can't take the airboat everywhere."

I frowned. "You're thinking of buying a fast car because we need a getaway vehicle? Do you realize how frightening that sounds? We're not bank robbers. We're not supposed to need a getaway vehicle."

"It is what it is," Ida Belle said and lifted the magazine up.

I opened my mouth to argue, but off the top of my head, I didn't have anything.

"Hey, should we have some fake names?" I asked.

"You think anyone here is going to care what our names are?" Gertie asked.

"Well," I said, "I get hit on by drunk men and non-drunk men."

Gertie frowned. "Oh yeah. Been a couple of years since I had that problem."

Ida Belle snorted. "It's been a century since you had that problem."

Gertie shot her a dirty look. "You can be Little Nicky and I'll be Icepick."

"Lord save us," Ida Belle mumbled behind her magazine.

"I was thinking something less 'mobster movie of the week,'" I said. "How about Tina and Mary? You can be either."

"Fine," Gertie said. "I'll be Tina."

"Then let's get this over with," I said and motioned Gertie toward the fray.

Despite the early hour, the party was in full swing. Country music blared from inside the bar, and I could see people inside sitting at the tables and dancing on the dance floor. A group of men sat on one corner of the porch playing cards and another group occupied the other end playing quarters. People gathered around several huge stainless steel pots on the front lawn, and I had to admit that whatever they were cooking smelled great. My vow to avoid eating anything went out the window. With any luck, investigating would offer up time for a snack.

"Everyone looks worse in daylight," I said.

Gertie scanned the crowd and grimaced. "The understatement of the year."

"Do you see Benedict?" I asked.

Gertie shook her head. "No, but he could be inside."

"I guess we should check, then find someplace to take up post."

"Have you noticed—no one has looked twice at us?"

I scanned the crowd again and realized she was right. A couple of people had looked up from their activities as we walked up, but no one had given us more than a glance. It was both encouraging and frightening all at the same time.

"Good call on the costumes," I said.

Gertie grinned. "I told you I had it handled."

"Let's just hope it holds."

We headed for the inside of the bar, but it only took a quick look to know that Benedict wasn't inside either. "We should get drinks," I said. "It will help us blend."

"Awesome," Gertie said. She strolled up to the bar, perched on a stool, pulled down her sunglasses, and smiled at the bartender. "Hey, cutie. How about getting a sexy woman a drink?"

I cringed a bit, waiting for the insults to fly, but apparently, nothing was new to the bartender.

"You bet, sweetheart," he said. "What's your poison? And please don't tell me anything that requires a blender. It's not that kind of bar."

"Please," Gertie said, "drinks shouldn't have an umbrella. Give me a scotch on the rocks."

The bartender smiled. "You got it. What about you, gorgeous?" He looked at me.

"Whatever light beer you've got," I said. "Gotta watch those calories."

The bartender gave me the once-over. "Whatever you're doing is working, so light it is."

He moved down the bar to retrieve the drinks and Gertie sighed.

"You got 'gorgeous.' I only got 'sweetheart.'"

"Yeah, but he's probably only forty or so. Wouldn't calling you 'gorgeous' be against one of those Southern rules about your elders?"

"You have a point. While 'gorgeous' is a bigger compliment, 'sweetheart' is probably more respectful." She sighed again. "Oh, for the days when men weren't concerned about being respectful with their compliments."

I grinned as the bartender placed our drinks in front of us. "What do I owe you?"

"First round is on the house," he said. "Enjoy the party." He moved off to the other side of the bar to serve a group of men arguing over fishing lures.

I took a sip of my beer and looked over at Gertie, who'd taken a gulp of her scotch and was making a face as though she'd drunk medicine. "Can I ask you a personal question?"

"Of course. God knows, I'm always trying to get into your personal business. It would be rather hypocritical if I didn't share mine."

"Why didn't you marry? I mean, you seem to like men and talk about the good ole days of the hunt, so what kept you from pulling the trigger?"

"That's a good question, and I have to admit, I thought about settling down a time or two, but I couldn't make that leap."

"Why not?"

She shrugged. "Lots of reasons. It was a different time then. Women were expected to fulfill a certain role in a marriage, and it wasn't one I was interested in. Don't get me wrong, I love to cook and knit for myself, but if I had to do it by demand and on schedule for someone else, then it would become work and not enjoyable."

"Surely there were men more progressive than that."

"Not in Sinful. And even if someone was willing to put in on the domestics and not heap it all on me, no man would have liked my independent streak. When Ida Belle, Marge, and I headed off to war, it scared a lot of people. Mostly men. Especially men who were praying they didn't get a draft call. And here we were, volunteering to go."

I nodded, thinking about the era and the mentality. I was certain I'd scare men today if they knew the real me. I suppose I couldn't blame men back then for being a little leery of women volunteering for Vietnam. "I guess it would be hard to wear the pants in that family, especially if they didn't serve."

"Exactly. But the biggest issue was kids. I never wanted them. I taught long enough to know it's not my calling. And not having kids wasn't really an option. Men wanted families. And other women expected you to have one if you were married."

"So it was easier to remain single and have the occasional fling."

She nodded. "I know other women look at Ida Belle and me and feel sorry for us. But that's because they don't know the real story. If people knew the lives we've led, they might change their minds."

"Why not tell them? The war was over a long time ago."

"We made promises to keep that information secret, and we take those promises seriously. It's about being a patriot. The only reason we shared our past with you is because you're a comrade. You understand the importance of secrecy more than anyone else we know."

I felt a swell of pride. These were extraordinary women who did a remarkable thing, and the fact that they considered my contribution equal was the biggest compliment I'd ever received.

"I think you and Ida Belle are incredible people," I said. "Everything you did was at a time when women weren't supposed to do anything even remotely like that. I could never feel sorry for you. You've lived more than anyone I know."

"Damn straight," Gertie said and lifted her glass of scotch to clink against my beer. "Now, let's go see if we can catch a criminal and live some more."

I hopped off the stool. "Let's go back outside. We can lurk off to the side and that way, we see everyone as they arrive. And then we'll know when the food is ready. It smells great."

"My mouth is watering for a mess of crawfish. I hope nobody gets stupid before I get at least a plate down. But don't tell Ida Belle we were eating."

"My lips are sealed."

"They probably won't be after you stick one of those crawfish in your mouth. I don't suppose you have lip balm on you?"

"No. I am armed only with a gun and a push-up bra."

"I managed to stuff Mace and my .45 in this outfit, but

there wasn't room for much else."

I looked over at her as we walked out of the bar. Where the hell did she have the .45? I was afraid to ask. "What about over there?" I pointed to a section of unoccupied weeds under one of the only scraggly shade trees surrounding the bar.

"Works for me," Gertie said. "We should have thought to bring lawn chairs."

"We can lean against the tree. I'm hoping we're not here forever. Carter's MRI appointment was this morning. I figure he'll be back sometime after noon."

"Do you have a cover story?"

I turned to face the crowd and leaned against the tree. "I texted him back that we were going out for a boat ride."

"At least that's the truth."

"Except for the part where we stop off at the Swamp Bar to look for a meth runner."

"Well, yeah, that part. Anyway, if you're not home when he gets back, he knows the reason."

"Yeah, but I have to get into the shower and get these tattoos off of me before he sees them. I don't have a legit way to link boating to tattoos."

"Crap. I forgot about that part."

I heard a boat motor behind us and turned to look out over the bayou. I've heard the expression "rolling total" for a car that needed to be sent to the junkyard, but in this case, it was a "floating total." The shrimp boat had definitely seen better days. Red paint was peeling from every square inch of wood, making it look like the boat had a killer case of the measles. The bench across the back was missing more vinyl than it had covering it, and foam was blowing out of it as the boat pulled up to the bank.

The driver climbed out and I felt my back tense. "That's Benedict."

Midthirties. Six feet two. A hundred ninety finely tuned pounds. Heavy drinker, but that might make him more dangerous, not less. Threat level medium without a weapon. High if he was packing a firearm, and I would bet anything he was.

Gertie casually turned enough to see him out of the corner of her eye. "Yep. Looks rougher and older than I remember, but that nasty scowl is still the same."

"Maybe he'll go talk to someone and things will get interesting." I pulled out my cell phone, preparing to snap some shots of anyone Benedict spent time chatting with. He headed straight toward the bar.

"I'll follow him," Gertie said.

"You sure?"

"Yeah. Stay here and hold our spots. I need to get a soda anyway. This cheap scotch tastes like Windex."

"You drink Windex often?"

"I did once, accidentally. It's not something I care to repeat."

She headed after Benedict and I studied the rest of the crowd gathering near the folding tables and steaming pots of heavenly smells. Some of the people looked familiar, but only in a vague way. When it was relevant, I never forgot a face, but these faces were those that had passed in front of me at the Swamp Bar on previous visits or maybe drove by my backyard in a bass boat…some sort of casual sighting. So they registered as people I'd seen in Sinful, but not as anything else.

About ten minutes later, I started to worry that Gertie had gotten into trouble. I was just about to make my way to the bar when Benedict stepped outside and headed for the pots of food. Gertie trailed behind him a couple seconds later.

"What took so long?" I asked as she handed me a plastic cup of soda.

"Benedict went straight for the men's room. I guess he can hang it over for the one thing, but the boat isn't the best place for the other."

I cringed. "That was way more information than I needed."

"It was way more information than any of us needed, but you asked and that's the explanation I have."

"Did he talk to anyone inside?"

"The bartender asked about work. Said he'd been working with some people out of New Orleans on a deal but if it didn't take off soon, he'd be heading back offshore."

"Interesting."

Gertie nodded. "And he asked about the best place to buy lumber. Claimed he was going to do some work on his boat, but you saw the thing. He hasn't put five cents into that floating shipwreck since he's owned it."

"You think he's shopping for lumber for a new lab. If he's in on it, that would make sense."

We sipped on our sodas and watched as Benedict lifted one of the pots of steaming food and dumped it on the table. People flocked over to the table and started piling red things onto plastic plates.

"Don't just stand there," Gertie said. "Get a move on."

We headed over for the tables as two more men dumped steaming containers of crawfish, corn on the cob, and potatoes onto the tables.

"Make sure you try the potatoes," Gertie said. "They are awesome."

I grabbed a plate and piled it up with potatoes and crawfish and corn on the cob, and followed Gertie to one of the folding tables set up for people to eat around. We took a position at the far end where we had a clear view of everyone loading up on lunch. I picked up the crawfish and pulled off the head, then started peeling the shell away from the meat. It took some wrangling but I finally coaxed the red-tinted meat out of the shell and popped it in my mouth.

"Jeez Louise, that's hot," I said, and reached for my soda. "But it's good," I managed once I'd put out the fire in my mouth.

"Told you."

"Looks like our friend isn't exactly Mr. Social," I said as Benedict fixed himself a plate, then moved off from the crowd and sat on a stump about fifteen feet away.

I nodded my head toward the parking area. "More people on their way."

"Good. I can't eat much more of this or I'll be on fire the rest of the day."

I watched as a group of people made their way in a cluster toward the tables, then they started to branch out and I got a look at the last two.

"Holy crap!" I grabbed Gertie's arm and she yelped. "It's Nelson and the hooker."

Chapter Fourteen

Gertie whipped around and then promptly dropped her plate on the table. "What the hell is he doing here?"

"Based on your description, wouldn't this be right up his alley?"

"Well, yes, but not if he's supposed to be upholding the law."

"No one really thinks he's upholding the law. If he recognizes us, the gig is up."

"What do we do?"

I watched as he grabbed a plate of crawfish and shoved it at the hooker. "I don't know. Just hold tight for a minute. Maybe they'll go inside."

Nelson started to walk toward the bar and I felt my anxiety tick down a notch, then he turned around and whistled. The hooker looked over at him, like a well-trained dog. "Hey, Lynne," he yelled. "You want a beer?"

She nodded and he continued to the bar. I frowned. Something wasn't right, but I couldn't put my finger on it. Something besides the obvious.

A couple minutes later, Nelson came out with two beers and handed one to the hooker. Then he grabbed his plate and looked around. He must have spotted someone he knew because he turned and headed in the opposite direction of where Gertie and I were standing. I was just about to let out a sigh of relief when he squatted down next to Benedict and took a seat.

"Lynne!" I said. "One of the known associates of Dewey was a Lynne."

"Oh," Gertie said, then her eyes widened. "Oh!"

"Let's not get ahead of ourselves. Maybe it's a coincidence."

"It's a coincidence that Nelson shows up in town as sheriff with a hooker named Lynne right when a meth lab explodes and he refuses to investigate it?"

"Okay, maybe it's not as big of a stretch as I originally thought."

"What do we do?" Gertie asked.

I pulled out my cell phone and snapped a picture of the three of them. "Watch and see if they do anything."

"Should we try to get closer?"

"I don't know if that's a good idea. I mean, the costumes are great, but Nelson has us in his sights. Do you really think he won't recognize us?"

Gertie blew out a breath. "You may be right, especially in your case. He always was a letch. He's probably already memorized every curve on you."

"Gross."

"Definitely, and because he doesn't know you, he wouldn't necessarily expect to not see you here. Does that make sense?"

I nodded.

"But he won't be expecting to see me."

"Oh no. You're not going any closer. That has disaster spelled out in neon."

"Look, they could be talking about the size of her breasts or running drugs, but either way, we need to know." Before I could say another word, she took off around the table, sauntering to the other side of the clearing.

I looked around the crowd, tapping my foot on the ground.

If I ran after her, it would attract attention. But if I let her go, chances are she was going to attract attention. It was one of those things you could just bet on.

Give her a chance. Maybe she'll find out everything you need to know.

And maybe the Swamp Bar would become a five-star restaurant by tomorrow.

She walked around the tables the long way, sidling up near Nelson and the hooker, a table with an ice cooler between them. I had to admit, it was a good spot. They couldn't see her and if she was within listening distance, she could actually get something. She looked back at me and gave me a thumbs-up. I smiled. This might work.

I munched on my crawfish and potatoes, keeping a close watch on Gertie. She held position near the cooler as Nelson chatted with Benedict. The conversation did not appear to be a pleasant one as they were both frowning. The hooker looked bored, but as I often wore the same look when men were talking, I couldn't attribute anything specific to it.

After about five minutes of conversation, Nelson rose from the ground and motioned to Lynne, who rose as well. The scowl on Benedict's face was a clear indication of how things had ended. Either that or he had heartburn.

As they turned to walk away, that's when it all fell apart.

Two women standing at a table near Gertie got into a yelling match. Apparently one thought the other was paying too much attention to her husband. The husband in question was a negative four on a scale of one to one billion, so I didn't quite understand the level of anger, but I suspected alcohol had something to do with it. And IQ.

The yelling escalated when one of the women threw her entire cup of beer in the other woman's face. The beer-drenched woman shoved the other woman so hard she flipped clean over the table and crashed into Gertie's knees. Gertie flew sideways onto the folding table and tackled the ice chest, pitching it off the table and into the lap of two men sitting behind it. The men jumped up and one of their lawn chairs flipped over backward, right in front of a man walking with a full plate of crawfish. The man tried to put on the brakes but couldn't manage it in time. He stepped right in between the legs of the chair and fell to the side, right on top of a Harley-Davidson, and they both crashed to the ground.

The two men drenched by the cooler looked back at the motorcycle, then turned around and glared at Gertie. "That's my bike!" one of the men yelled. "You're going to pay!"

Gertie whipped around and took off running for the boat. I was a good thirty feet behind but made up ground fast, passing the angry men and sprinting around Gertie. "Move it!" I yelled as I passed.

Gertie picked up speed and we rounded the corner of the Swamp Bar to the bank where the boat was parked. Ida Belle, true to her word, must have been listening for the fray and already had the boat untied and was in the driver's seat, ready to go. I slowed to let Gertie pass me and she bailed into the boat, crashing on the bottom. I shoved the boat away from the bank with my foot and jumped in after her.

I paused long enough to help her to an upright position in the bottom of the boat and jumped into my seat. Ida Belle didn't hesitate a second before slamming her foot down on the accelerator. The boat took off from the dock like a bullet shot from a gun. The bandanna flew off my head as I turned to see the angry men jumping into a ski boat.

"How fast can they go?" I asked.

"Not as fast as us," Ida Belle said, but a tiny crease of worry inched across her brow.

I had no doubt the airboat was faster in a drag race, but the problem with bayous is they weren't very straight or wide. I turned around to watch as the men launched their boat from the bank and took off. The boat leaped on top of the water and pursued at an alarming rate. Gertie leaned over the side of the boat and looked behind us.

"They're gaining on us!" she yelled. She moved back to the center of the boat and lost her grip on her bandanna that she'd been clutching in her hand. It shot between Gertie and me and into the giant fan, then came out of the back of it a second later in pieces.

"Hold on," Ida Belle said and made a sharp left into a narrow channel. I clung to the bars, barely managing to keep my seat. Gertie didn't even try to stay upright. She simply flopped over in the bottom of the boat and waited until we had straightened out again before inching back up to a sitting position.

I looked back, thinking surely we'd lost them with that move, but the ski boat was speeding along behind us. Ida Belle glanced back and frowned.

"I can't lose them," she said. "We're almost back to town. I can't just dock behind your house with them on us."

"I have an idea," Gertie yelled. She flipped open the top to the bench and disappeared behind it. A couple seconds later, the top dropped back down and Gertie emerged.

Holding a fire extinguisher.

Ida Belle's eyes widened. "No!" she yelled and threw her hand over her eyes.

But it was too late.

Gertie let loose a stream of spray right onto us. I felt the white foam hit me and threw my hands up to keep it from pelting my face. My sunglasses were completely covered and I couldn't see a thing. But I could hear yelling behind me. I whipped around in my seat and ripped off the sunglasses in time to see a blizzard of foam hit the guys behind us.

Ida Belle made a hard right and we shot into the bayou behind my house. The man in the passenger side of the ski boat had managed to duck behind the console and avoid the worst of the spray, but the driver looked like the abominable snowman. He wiped his hand across his eyes and slung a handful of the foam over the side of the boat, then opened his eyes.

But it was too late.

He'd missed the hard right and was now barreling straight for the bank. I heard both men scream like girls as the ski boat hit the bank and ran straight into someone's backyard clothesline. White sheets from the clothesline hit both of the men and wrapped around them. It looked like something from a Scooby-Doo cartoon—ghosts driving a boat on land.

Ida Belle let out a hoot but never slowed. Minutes later, she drove the airboat halfway up the bank in my backyard and we bailed out. The back door to my house flew open and Ally ran outside, her eyes wide.

"Oh my God!" Ally cried. "What happened to you?"

"It's a long story," I said.

"Well, there's no time for it," Ally said. "Apparently Carter has been trying to reach you and couldn't. I just got off the phone with him. He's on his way over here."

"Now?"

"He'll be here any minute. And I have a feeling that whatever this is, he won't be happy about it."

Panic set in. No way did we have time to change clothes and shower.

"Sit down," Ida Belle said.

"What?" This was no time for sitting. This was time for

running all the way back to DC.

"I have a plan," Ida Belle said and pointed to the lawn chairs. "You and Gertie sit down."

She jumped into the airboat and grabbed the fire extinguisher, then jumped back onto the bank and shoved it in Ally's hands before taking a seat next to us. "Spray us with it," she said.

Ally's mouth dropped open. "What?"

"Hell no!" I said. It was already going to take an entire tube of toothpaste and maybe even an electric sander to get the taste out of my mouth.

"Spray us," Ida Belle said. "Trust me."

Ally's expression said we'd clearly lost our minds, but she directed the hose at us and sprayed. I squeezed my eyes and mouth shut and forced myself to stay seated as the foam pelted my face and upper body.

"What the hell is going on here?" Carter's voice sounded behind us.

I prayed that whatever Ida Belle had in mind made any kind of sense, but I didn't hold out much hope. I wiped the foam from my eyes and squinted as Carter stepped in front of us. The look on his face was a mixture of disbelief and fear. He looked over at Ally.

"What are you doing?" he asked.

Ally froze for a moment, then shook her head. "Don't look at me. I'm just following orders."

Ida Belle wiped the foam from her mouth. "Skin treatment," she said.

"What?" Carter sounded as incredulous as I felt.

"I read it on the Internet," Ida Belle said. "It's supposed to make your skin look ten years younger."

"Fire extinguisher foam?" Carter asked. "You've got to be

kidding me."

"Makes sense, really," Gertie said, spraying foam as she spoke. "It's moist enough to put out fire."

"You're fully dressed," he said.

"Would you prefer we sit out here naked?" I asked.

"I…uh…of course not."

I struggled not to smile. He probably wouldn't mind if one of us sat out here naked, except for the legality of it. "Besides, we're just treating our faces," I said.

"You've got it all over you," he argued.

"Have you ever tried to apply fire foam in a small area?" Ally asked, getting into the act. "We started in the kitchen and it took us an hour to clean up the mess."

I nodded. "Not to mention we scared the cat half to death. He's probably packing a bag as we speak."

Carter stared a couple seconds more. "I…well. I need a beer." He headed back toward the house. We all turned around to look as he walked and waited until the kitchen door was closed before we started laughing.

"Oh my God," Ally said. "That's the funniest thing I've ever heard."

"The funniest part," Gertie said, "is that he bought it."

"I'm not convinced that he did," I said, "but he can't come up with any logical reason to explain what we would have been up to that resulted in this."

Ida Belle nodded. "And with luck, he never will."

"I don't think anyone's imagination stretches as far as Gertie's reality," I said. "And it's not likely those two goons are going to report what happened."

"Even if they do," Ida Belle said, "what proof do they have?"

"There's not many airboats in Sinful," Gertie said. "But on

the other hand, it's their word against ours."

"Okay," Ally said, "someone please tell me what happened, because I can't stretch my imagination to come up with any explanation for this."

"Grab the water hose and spray us off," Gertie said. "We'll tell you while we're drip-drying."

"Tell her while she's spraying," Ida Belle said. "A quick trip up the bayou in the airboat and we'll be dry."

I flicked some foam off my arm and felt my stomach clench. "I can't do either."

"Why the heck not?" Ida Belle asked.

"The tattoos. I've got to get in the shower and get these tattoos off of me. The foam was covering them when Carter was out here, but I can't rinse off and stroll inside wearing sleeves. Carter will freak. And a boat ride is no explanation for these."

"You've got tattoos?" Ally asked and leaned forward to inspect my arms. "I thought that was a long-sleeved shirt with designs. Now I really want to know what you guys were up to."

"We can fix this," Gertie said. "Just hurry inside and upstairs for a shower."

A huge glob of foam ran off my arm and plopped onto the grass. "Too late for that," I said. "Carter's probably sitting in the living room watching TV. I can't get by him without him seeing."

"What do you need to take it off?" Ally asked.

"Soap," Gertie said.

"Okay," Ally said. "I'll go get some soap and a sponge from the kitchen and we'll scrub them off out here."

"And if Carter comes back outside before we're done?" I asked.

"Then we're out of luck," Ida Belle said.

"I think our luck ran out about twenty minutes ago," I said.

"I'll be right back," Ally said, and hurried off.

Ida Belle put her hands on her hips and looked at Gertie and me. "I'll wait for Ally to hear what prompted our great escape, but what I want to know now is if you found out anything."

"Oh, yeah," I said and filled her in on Benedict asking the bartender about lumber, and Nelson and his hooker friend Lynne.

"You think it could be the same Lynne?" Ida Belle asked.

"If she's not, it's a hell of a coincidence," I said.

"True. So Nelson and his hooker could be our New Orleans connection," Ida Belle said.

"Once we saw them talking to Benedict," I said, "Gertie sneaked over to try to overhear their conversation."

"And?" Ida Belle asked.

"I don't know," I said. "Things got hairy and we bailed before she could tell me anything."

Ida Belle looked at Gertie. "Spill, woman. And this better be good because I'm assuming this listening adventure you were on is also what caused our need to flee."

"How come everyone always assumes it's something I did?" Gertie asked.

"Was it?" Ida Belle asked.

"Yes," Gertie said, "but that's not the point."

"Who cares?" I said, trying to stop the argument before it got off the ground. "Just get to the good stuff."

"Okay. Benedict was bitching about a delay in getting business off the ground, and Nelson said that some things couldn't be helped but now that he was here, he would take care of potential problems."

"The delay being due to the explosion," I said.

"That's what it sounds like," Ida Belle said. "What else?"

"Nelson said he had some things he had to take care of for

Celia," Gertie said, "and that if he managed to get them done, he'd have carte blanche over Sinful and with her blessing."

"Do you think he's talking about us?" I asked.

"Maybe," Ida Belle said, "but there's also Carter and Deputy Breaux to consider. As long as they're in place, Nelson is under watch."

"True," I said. "Did you hear anything else?"

Gertie nodded. "Benedict said he needed cash to buy supplies, and Nelson told him to 'come by tonight at nine' and he'd give him the funds and they could discuss the plan."

"Come by where?" I asked. "Surely Nelson isn't staying with Celia."

"I can't imagine she'd allow that," Ida Belle said. "Celia is more than willing to use Nelson for her own gain, but I don't think she harbors any illusions as to what kind of person he is."

"She's just mistakenly assumed she can control him," Gertie said. "She doesn't know how deep he's gotten into the criminal end of things."

"Does he have friends in Sinful?" I asked.

"I doubt he has friends anywhere," Ida Belle said. "Even if he did, he wouldn't conduct criminal business in someone else's house. Even Nelson isn't that stupid. My guess is he's staying at the no-tell motel."

"Is that really a thing?" I asked.

"Technically, it's the Bayou Inn," Gertie said, "but decent people avoid it like the plague. It's located off the highway about twenty minutes from Sinful, but most people choose to drive into New Orleans to stay. The sheriff's department gets called out there a couple times a month, and that's probably only when the motel employees get desperate. God only knows what's going on there every day."

"Sounds like Nelson's kind of place," I said.

"So what do we do?" Gertie asked. "We have some damaging leads but no evidence. For all we know, Nelson and Benedict could be starting an online porn business starring Lynne the Happy Hooker Dispatcher."

"She's right," I said, "and despite the fact that giving Nelson's name to Little Hebert would kill two birds with one stone, we have to make sure he's both birds. If you know what I mean."

Ida Belle nodded. "Unfortunately, I do. If only they'd said something at the crawfish boil that indicated the money was to build a new lab."

"I'd be willing to bet it is," Gertie said.

"But are you willing to bet lives?" Ida Belle asked. "This is not going to turn out well for anyone whose name makes it to Little Hebert."

"If we can get enough evidence," I said, "we can turn it all over to the state police. If the key players are in prison, I don't think the Heberts will take any action."

"That's true," Ida Belle said. "No use sticking your neck out if the problem has been eliminated. But the state police are going to require even more evidence than the Heberts."

"To get a conviction, sure," I said, "but if we give them enough to launch an investigation, they should be able to put the pieces together. Nelson can't be a criminal genius. I'm sure he's left a trail of evidence."

Gertie nodded. "And at least one of them will roll on the others once they're arrested."

"Then it sounds like a plan," Ida Belle said.

Ally hurried over to us, dish soap in one hand and a sponge in the other. "Sorry it took so long. Francine called while I was inside and I made the mistake of answering. She is in the worst snit I've ever seen. Not that I blame her."

"She's pretty upset over the church release time thing, isn't she?" Gertie asked.

"Yeah, but that's not the worst of it," Ally said as she wet my arms and started soaping them up. "Today, Celia showed up at the café after I got off and told Francine that if she stopped serving banana pudding, the city would revoke her business license."

"What?"

"Are you kidding me?"

"She's lost her mind!"

We all started yelling at once.

"I don't understand Celia at all," Ally said. "She's going about everything wrong. Francine's is the only good place to eat in town, and anyone who tried to open if Francine is forced out would never do a dime of business with the residents."

"She thought if she was mayor," Gertie said, "that she could control everything. And she's finding out that people have their own minds."

"If she's not removed from office soon," Ida Belle said, "this could get really bad. They may start with rocks through her windows, but that's not where things will end if she keeps running roughshod over this town."

"We might have a more immediate problem," I said.

"What?" Ida Belle asked.

"These aren't coming off." I pointed to my now-squeaky-clean arms, complete with dark tattoos.

Chapter Fifteen

"What?" Gertie leaned over and rubbed her thumb on my arm. "That's not possible. Look, mine are already starting to bleed from the fire foam."

"We're all looking at it," I said, "so clearly it's possible."

"Maybe different skin types have a different reaction to the dye," Ally said.

"You're sure the tattoos came from the same place?" Ida Belle said.

Gertie's eye widened. "Uh-oh."

"What?" I yelled. "No. 'Uh-oh' is not an acceptable response."

"I ordered them months ago," Gertie said. "I forgot that the one company only had this set that I liked."

"So the tattoos I'm wearing are from a different company?" I threw my hands up in the air. "Great. At the rate my luck is going, I'll be wearing these things all summer."

"I don't think it will be that long," Gertie said, "but maybe a few days, if you shower a lot."

"How am I supposed to explain this to Carter?" I asked. "It's not like I can wear long-sleeved shirts until they fade."

The three of them looked at one another, then at the ground.

"You're all a big help," I complained.

"My hip is hurting," Gertie said. "I think I'm going to finish the rest of the cleanup at home."

Ida Belle nodded. "I rode over here with her. We'll check in later about the other thing."

The two of them hightailed it around the house and I looked at Ally. "Are you abandoning me, too?"

She bit her lower lip. "I won't, but I'm not sure what I can do to help. I don't think my being there is enough to keep him from losing it."

I sighed. "I know. Please tell me there's something delicious and sweet in the kitchen that I can use to soften the blow."

"We baked lemon pies this morning at the café. I brought one home for you."

"Okay, that helps. Go on. Take a walk. Rob a bank. Anything is probably more pleasant than what I'm about to do."

"Sorry," she said. "Send me a text when it's safe. I'm going to take a walk over to my house and see how the construction is coming."

She hurried off without so much as a backward glance. Probably trying to get out of sight before I changed my mind. I turned off the water hose and headed inside to face the music. I didn't have a single idea of how to explain the tattoos, so I'd have to wing it. I stopped in the kitchen long enough to grab another beer from the refrigerator, then headed into the living room.

I handed Carter the beer, and he glanced over long enough to take it. "Thanks."

"I thought you might be due for another. I'm going to head upstairs for a quick shower."

He looked up at me and his eyes widened. "What the hell? Your arms? Is that…you didn't get—"

"They're only temporary," I said. "Unfortunately, they're not quite as temporary as Gertie thought."

"You trusted Gertie to decorate your body?" He stared at me as if I'd lost my mind. Then I saw his lower lip quivering.

I punched him in the arm. "You think this is funny."

"Well, yeah. Gertie is a total disaster. Why in the world would you trust her to put ink on you without reading the instructions?"

"I guess for the same reason I let Ida Belle talk me into being sprayed down with a fire extinguisher?"

"Yeah, I totally don't get the skin care thing, but if Ida Belle thinks it's a thing, I can kinda understand that move. But what in the world possessed you to try tattoos?"

"I don't know. Gertie got the idea that tattoos would make us look tough."

His eyes widened. "Gertie did the tattoos as well?"

"Yeah, but hers are the kind that washed off, so they're already in the Sinful sewage system. Apparently, she wasn't as diligent with the product description reading on mine."

"And you need to look tough, why exactly?"

"We don't, I guess, but it sounded cool at the time."

He studied my arms for a minute. "It's kinda cool, I guess. Except for the part where you look like a regular at the Swamp Bar."

I felt my back tense. "I didn't think about that. I guess people might look at me a little weird for the next week or so."

Carter shook his head. "I'm not sure which is worse—the things you get into when you're sticking your nose into police business or the things you get into when you're not."

I just nodded. That conversation was fraught with issues. Besides, I was so relieved that he was amused rather than suspicious that I didn't even care if he thought I was a fool. I headed upstairs, shaking my head. Where the hell had I gone so wrong that being thought a fool had become the good option?

I had a feeling the answer started with coming to Sinful.

Despite a thirty-minute shower in scalding hot water and three rounds of soap, two of shampoo, the tattoos didn't fade even a little. I spent an afternoon watching television with Carter and slowly losing my mind. How did people just sit in front of a television when there were so many things to be done?

I kept having to remind myself that Carter was under doctor's orders to sit in front of the television and specifically restricted from doing things. Not to mention I'd chewed him out for not doing so the night before. Several times I looked over at him, expecting to see some look of frustration or boredom, but he seemed perfectly content to take up space in my recliner and watch reruns of *Gunsmoke.*

And who was I to judge? If my entire life was being sidelined by idiots, I might retreat to a recliner with a beer as well. It was a better option than beating your head against a brick wall, and right now, that was an accurate description of Celia.

Halfway through the ten millionth shootout, I got a text from Ida Belle saying she'd confirmed Nelson was staying at the motel. They wanted to regroup tonight to plan our next move, assuming I could find a good reason for ditching Carter on a Saturday night. As it turned out, luck was on my side once more, and Carter had his monthly poker game that night. And an old high school friend of Ally's was having a baby shower, so I was free and clear to do any and all of the things I was not supposed to do.

Ida Belle and Gertie showed up around seven and we headed right for plotting headquarters, also known as the kitchen.

"What did Carter say about the tattoos?" Gertie asked.

"He thought it was funny," I said.

They looked at each other, clearly confused.

"Why would he think tattoos are funny?" Ida Belle asked.

"Not the tattoos themselves," I explained, "but the fact that I trusted Gertie and now they won't wash off."

"Why is everyone always picking on me?" Gertie asked.

"I don't know," Ida Belle said. "It can't possibly be because of the things you do."

"Why did you tell him I put them on you?" Gertie asked.

"Because I couldn't have done it myself and you're the only person who would talk me into something that stupid."

"There is that," Gertie agreed.

"Anyway," I said, "the good thing is the tattoos didn't cause him to question anything but my judgment, so we got away with this one."

"We're lucky he's on medical leave," Ida Belle said. "If he'd gotten the call on the runaway boat, he would have known it was us."

"He's bound to hear about it sooner or later," I said. "I don't think I've heard the end of this one."

"At least we're clear for tonight," Gertie said. "If he'd clued in that we were after the meth producer, he would have canceled poker and sat watch. What did you tell Ally?"

"Nothing," I said. "By the time she got back here, she had to get ready for the shower. I told her I'd fill her in later."

"Good," Ida Belle said. "The fewer people who know about this, the better. I know we can't keep her out of it forever, but maybe by tomorrow, it won't be an issue."

I looked at Ida Belle. "You have a plan?"

She nodded. "The motel rooms all face the parking lot and the only rear window is one of those little ones over the bathtub. Given the regular criminal activity happening there, the parking lot has security cameras that show everyone entering and exiting the rooms."

"Do I even want to know how you know that?" I asked.

"One of the ladies from choir had her attorney subpoena the footage to bust her husband cheating."

"Nice."

"So given the security cameras," Ida Belle said, "I didn't think we could risk breaking into his room to bug it."

"Ha," I said. "If we got caught breaking into the new sheriff's motel room, Nelson would put us under the jail. And we wouldn't have a leg to stand on."

Ida Belle nodded. "But there's nothing to stop us from renting the room next door."

"You think the walls are that thin?" I asked.

"I'm sure the construction is shoddy," Ida Belle said, "and we might be able to hear through the wall, but I'm positive we'll be able to hear through the ceiling."

"Oh!" I clued into what Ida Belle had in mind. "It's those ceiling tiles like in the sheriff's department. So we could slide one to the side on our end, inch one over on theirs, and have a bird's-eye view of the room and the conversation."

"That's what I'm hoping," Ida Belle said.

"Wait. You don't know for sure it's the ceiling tiles?"

"Of course not," Ida Belle said. "Why in the world would I have been in one of those rooms? But given the year of construction, it's likely."

"What's the worst thing that can happen?" Gertie asked. "We get nothing?"

"I guess so," I said. "But we have to be extra careful that Nelson doesn't see us."

"Goes without saying," Ida Belle said.

"So what's the plan?" I asked.

"We head out now for the hotel," Ida Belle said. "We'll take Gertie's car. It's so beat-up it won't stand out in the parking lot."

Gertie frowned but didn't argue.

"You and I will go into the room and handle the recording part." Ida Belle reached for the backpack she'd brought inside and pulled out a tiny camera that looked like nothing more than a small plastic tube. "This will record to a cell phone. All we need to do is put it in place and wait for Benedict to show up."

"What am I supposed to do while you're having all the fun with high-tech gadgets?" Gertie asked.

"You're going to stay in the parking lot and make sure no one gets the jump on us. We need to be certain the coast is clear before we leave the room."

"I guess it's only fair since you had getaway boat duty on the last mission," Gertie said.

"So that's it," Ida Belle said. "We get the footage, get out, and send the whole lot to the state police. I've already gotten information on the lead detective on the drug task force."

"I hope they jump on it quickly," I said. "We can't hold off the Heberts forever."

"I think they will," Ida Belle said. "I know they can't use the video in court, but I would bet everything I have that Nelson's been sloppy."

"I think we both agree on that one," I said. "Well, if that's it, then let's get this show on the road."

Gertie stuck her fist out. "Don't leave me hanging."

The three of us bumped our fists together.

Swamp Team 3 rides again.

Chapter Sixteen

It was still daylight when we arrived at the motel. Ida Belle hadn't been exaggerating about the place. It looked as if it had been condemned decades ago, and that was the nice description. The parking lot had a couple of cars in it, each one in worse condition than the other, and none of them Nelson's Mercedes.

Ida Belle hurried into the office with cash and came back out with the room key a couple minutes later.

"I guess it doesn't take long when there's no paperwork," I said as she hopped back into the passenger seat.

"You can't be called to testify on what you don't know," Gertie said.

"Nelson's room is 106." Ida Belle pointed. "The one next to the breezeway. Ours is on the other side."

"Cool. Gertie, drop us off in front of our room and park at the other end of the parking lot away from the light pole. Make sure you give yourself a clear view of the rooms."

Ida Belle nodded. "And remember to stay crouched down until dark. If someone sees you sitting there, it will raise alarms."

Gertie waved a hand at us. "I know. I'm not an idiot."

I grabbed the backpack, jumped out of the car after Ida Belle, and hurried to the room. I stepped inside, closed and locked the door behind us, then turned around and froze. "Good God!"

The room was something straight out of a horror movie.

The bedspread was gold and red and had been washed so many times that it no longer completely covered the mattress. The mattress sagged so much in the middle that I could see it touching the green shag carpeted floor. The walls were covered with gold wallpaper that had some sort of felt-looking texture to it. Everything in the bathroom dripped and the fixtures were so rusty, I would be surprised if the faucets turned at all.

"Not exactly the Ritz," Ida Belle said.

I shook my head. "I'm afraid to touch anything. I had better quarters the last time I was in Iraq."

"There's some nice hotels in Iraq."

"Yeah, but I was sleeping in a dugout."

Ida Belle glanced around. "You've had a tetanus shot, right?"

"Requirement of the job. You?"

"Requirement of being friends with Gertie."

The desk appeared to be the least sketchy spot in the room, so I put the backpack down there and pulled out the camera.

"Can you reach?" Ida Belle asked.

"Oh yeah." I climbed up onto the dresser and pushed one of the ceiling tiles to the side, praying that the wall between the rooms didn't go all the way up to the ceiling. I smiled when I saw the long line of ceiling tiles. "It goes straight through."

"Thank goodness."

I reached over the wall and pushed a ceiling tile in Nelson's room over a half inch in one corner and slipped the tube into the hole. "Hand me the duct tape."

Ida Belle pulled the duct tape from the backpack and tossed it up to me. I secured the tube with a little piece and jumped off the dresser. "I should be able to dislodge the camera with a good tug. Just in case we need to leave in a hurry."

"For once, I'd like a leisurely stroll away from one of these situations."

"Me too, but I'm not counting on it."

I plugged the other end of the camera into my cell phone and brought up the app. A view of Nelson's room flashed on the screen. "We have picture. Now let's see if we have sound. Hold this."

Ida Belle took my phone and I climbed back up onto the dresser. "Watch the indicator on the bottom of the screen and see if it spikes up." I tapped my finger on the ceiling tile near the camera.

"We're good," Ida Belle said.

I hopped off the dresser again and pulled out the desk chair. "Then I guess there's nothing left but the waiting."

Ida Belle dragged a chair from the corner over near me and sat. "It's eight thirty now."

"Thirty minutes to wait, and that's if Benedict is on time." I tapped my fingers on the chair. That thirty minutes was going to feel like forever. I wished I had brought a book. Even if the ancient television worked, we couldn't afford to have the noise.

"Hand me the backpack," Ida Belle said.

I passed the pack over to her and she pulled out two sodas, individual bags of chips, and a deck of cards.

"Will you marry me?" I asked.

Ida Belle laughed. "I thought you'd already proposed to Ally."

"Maybe I'll become Mormon and have several wives."

"It's probably easier and a lot cheaper to have good friends."

I lifted my soda can in the air. "I'll drink to that."

We finished off the chips quickly, and I owed Ida Belle forty-two dollars when I finally got a text from Gertie.

Nelson just pulled into parking lot.

"Nelson's here," I whispered.

"Fifteen 'til," Ida Belle said. "I hope he and the hooker don't decide to get happy before Benedict gets here."

"Yuck. Thanks for putting that image in my head."

"That's what friends are for."

I lifted my phone and sent a text back to Gertie.

With hooker or alone?

Alone.

"We're in luck. The hooker must be working or something."

I switched my phone over to the video app and watched as Nelson entered the frame. Ida Belle moved her chair over closer and we watched as he flipped on the television and flopped on the bed. I cringed and closed my eyes. "Please tell me he's not renting porn."

"No, looks like car racing."

"Thank God." I opened my eyes and plugged in a set of earbuds to the phone. I handed one to Ida Belle and popped one in my ear. The sound of car racing instantly filled my head. I looked over at Ida Belle, who gave me a thumbs-up. I checked the flashing red recording button and then the time. Ten more minutes. I pressed the button to pause the recording.

"I'm preserving memory," I said. "I'll start it up when Benedict arrives."

"Good thinking."

We sat for another ten minutes, me drumming my fingers on the desk and Ida Belle tapping her foot on the green carpet. I was so on edge that when my phone vibrated, I almost dropped it. I checked the screen.

Benedict just arrived.

"Showtime," I said and started recording.

We stuck the earbuds back in our ears and I lifted the

phone up so that both of us could see the video feed. Nelson got up from the bed and walked toward the door. A couple seconds later, he walked back into view, followed by Benedict. Nelson sat in the chair in the corner and Benedict sat in the desk chair.

"I priced out the lumber this afternoon," Benedict said. "Everything I need to rebuild will run about two grand."

"Not a problem," Nelson said. He opened the desk drawer and pulled out an envelope, then counted out a stack of cash and handed it to Benedict.

"What's the deal with the cooker?" Benedict asked.

"I've got someone lined up," Nelson said. "He should be available next week."

"I hope he's better than Dewey," Benedict said.

"Dewey was a good cook. He just got impatient. I should have monitored him more closely."

"You sure there's no one looking into the explosion?"

"I'm the sheriff. Deputy Breaux is a fool, and Carter is out on medical leave. Who else is there?"

"I guess, but I don't like surprises. I agreed to build and run security for you because I'll make enough money to get to Mexico and live like a king, but I'm not interested in making a stop-off in prison."

"Stop worrying. I'm telling you, no one's investigating. Everyone thinks it was a still, and since it's an unwritten rule that no one in Sinful talks about their stills, I haven't heard so much as a peep about it."

"What about Lynne? She seems a little on edge."

"Lynne's not a problem."

"I'm more worried about her husband."

What the hell? I looked over at Ida Belle, who shrugged. What kind of hooker had a husband?

"He's in too deep to back out now. If it looks like he's

becoming a problem, I'll take care of him."

"If the cooker starts next week, what are you going to do about transport?" Benedict asked.

"The trailer has been ordered but it will take a while," Nelson said. "I'll improvise for now. If I have to, I'll drive the meth to New Orleans myself." He smiled. "Maybe I'll take it in the sheriff's department's SUV. Wouldn't that be a ripper?"

Benedict laughed. "I guess you could always claim you confiscated it if you get stopped, right?"

Nelson started to say something, then paused and pulled out his cell phone. He frowned and motioned to Benedict. "We got a problem."

They both jumped up and headed off camera. I heard the door to the room open, then slam shut. I switched my phone over to text and sent Gertie a message.

What's going on?

Nelson is outside talking to Benedict. Lots of arm flapping.

"Wrap this up," I said. "Something's wrong. I can feel it."

I tugged the wire and the camera popped out of the ceiling. Ida Belle shoved the equipment in the backpack and I checked the magazine on my nine-millimeter. My cell phone buzzed again.

He's pointing at your door. Get out!

How were we supposed to get out? There was only one door and a tiny window over the bathtub. "They're coming," I said. "Go out the back window."

"What about you?" Ida Belle asked.

"I'll be right behind you as soon as you're clear."

Ida Belle hurried to the bathroom and opened the window. I stood in the bathroom doorway, my nine pointed at the room door. Ida Belle tossed the backpack out the window, climbed on the edge of the tub and pulled herself headfirst through the window. I heard a *thud* and thought she'd hit the ground, but when I glanced back, I saw her feet disappearing over the ledge. Then I realized the thud was Nelson and Benedict trying to break down the door.

I whirled around and leaped onto the edge of the bathtub, then pulled myself through the window. As my body weight tipped over the ledge, I dropped my pistol to the side and put my arms out to slow my fall, then tucked and rolled. Broken glass pierced my hands and body as I rolled and weeds slapped against my face. I popped up and reached back for my weapon but before I could bend down, I heard a woman's voice.

"Try it and the old lady gets it."

I knew that voice!

Chapter Seventeen

I looked up and saw Kayla standing in front of me, holding a .45 against Ida Belle's head.

Blood rushed to my head as it hit me at once—the huge miscalculation we'd made. The big weight loss, all the dental work…Kayla was a meth addict. And I'd bet anything that the trailer on order that Nelson had just mentioned was the food trailer to replace the one that had burned. It was the perfect cover for transporting drugs. They traveled to different cities every week and with the huge refrigerators could carry a ton of meth without sacrificing the quality of the drugs.

"It doesn't have to be this way," I said.

Kayla sneered. "What way is that? The one where I have the upper hand?"

"You don't have to hurt either of us."

"That's where you're wrong. Nelson blackmailed me into doing this gig, but I'll be damned if I'm going to prison for it. If you would have minded your own business, killing you wouldn't be necessary."

"You're Lynne Fontenot," Ida Belle said.

"Yep. Known associate of Dewey Parnell," Kayla said. "I went by my middle name then."

"And you married the Fontenot twin," Ida Belle said.

"He didn't like the extracurricular activities I picked up freshman year, so we had to part ways."

"Why Nelson?" Ida Belle asked. "You know better."

"Yeah, well, Nelson works for some suppliers in New Orleans and he had the goods on me. I'm at my limit for arrests, and not interested in going to prison. With the payout from a job, Colby and I could have skipped town and started over."

I appreciated that Ida Belle was keeping Kayla talking. Buying time was never a bad thing when you had a gun pressed to your head, but my options for a rescue were essentially none. Even if I dived for my gun and got off a perfect shot, it would take me at least two seconds to execute the move. Kayla could squeeze the trigger in less than a second, and even though I would get her in the end, it would be too late for Ida Belle.

"Kayla!" Nelson's voice sounded to the side of me as he came through the breezeway and into the weeded plot of grass that separated the motel from the swamp.

"You were right," Kayla said. "They've been watching you."

Nelson walked closer, smiling. "Those tattoos. I recognize them from the Swamp Bar. I had a feeling about you two."

"This is bullshit." Benedict walked out of the breezeway and stared. "I didn't sign up for this."

"Actually," Nelson said, "this is exactly what you signed up for. You're security, remember?"

"I ain't killing no old lady," Benedict said.

"Then I'll do it myself," Nelson said. "Where's the other one? They travel in threes."

"She was sitting in the beat-up Caddy at the far end of the parking lot," Kayla said. "I clocked her good. She'll be out for a while."

Nelson grinned. "Like forever."

"I say we do this here and dump the bodies in the swamp," Kayla said. "There's cameras up front."

"Sounds good." Nelson pulled a pistol out of his waistband

and started to lift it at me.

The shot came out of nowhere and I crumpled to the ground, certain that Kayla had shot Ida Belle, but when I forced myself to look, I saw Kayla staring at us, mouth and eyes wide open and a single exit wound in the middle of her forehead. She pitched forward on the ground and I sprang for my nine, yelling at Ida Belle to run.

Nelson fired a round at me and as I rolled, I could hear the bullet whizzing by me. I jumped up and fired back, then dashed into the swamp after Ida Belle.

"We have to circle around for Gertie," I said, and pointed to the right.

We changed direction and ran through the brush. I could hear Nelson and Benedict thrashing behind us and hoped they didn't start firing. Even an idiot could get off a lucky shot. I could see the parking lot lights through the top of the trees and veered right again when I saw the last light pole.

"Who shot Kayla?" Ida Belle managed to huff out as we ran.

"I don't know, and we're not waiting around to see."

I burst out of the swamp and hit the edge of the parking lot, but Gertie's car wasn't parked where it was supposed to be. I looked over at Ida Belle, panic setting in. A second later the ancient Cadillac screamed around the corner of the motel and squealed to a stop beside us. The passenger door flew open and Mannie yelled, "Get in!"

I'd never been more confused in my life, but I dived into the front seat, Ida Belle right behind me. She didn't even get the door shut before Mannie floored it and shot across the parking lot and out the entrance. I turned around and saw Gertie slumped over in the backseat.

"Gertie!" I yelled.

"She's just unconscious," Mannie said.

I looked up as Nelson and Benedict burst out of the swamp. They both started firing but neither was a good enough shot to make it count. Mannie swung the car around the corner and we disappeared from line of sight.

"They'll come after us," I said.

"No they won't," Mannie replied. He made a hard left and launched the car into the swamp, then killed the engine.

"What the heck are you doing?" I asked.

Mannie pointed to the road, and that's when I realized sirens echoed across the swamp. Seconds later, two cars with red flashing lights on the dashboard and the words "Louisiana State Police" on the door sped by.

"Only one way in," Mannie said and winked. He started the car and backed out of the weeds, then floored it, not slowing at all when he took the turn for the highway. As soon as we hit the paved road, he pressed the accelerator even harder and we sped off toward Sinful.

So many questions raced through my mind that I didn't even know where to begin. "How did you know where we were?"

"Little thought you might take risks," Mannie said, "and if you did, you'd need backup."

"You were following us?" Ida Belle asked.

"Actually, we put trackers on all your vehicles back when you broke into the storage facility. Given the things you tend to get involved in, Little thought it would be a good idea to keep tabs on you."

I wanted to be mad, but it was hard to be when Little's paranoia had just saved our lives. "Who shot Kayla?" I knew it couldn't have been Mannie, because the shot had come from the swamp, and he couldn't have made the shot, then gotten to the car that quickly, not with Nelson and Benedict right there.

"You don't need to know that," Mannie said. "What you need to know is that the state police got an anonymous tip that a drug deal was going down at the motel. One of the drug dealers shot another one."

"But the gun…" How in the world could Little make that one work?

"The gun was appropriated from Nelson's private collection when he took the position of sheriff…insurance for Little in case he decided to occupy the position for too long."

"Looks like Little got a two-for-one deal on this one," I said.

Mannie grinned. "He's really happy about that."

I stiffened. "The backpack! We left it on the ground behind the motel."

"Don't sweat it," Mannie said. "My associate retrieved it."

"We have video of Benedict and Nelson talking about the explosion and the meth deal," Ida Belle said.

"Really?" Mannie glanced over at us.

"Yeah," I said. "We know it's not admissible in court, but it should encourage the state police to build a case."

"Where's the footage?" Mannie asked.

I held up my cell phone.

"Send it to the number Little gave you," Mannie said. "We'll handle the rest."

I wondered what Little's plan for delivering evidence to the state police involved, but I wasn't about to ask. All that fell under things we were better off not knowing.

"So we're in the clear on this," I said, not quite believing it.

"Looks like," Mannie said. His cell phone rang and he answered. "Yep, got them right here. One down, two on site." He paused for a minute and I could hear Little's voice, but couldn't make out what he was saying.

Finally, he hung up. "Little says to tell you it was excellent work. And he'd like you to keep the airboat as a token of his thanks."

"Oh, I really appreciate it," I said, "but I can't do that."

Ida Belle elbowed me in the side.

"I'm afraid he insists," Mannie said.

"Well, if he insists." I looked over at Ida Belle, who was grinning from ear to ear.

Who was I to argue with the mob?

It took Gertie another ten minutes after Mannie delivered us to her house before she started to stir. Or maybe "stir" wasn't a good description. Mannie had carried her inside and placed her on the couch per Ida Belle's instructions before hurrying back outside and jumping into a black sedan that disappeared as quickly as it had materialized.

When Gertie came back to life, she flew straight up off the couch, grabbed a lamp, and darn near clocked Ida Belle with it before she got a good look at her surroundings.

"What happened?" she asked. "I was reaching into my purse to get my gun and someone hit me across the head." She reached up to touch the back of her head and swayed.

I grabbed the lamp and Ida Belle hurried to the kitchen. "Sit down," I said, "before you fall down."

Ida Belle came back with aspirin and a glass of ginger ale. "Take these. I think we should take her to the emergency room."

"No way," Gertie said. "It's just a knot."

"You've been out for a while," I said.

"If I still have a headache tomorrow, we'll go then," Gertie said. "Now will someone please tell me what happened before I explode?"

Ida Belle and I took turns filling Gertie in on everything that had transpired at the motel, and played the video for her. She was shocked when we told her that Kayla was involved and was the one who'd knocked her out.

"I can't believe it," Gertie said. "She was never a wild one. Always kind of quiet and, I don't know, forgettable. I can't connect the girl I knew with meth dealing."

"I think she's an addict," I said, and told them my theory about the weight loss and teeth replacement.

Ida Belle nodded. "That makes sense. She'd been busted for using and Nelson knew about it. So he blackmailed her into helping him transport through Sinful."

"She was the perfect choice. With her mother still living here, no one would question frequent visits to town, and then they would be off to the next festival."

"The next delivery location," Ida Belle said.

"I don't think Colby was happy about it," I said. "Remember, he made the comment after the fire that the only reason they were here is because of her. At the time, I thought he meant they took the gig because she was from Sinful, but I don't think that's it."

Ida Belle nodded. "And Benedict was afraid he was a weak link."

"Maybe he'll roll on them," Gertie said. "That would certainly make the state police's job easier."

"With Kayla dead," I said, "he has nothing to lose."

Gertie shook her head. "It's all so surreal. And I slept through it all. What a ripper."

"Just be glad we're out of this one clean," Ida Belle said. "I can't imagine trying to explain to the state police why we were even at the motel bugging Nelson's room, much less being involved in a shootout where someone was killed. We'd be in jail until next week while they sorted it all out."

"Yeah," I said, "and jail is definitely not a good option for me."

We were all silent for a minute, and then someone banged on Gertie's door and we all jumped.

"No one knows we're here," Ida Belle said.

"Ally does," I said as I headed for the door. "I texted her earlier after I sent the video to Little."

I peered out the peephole and saw Ally standing on the porch, looking ready to explode. I opened the door and she ran past me and turned on the television.

"You're not going to believe this," she said and pointed to the special news report in progress.

We all looked at the screen and saw the state police shoving a handcuffed Nelson and Benedict into the back of police cars. The female reporter turned around with the microphone and looked at the camera.

"We're on location at the Bayou Inn, where the drug enforcement task force with the state police acted on a tip and have arrested Nelson Comeaux and Benedict Granger, both suspected of cooking and distributing meth. This news comes as an even bigger shock because Comeaux was recently appointed sheriff of Sinful, Louisiana, by his cousin Celia Arceneaux, who was just elected mayor with a vote that is being contested by her opponent. The police aren't giving more details at the moment, but we'll be reporting as this story unfolds."

Ally turned to look at us, her face flushed. "Can you believe it?"

"Wow!"

"That's unbelievable."

"I never would have guessed."

We all spoke at once, and I had to admit, our surprise sounded darn convincing.

"I bet Celia is having kittens," Gertie said gleefully.

"I know for a fact she is," Ally said. "She was at the same shower I was. When the first report came on the news, one of the husbands yelled for us to come in the den. Celia passed out right there in front of the television, and I took off for Gertie's house to make sure you guys saw it."

Ally flopped onto the couch on the opposite end from Gertie and let out a breath. "I broke forty major laws on the drive over here and I was only three blocks away. I still can't believe it. I mean, we all knew Nelson was a piece of crap human being, but even I wouldn't have pegged him for the meth business."

Suddenly, she stopped talking and narrowed her eyes at us. "You guys weren't involved in any of this, were you? I never did find out what you were doing with the tattoos and wearing the fire extinguisher foam."

"We overheard Nelson saying he was going to the Swamp Bar for the crawfish boil," Ida Belle said. "So Gertie and Fortune went undercover to see if they could catch him doing anything that would get him thrown out of office."

"Oh." Ally looked slightly disappointed. "And the foam?"

"There was an incident with Gertie falling and a Harley-Davidson," I said. "She might have sprayed them and got a little on us."

Ally smiled. "There's never a dull moment with you guys. But I'm glad you didn't find out anything while you were there. Can you imagine if you'd clued in on Nelson's drug dealing? He would have killed you."

"He would have tried," Gertie said.

We all laughed.

My phone buzzed and I looked at the display. It was from Carter.

You see the news?

Yeah. Ally just busted into Gertie's house and turned on the television.

One problem down. ☺

I sat down in a recliner and leaned back, all the tension leaving my neck. This was going to work out. Nelson and company were going down, some of Sinful would revert back to normal, and Swamp Team 3 would come out smelling like a rose.

We were getting better at this.

Chapter Eighteen

I had barely opened my eyes when I heard a knock at my front door. I forced myself out of bed and into a pair of shorts and trudged downstairs, desperate for coffee and with no desire at all to address whoever was on my porch. I swung open the door and squinted at the bright sunlight. I finally managed to get one eye partially open and saw Carter standing there staring at me.

"You awake?" he asked.

"Not really." I stepped away from the door and headed for the kitchen. Coffee was a necessary thing. Like ten minutes ago.

"It's almost noon," he said as he took a seat at my kitchen table.

"Sunday or Monday?" I poured water into the coffeepot and yawned.

"Sunday. Did you really think you'd slept through an entire day?"

"I kinda wanted to." I plopped into a chair and slouched back. "No banana pudding equals no race equals no church equals sleeping as long as I want."

He frowned. "Are you feeling all right?"

"I'm not sure. I'll let you know when I can feel again."

He chuckled. "Too much wine?"

"Champagne. Ida Belle, Gertie, Ally, and I might have celebrated a while last night. And well into the morning."

"What time did you go to bed?"

"I think it was around four, but my phone was blurry."

"No wonder you don't want to move. Stay there." He got up from the table and poured two cups of black coffee and placed them on the table.

I took a sip and waited for the coffee to spike my system. It didn't take long. By the time I finished the cup and poured myself another, I was well on my way to feeling human again.

"Hey," Carter said. "You've got both eyes open. That's an improvement."

"What a day. Between the boating and the whole Nelson thing, I need a vacation."

Carter leaned back in his chair and looked at me. "Yeah, about that boating thing. Deputy Breaux said he heard that two women with tattoos caused a brawl at the Swamp Bar."

"And?" I forced my body to remain limp and my voice casual. "Deputy Breaux needs to be a little more specific, doesn't he? I mean, were the tattoos spelled correctly? That might narrow things down."

"They were sleeves, not words, and the description of the two women sounded oddly like you and Gertie."

"Video or it didn't happen."

He raised one eyebrow.

"Fine," I said, deciding to use Ida Belle's lie to Ally from the night before. "Gertie overheard Nelson saying he was going to the Swamp Bar for the crawfish boil, and we went hoping to catch him doing something that could get him removed from office."

"Uh-huh. And the fight?"

"That was an accident. Two women started fighting over one ugly husband and the end result was a Harley-Davidson biting the dust and Gertie getting the blame."

Carter shook his head. "It's all a moot point now, but did you see anything damning?"

"Just Nelson and the hooker. Oh, and they were talking to that Benedict dude who was arrested with him last night."

"Didn't you promise me you wouldn't get involved in this sort of thing?"

"No. I promised you I wouldn't get involved in the meth lab explosion. How the heck were we supposed to know Nelson was in it up to his neck?"

Carter sighed. "You weren't. Hell, that one came as a surprise even to me. I knew the guy was worthless but I never saw this one coming." He sat up and leaned forward. "Deputy Breaux also told me that two men wearing sheets drove a boat into Mrs. Pickens's backyard. They're lucky Mrs. Pickens is a bad shot."

"That would have been worth seeing. What happened to them?"

"They're in jail right now, but Mrs. Pickens wants them charged with a hate crime."

"Driving a boat into someone's backyard isn't a hate crime."

"Mrs. Pickens is black."

"Oh." I sat up straight. "OH!"

"And the boat had fire extinguisher foam all over it."

"Maybe they were trying to put out an engine fire and lost control."

He grinned. "I suppose anything is possible."

"So," I said, ready to change the subject while he was in a good mood, "have you heard any details on Nelson's arrest?"

He nodded. "I have a friend with the state police. I gave him a call this morning and got the skinny. He said they got a tip from an informant yesterday about Nelson running meth."

I stiffened. An informant? Surely not the Heberts? Informants for the state police? But the more I thought about it, the more it made sense. And it certainly explained a couple of things—like how Little got the print check on Dewey, and why he wasn't worried about how to get the video to them, and how they showed up at the motel based on a "tip."

"Our buddy Nelson wasn't all that careful covering his tracks," Carter said, "and they did the bust last night figuring they'd have enough evidence for a conviction by trial."

"You think they'll get it?"

"I don't think they need it. Ballistics proved Nelson's gun killed Kayla, and his were the only prints on it. And Colby rolled on them. Apparently, Nelson blackmailed Kayla into distributing. Colby admitted they were both addicts, but said he never wanted to be involved with Nelson. He's telling everything."

"Sounds like an open-and-shut case."

Carter nodded. "I can't imagine him or Benedict walking on this."

"Doesn't sound like it. Good for you and Sinful."

"Not to mention another chink in Celia's armor. This isn't going to look good for her, bringing the meth trade to town."

"Nope. If this election audit doesn't put Marie in office, I bet enough has gone wrong to get Celia ousted. Any word on the man who lost his leg?"

"Yeah, Colby said it was the cooker, Dewey Parnell. He was a local who left for New Orleans after high school. I don't think I've seen him since, but I'd heard he wasn't up for citizen of the year."

I opened my mouth to reply but before I could, I heard my front door open and bang shut. A couple seconds later, Ida Belle and Gertie came running down the hall and into the kitchen, blocking each other on the way. When they came to a sliding stop in front of Carter and me, they were both winded.

"What is wrong with you two?" I waved at chairs. "Are you being chased by wild animals?"

"Gertie's car is broke so we walked to church," Ida Belle said, "but then we saw something at Francine's that you're not going to believe. We ran all the way from the café."

"I want to tell them," Gertie pouted.

"Then tell, but hurry up before I burst," Ida Belle said.

Their excitement was contagious. "Someone tell. Please."

"You're not going to believe who walked into the café," Ida Belle said.

"Who?" I asked.

Ida Belle and Gertie looked at each other and grinned.

"Celia's husband!" Gertie said.

Carter bolted out of his chair. "What? You're lying."

"Gertie doesn't lie on Sundays, remember?" Ida Belle said.

"But he's been missing decades," I said, completely confused.

Ida Belle nodded. "When he didn't turn up for Pansy's funeral, we all figured he was dead."

"Well, yeah, because that's the only thing that makes sense," I said.

"Not really," Gertie said. "He could have been at the North Pole, or in prison, or living completely off-grid in the mountains of Tibet."

"Tibet non-withstanding, why come back now?" I asked.

"Maybe he wants to be first man of Sinful," Gertie said.

Ida Belle looked up and mumbled, probably praying.

"I don't get it," I said.

"Nobody gets it," Ida Belle said.

"Especially Celia," Gertie said. "She passed out right there in the middle of Francine's. Tipped an entire tray over on Pastor

Don."

Carter stared back and forth from Ida Belle to Gertie, clearly dumbfounded and waiting for the punch line that wasn't coming.

"But," he said finally, "he never saw his daughter again, even at her own funeral. And he left his boat. I always thought he'd come back for that boat. I wonder where he's been all this time."

Ida Belle shook her head. "I don't know, but I have the feeling things are about to get really interesting around here."

"Good," I said. "I was getting bored."

The End

About the Author

Jana DeLeon grew up among the bayous and gators of southwest Louisiana. She's never stumbled across a mystery like one of her heroines but is still hopeful. She lives in Dallas, Texas with a menagerie of animals and not a single ghost.

Visit Jana at:

Website: http://janadeleon.com
Facebook: http://www.facebook.com/JanaDeLeonAuthor/
Twitter: @JanaDeLeon

For new release notification, to participate in a monthly $100 egift card drawing, and more, sign up for Jana's newsletter.

20414716R00146

Made in the USA
Middletown, DE
27 May 2015